DRAWING DOWN THE MIST

Praise for Sheri Lewis Wohl

She Wolf

"I really enjoyed this book—I couldn't put it down once I started it. The author's style of writing was very good and engaging. All characters, including the supporting characters, were multi-layered and interesting."—*Melina Bickard, Librarian, Waterloo Library (UK)*

The Talebearer

"As a crime story, it is a good read that had me turning pages quickly...The book is well-written and the characters are well-developed."—*Reviews by Amos Lassen*

Twisted Echoes

"A very unusual blend of lesbian romance and horror...[W]oven throughout this modern romance is a neatly plotted horror story from the past, which bleeds ever increasingly into the present of the two main characters. Lorna and Renee are well matched and face ever-increasing danger from spirits from the past. An unusual story that gets tenser and more interesting as it progresses."
—*Pippa Wischer, Manager at Berkelouw Books, Armadale*

Twisted Screams

"[A] cast of well-developed characters leads you through a maze of complex emotions."—*Lunar Rainbow Reviewz*

Vermilion Justice

"[T]he characters are so dynamic and well-written that this becomes more than just another vampire story. It's probably impossible to read this book and not come across a character who reminds you of someone you actually know. Wohl takes something as fictional as vampires and makes them feel real. Highly recommended."
—*GLBT Reviews: The ALA's GLBT Round Table*

By the Author

Crimson Vengeance

Burgundy Betrayal

Scarlet Revenge

Vermilion Justice

Twisted Echoes

Twisted Whispers

Twisted Screams

Necromantia

She Wolf

Walking Through Shadows

The Talebearer

Drawing Down the Mist

DRAWING DOWN THE MIST

by

Sheri Lewis Wohl

2019

DRAWING DOWN THE MIST
© 2019 By Sheri Lewis Wohl. All Rights Reserved.

ISBN 13: 978-1-63555-341-3

This Trade Paperback Original Is Published By
Bold Strokes Books, Inc.
P.O. Box 249
Valley Falls, NY 12185

First Edition: February 2019

Credits
Editor: Shelley Thrasher
Production Design: Stacia Seaman
Cover Design by Melody Pond

To my family.
You might not always get me, but you always have my back.

To me belongeth vengeance and recompence;
their foot shall slide in due time:
for the day of their calamity is at hand,
and the things that shall come upon them make haste.

Deuteronomy 32:35
The Holy Bible (King James Version)

PROLOGUE

Fifty Years from Now

"You have to do it." The old woman with the snow-white hair lay back against the soft, green pillows and closed her eyes. "It's critical." A fire was blazing in the big stone fireplace, and even though she was covered with blankets, she still shivered.

"No one will believe me." It wasn't that she hadn't thought of the very same thing at least a hundred times. She just couldn't shake the feeling that it was pointless. No one wanted to remember what had happened all those years ago, and that included her.

"Oh, my darling. When exactly have you ever cared whether anyone believed you?" She laughed, though the sound came out more as a cough. Her frail body shook with the effort.

She had a point. Once she'd cared about a great many things. Friends, family, honor. A long, long time ago. For many years now the only thing…the only one…she cared about was the woman on the sofa. She was her whole reason for existence. She made this interminably long life bearable. She made everything that came before and after important.

Now, this phase in life was ending. They had lived and loved and shared the moments that made what their world had become something worth enduring. They had helped to save so many, though the ghosts of those who had perished still haunted her. No matter how many years rolled by, she could still see their faces as if they were standing in front of her right now.

Her own single-minded, blind revenge had been sweet yet at

the same time bitter. She had won a battle waged over the course of a century, but in the years since, she'd wondered too many times to count if the cost had been too high. Her victory had come at a very high price, and for that reason, regret had been her constant companion.

Her gaze fell upon the old, frail woman. As she looked at her familiar face, she didn't see her age or infirmity, for in her mind's eye she could still glimpse the youth and vigor that had first captured her interest. The smile and the sparkling eyes. The quick wit and the sharp mind. Exciting didn't even begin to describe the relationship they'd had. Still had. It was different these days, but it had lost none of its shine, at least not to her.

"I care what you think."

The old woman pushed herself up to a sitting position and with bony hands tucked the blankets beneath her legs. Wispy white hair floated around her face, feathering against her high cheekbones. Tiny red stones hung from her ears, reminding her of a day many decades past when she'd walked into that strange room and seen her for the first time. Even then, when everything in her world was going sideways, she'd known that the beautiful woman with the sweet little earrings was someone special. And it hadn't taken her long to discover exactly how special.

Coughing interrupted her foray into the past, and she jumped up to bring her companion a glass of water. She held it to the old woman's lips as she took a sip. Despite the fire, the hand that patted her on the cheek was as cold as if she'd just come in from a blizzard. "Thank you, my sweet. Now, sit down and write. I won't rest easy until you've finished it."

It wasn't an idle threat. If she didn't finish it, neither of them would have any respite. She returned to the table and stared down at her hands. Unlike the woman on the sofa, hers were strong and unlined. "I still don't think it will make a difference to anyone. It was all in the past, and it should stay there. No one wants to remember."

The old woman slid back down on the sofa, and her eyes fluttered shut. Her voice was soft as she spoke. "It matters, and people need to know. They need to remember whether they want to or not. You can tell them. You have to tell them. For me."

Chapter One

Present Day

She was born a princess and should have died one too. The universe, it seemed, had a different idea, for she hadn't died at all. Or at least not yet. Sasha Rudin sat alone in her living room with a glass of wine in one hand and a gourmet cupcake in the other. Some things had changed in the last century, the quality of the baked goods she held being one. For her first nineteen years, her father had celebrated her birth with a lovely cake the harried staff prepared, but this—she breathed in the intoxicating scent of chocolate and salted caramel—was light-years away from those celebratory cakes. And she suspected the baker who made it did so with far more joy than her father's obedient staff.

Yet, even the luscious treat with the delicate whipped frosting didn't chase away the shadows that plagued her every year when the fourteenth of June rolled around. Time didn't lessen her sorrow. She stood alone with her cake, missing them as she celebrated in solitude once again. She missed them all, even that horrible creature who'd sucked in her mother with his empty promises. What a strange paradox. In life she'd hated that man, and yet in death, she would give anything to see his face once more.

"Happy birthday to me," she whispered before she devoured the cake and drank the wine. For anyone else, it probably would have been a sensory delight. For her, both tasted more like sawdust than gourmet items, and she still didn't feel any better.

How she wished to. Her wishes never came true, and in the back of her mind she knew they never would, for so many reasons. Perhaps if the one who evaded her was finally brought to justice, then she could enjoy these simple pleasures. She had her doubts that the taste of the delicate cake would ever delight her again, but meting out the justice the monster deserved would at least bring her a measure of peace, and she would give anything for peace.

Instead, it was to be another lonely birthday filled with sadness and frustration, and the knowledge that one more year had passed in failure. She set down the now-empty glass and went to stand before the floor-to-ceiling windows that covered one full wall of the living room. Others like her would never consider building a wall of windows that would allow unfiltered light into their personal space. Sasha was different. She wanted to know it was here, to know that her home was filling with the warmth and rays of the daylight sun.

Even if she couldn't enjoy it.

Knowing that her world still had it was enough. She could sleep in her space and remember what it was like to have that sun on her face, to feel it warming her skin. To sit on the patio with her sisters and laugh as the dogs ran through the grass barking and playing. To hold another's hand and let love fill her heart.

Yes, she wanted to remember it all. Remember it and stoke the fury that had been with her every single day for well over a century. She would pay—the one who took it all from her—and that was a promise. This birthday was unlike the others because after all the empty years, something felt different, and she believed it was the universe letting her know that the time was upon her. Hard work, persistence, and single-minded ambition had brought her to this place and this time. They had prepared her for the battle that was coming. Payment was due, and she was the one who would stand before her to collect.

More than revenge had her stirred up. Even though the year just past had been frustrating, tomorrow was the start of a new year, and it was going to be different. Things in the world were not as they should be. Every corner was shadowed as though danger lurked just around it. When she walked the streets at night, they felt darker and more ominous than usual. On the air were whispers that left her uncomfortable. It was time in more ways than one for a revolution of sorts. As she had used the years to prepare herself, so too did others, and that had her worried.

It was why she had not come to this birthday unprepared. It would not be the first revolution for her, though she truly hoped it would be the last.

The fact that she continued to celebrate her birthday year after year, decade after decade, said something about her, and she was under no illusion what it was. She'd been waiting for this shift for over ten decades. For some reason she couldn't explain, she'd believed all along that a day would come when the fight would commence, when all her hard work would come to fruition.

This birthday was that day, and the realization made her square her shoulders and bring her chin up. The posture displayed more than resolution and strength; it was her birthright. Her sisters would be proud of the woman she was today, and how she wished she could share with them. She had gone to what should have been her death with the same posture, and if that day was to come now, she would once again stand before the instrument of her death with pride. Some things could not be taken away.

Her phone rang, and she turned her back on the windows as she reached for her cell. "Talk to me."

Only select people had this number. The calls were infrequent and always critical. This one didn't surprise her.

"Something's cooking." Rodney Cornell never wasted words, an admirable trait. She didn't have time for extraneous details and justifications.

"I feel it. What have you found?"

When one was a survivalist, most assumed that person was also off the grid. Not so for Rodney. He managed to juggle his underground lifestyle with an intricate system that allowed him to monitor everything on the grid while staying undetected and keeping his location secure. Perhaps it might be more appropriate to characterize him as a spy. Nothing got past this genius of a man, and she was proud he was her ally and not a foe. The fact that she also quite liked him was a bonus. He knew exactly what she was, what she was looking for, and had been at her side for almost two decades. He was as ready as she was.

"They're mobilizing."

Even though she was expecting the news, his words still startled her. Theorizing about something and having it become reality were two very different things. "Bastards."

"Yeah. Motherfuckers, if you ask me, but it's what we've been waiting for. We got this, Sasha. They're not going to know what hit them."

She gripped the phone. He was right, of course. They were prepared. Regardless, it had the same feel to it as all those years ago when they were herded from the palace and into house-arrest seclusion. The experience had been disconcerting. Back then, none of them had an inkling of what was to come. Today she knew what was just beyond the horizon. "Yes, it is the moment, and I'm ready."

To kill them, she didn't add. Then again, she didn't have to.

❖

"Look, Lydia. I've got to have more of a challenge. I don't want to do another Marla book. She's wearing me out. I want exciting and edgy, not more of the same thing I've been writing for the last decade. Not to sound trite, but I'm bored to tears."

Dee Arkin paced as she talked to her editor, Lydia Lyons, on speakerphone. Her hands were pushed into her pockets so she could resist the urge to run her hands through her hair and destroy the blue-tinged Mohawk she'd spent half an hour perfecting. It said a lot that she spent more time trying to get her hair right than working on a new book. At the moment, she'd do anything to stay away from her computer.

"Marla has made you rich." The near whine in Lydia's voice got on Dee's nerves.

Yeah, yeah, yeah. Her Marla Watty detective novels had indeed made her stinking rich, no argument there. But she'd been working on a book much darker and more edgy. She desperately wanted Lydia on board with her for the project but doubted she could get her there. Her ace in the hole was the fact that she'd made Lydia and the publishing house a lot of money, and in her mind, they owed her the time to do this. If it failed, so what? Everybody was entitled to a bomb now and again. If it didn't, well then, they should all be happy.

"I want to do this." She stopped pacing and stared at her computer, where research files beckoned. It had been years since she'd enjoyed the process this much. "I'm going to do this, with or without you."

Over the phone, Lydia's sigh was faint and not intended for Dee to hear. She smiled. Her point had been made, and Lydia was smart enough to know when to give in. The high-powered and ambitious editor didn't want to lose her cash cow. "Fine. I'll send you a contract for this *one* book, and then you have to promise to send me another Marla installment. Deal?"

Not quite. "With an option for a second book." She could push too. People tended to think she was easy to manipulate because she was a typical writer: a bit introverted and quiet. She spent so much time inside her head and by herself, they regarded her as passive. They'd be wrong in her case. Pushover just wasn't in her DNA.

"Come on, Dee…"

"An option, Lydia, or I'll go somewhere else." It wasn't an idle threat. She had enough money to do what she wanted, and right now she wanted to write this new book.

"Fine. Don't be talking crazy now. We'll make this work. You want to write a new book, write it, and I'll publish it."

Dee smiled broader, glad Lydia wasn't here. Lydia always liked to believe she was the one driving the deals. "Email it to Don." She'd already briefed her agent, Don, and he was expecting both a contract for the new book with the option and the Marla book. Lydia wasn't going to risk losing her by turning down the new proposal.

Now that she had what she wanted, the computer didn't seem like such a demon anymore, and she was eager to pick up where she'd left off. She ended the call and sank into her desk chair. Lydia and Don could hammer out all the minute details; she was free to write.

Dee rested her chin on her hands as she pulled up the files she'd saved earlier. It had struck her the first time she'd been through the multiple pages, and the second time around didn't clear it up any more. How could it be right? She didn't particularly believe in conspiracy theories, yet this sure felt like that's exactly what it was. And it was exactly the thing that made her crave time to work.

Her Marla Watty detective series had started out pretty fun to write, and she'd made some great friends in the local law-enforcement community who had helped her keep realism in the work. What she'd come across as she researched for her new novel was outside her norm by a long stretch. She was working on what she thought of as a paranormal book and, more specifically, a vampire book. She'd always wanted to do something along those lines, being a big fan of the nineteenth-century vampire stories *Carmilla* and *Dracula*. Joseph

Sheridan Le Fanu,and Bram Stoker had captured her imagination the first time she read their works. Then the success of the Marla series had swept her life away, and she hadn't been able to get back to the germ of an idea that had been percolating since the first time she seriously considered becoming a writer.

The moment had come to take the idea and make it a reality. She couldn't turn away even if she wanted to. Of course, she didn't intend to do that. She'd waited too long to do this.

She was puzzled too. She was coming up against the strangest things as she researched. Typically she used historical information to craft the heart of a story. Yes, it was fiction, but she wanted her fiction to feel real, which meant doing her homework before she began to write. In her mind the best fiction started with a solid base of reality.

Writing a vampire story was counterintuitive to her normal starting point. After all, vampires were strictly an invention of folklore and fiction. Granted, folklore often had its birth in reality, but from what she'd learned thus far, vampire legends were rooted in misunderstandings of the decomposition of human remains and premature burial. The former made perfect sense to her. The latter gave her the creeps. Really, how did one accidentally bury someone who was still alive? Yet she came across the situation again and again in her research. Apparently it wasn't as difficult as she thought. She shivered, grateful she lived in an era of great scientific knowledge.

The misinterpretations at the root of vampire lore weren't what was bothering her right now. The rest of what she'd stumbled on had her scratching her head. It had all started with a single name, and no, it wasn't Vlad Dracula. It was a Hungarian nobleman named Imre Thurzo, born in 1598. Nothing too unusual about him except that he was noted to be the last male member of his family, and he reportedly died in 1621 at the ripe old age of twenty-three. Again, no biggie, given the times. People often died at tragically young ages. Many family lines petered out when the male heirs were unable to produce offspring.

So, why did Imre catch her attention? Easy. The deeper she dug, the more he kept popping up. In 1708, in 1845, in 1927, and most recently, in 2016. Had to be a relative, right? The historical data that pegged him as the last of his family lineage had to be wrong, and he'd left some descendants out there somewhere. That's what she thought until she dug and found his likeness again and again. The guy obviously loved himself, because she found at least a dozen images, and each and every one of them showed exactly the same face. Different clothes and hairstyles, same face. Same smile that, to her mind, suggested a bit of narcissism. Something about his expression sent a chill through her. This guy liked himself way more than the average mirror-loving pretty boy.

Now she wanted to know more. Dee loved the search engines available to her these days, including the services she paid for that gave her access to more in-depth information, and she continued her archeological dig. She'd already saved what she'd found so far, and it was like a treasure map leading to a fascinating mystery. Imre was her starting point, and he sparked her imagination even more than it already was. She could picture him, with his blue eyes and arrogant smirk, as the perfect vampire. The man of royal birth who became an immortal. Yes, this was exactly the kind of thing that got her blood pumping and her mind working furiously. A novel was almost writing itself inside her head.

The discovery of the improbable immortal Imre led her to the model for her next character. This time it was a woman named Katrina Petrin. Like Imre, she appeared to have been around far longer than was possible for a human. The first mention of her name came up in 1766, then six or seven more times all the way up to and through the twentieth century. Like with Imre, her first inclination was to believe that the subsequent mentions were of Katrina's family members. Also like Imre, the images weren't just similar; they were identical. Her gut told her that they were relatives while her eyes insisted they were the same person.

She tried to discover if anything linked the two anomalies, and nothing did, at least that she could find, except that they came from adjoining geographic regions. She kept thinking that if they had truly been alive all that time, surely they would know of each other. Then again, in totality it was pretty crazy, so maybe she was just making up what she wanted to see. Writing the story the way she wanted it to go. Wasn't that a writer's prerogative?

By the time darkness blanketed the house, her office was lit only by the glow of her laptop screen. The words flowing across her screen were too engrossing for her to even bother to reach up to turn on the desk lamp. She kept her head bent, her fingers flying over the keys, but couldn't run the queries as fast as she wished. Once she figured out where to dig, she found a gold mine.

Ignoring the lights was one thing, but her back was another, and it was telling her or perhaps more accurately was screaming at her that enough was enough. When she tried to sit up in her chair, her shoulders remained drawn together, and her back arched forward like she was a crippled-up hundred-year-old instead of not quite forty, with a straight spine and shoulders. Her physical-therapy friend would kick her butt for sitting all hunched over a keyboard for God only knows how long. She'd neglect to tell her that the next time they hung out. By then she might actually be able to straighten up again.

When the sharp pains faded, Dee reached out and flipped on the desk light. It was like suddenly being hit by the stereotypical interrogation spotlight. First she'd had needles in her back and shoulders, and now she had needles in her eyes. If this happened at almost forty, she could hardly wait to see what the next few decades held.

It took a couple of seconds for her eyes to adjust, and when they did, she glanced over at the clock. Then she snapped her gaze down to her computer and the tiny clock in the right-hand corner of the taskbar. Wow. Where had the time gone? She'd sat down here at a little past two, and it was now a quarter of eight. She couldn't remember the last time she'd gotten so wrapped up in her work that she completely lost track of time. The one thing it told her was that she was on the right path. It was the kind of thing that made her mind whirl, and it had been a long time since she'd felt this way.

Most of what she'd dug up was in digital files on her laptop, but she'd found at least twenty pages of information intriguing enough to go old school and print out. Now that she was shaking out the kinks, she realized she was starving. There had to be something to eat in the kitchen, and she could peruse the stuff she'd printed while she chowed down. Old school had its uses. Besides, she was on a roll and saw no sense in quitting now.

She grabbed the pages from the printer, turned off the desk light, and headed toward the kitchen, flipping on overhead lights as she went. It was a little weird to do that, yet for some reason she was compelled to have lots of light. Brought back memories of childhood when she was scared of the dark. A little laugh escaped her lips as she hit yet another light switch.

In the kitchen, she laid the sheets on the island and pulled open the refrigerator door. A pathetic sight greeted her. The shelves were nearly empty of any food of substance, while the door held six bottles of really good beer and a nice, unopened bottle of pinot. Yeah, if she didn't get this thing filled up with something decent to eat, AA would be knocking on her door.

But what the heck. Since her choices were slim, she grabbed one of the bottles of beer and the two sharp-cheddar cheese sticks that remained from a family-sized bag. Seriously, one couldn't go wrong with cheese and beer, right? She snagged her papers and headed out of the kitchen without turning off the lights.

In the living room, she sat down on the power sofa and pushed the button to bring up the footrest. She clicked on the television, not because she felt like watching it but because it was great white noise. She opened the beer, peeled the plastic off the cheese sticks, and began to nibble as she started to read. This was some seriously interesting shit. The research, not the food.

She'd finished both cheese sticks and most of the beer when her head came up. It sure sounded like someone had pulled into her driveway, which was unusual given that her house was at the rear of a two-acre parcel. If people used her driveway to turn around, their lights were a mere whisper in her windows. Tonight it was different.

Dee stood up and stared out the window. A car pulled up slowly in front of the house, its lights illuminating her brick steps and beautifully maintained shrubs. She waited to see who it was, given that she didn't recognize the car. Nothing happened. She set the bottle down and was just about to head to the front door when the car continued through the circular drive and left.

"Well, wasn't that strange as all get-out," she muttered. Was it finally time to install the driveway gate all of her friends kept urging her to get? She'd never wanted to make her home a fortress, yet right now she had an uncomfortable feeling that maybe her friends were right. Random cars driving all the way into her personal space just didn't happen, until tonight anyway.

A ding from her pocket let her know an email had just come in. She was still staring out the front window thinking about the car and the gate as she pulled the phone out. One new email from an address she didn't recognize. She thought about sending it immediately to the trash without bothering to look at it. Curiosity won, and she opened it and read.

Leave it alone or we'll kill you.

Katrina was pissed. Stupid humans didn't know when to leave well enough alone. She shouldn't be surprised, or even upset, for that matter. It wasn't like this hadn't happened before, and on multiple occasions. Most of the time she operated quite nicely under the radar, even with today's technology that gave everyone global reach. She, and others like her, did their business and built their empires on the down-low while the humans went about their lives fat, dumb, and happy. It was safer for her and her kind, and those fat, dumb, and happy humans made for an excellent source of untainted blood.

Every once in a while a human came along with too many questions and too much tenacity. They grabbed what they shouldn't and refused to let it go. It was such a pain in the ass when this happened, and now was the worst time to have someone sticking their nose into her business. It was far easier when the humans kept their attention on their own world and didn't worry about things like the very long lives of those like her.

When Eli had brought her the news earlier tonight, she'd been furious. She'd wanted to race down to the garage, jump into her fastest car, and go wrap her fingers around the woman's neck right before she sank her teeth into her flesh. After she'd drained her, she'd dump her body in the middle of the street as a cautionary tale for anyone else who thought it was a good idea to dig into her affairs. Fortunately, age and wisdom paid off, and she stayed put. Violence had its place, but in this day and age it had to be wielded with a very deft hand. This was not the moment to go old school, even as satisfying as that would be. She had to deal with this threat quietly and effectively, utilizing the tools the twenty-first century had to offer.

"I've got the details on her." Eli came through the open door and dropped a file folder onto her antique desk. "She could be a problem that we don't need right now. We're going to have to do something about her sooner rather than later."

She opened the folder on top of the massive hardwood desk she'd been using since Woodrow Wilson was in office. It didn't really fit in with the way people worked these days, but she couldn't get rid of it. Even she had moments of sentiment, and this represented one of them. The woman who'd given it to her was one of her most satisfying human lovers, and the desk brought back fond memories. She didn't have many of those.

"Let's take a look at this pest." She was flipping quickly through the pages, scanning for anything that jumped out at her. Typically, it took only a quick perusal to find a human's Achilles heel, and then it was an equally quick matter to use it to shut the problem human down.

"Sort of a double-edged sword, Boss." Eli was standing behind her gazing over her shoulder.

She cringed and wanted to backhand him. It wasn't the way he stood so close that he was infringing on her personal space; it was his insistence on calling her "boss" that irritated the hell out of her. She'd talked to him about it no less than a hundred times. After each lecture he'd be good for a day or two, and then it would be right back to "boss." A man...a vampire...his age should be able to get it and stop the annoying behavior. He wasn't stupid. Truthfully, she suspected he got it all right. He just didn't care. In the vampire world, he was young, and that was the problem with the younger generation. They could be incredibly impertinent.

Ignoring the irritation, she tapped the folder. "Explain." She had to let it go for now. She had bigger things to concern herself with. They'd have another lesson on respect once this was all done. Perhaps a permanent lesson.

"She's a *New York Times* best-selling author."

Seriously? That's what he was worried about? "She's a writer. So what? We've dealt with more powerful humans than that before. She makes her living on lies, not a big threat to us. What else have you got?"

Eli was shaking his head. "I have to disagree with you. I know you've cut the legs off some bigwigs. That was in another time. In this century, things are a lot different. This writer could be a big deal because she's stinking rich and what they like to call a bulldog. Once she's on to something, she doesn't let go. With her resources, she could cause the kind of problems we can't afford."

"Like the Consortium."

"Like that. However she's done it, she's beginning to put the pieces together, and I don't believe she'll let go until she figures it all out. No one on the council is going to take that well, and they'll blame you."

He was right, even though she had nothing to do with her. It was a case of proximity, and she was in her region. That alone made her Katrina's responsibility. "Then we will make her let go before she causes us any of said problems."

He nodded, which didn't surprise her. After all, he'd been around her long enough to understand she took care of issues without a single second of hesitation. It had been that way for her since the beginning. When she said she was going to do something, she did. Emotions didn't enter into any decision. "Agreed."

"But what?" She could hear the *yeah but* in his voice, and that surprised her. The little "boss" issue aside, Eli didn't challenge her. Ever. He was a very good boy.

He leaned over her shoulder and began to flip pages. On each one, he'd point to something. "Look at this. Everything in this report here indicates she's not likely to give it up without a fight. She thrives on challenge. She wasn't gifted with success. This woman fought for it and earned it. That tells me she's not going to let this go. Look at the time she's already spent on her research. She's getting close to putting the pieces together."

In some respects she could admire that particular quality in the woman. In any woman who had daring and determination and who fought against the status quo. She also hated it. She herself was exactly that kind of person, and for her, it worked. It better, given how many years she'd had to sharpen her skills. She wouldn't be in the position she was right now if she hadn't herself been a bulldog.

In her foes, it was a different story. She much preferred those who knew when they were up against their betters and retreated. It didn't sound like that was the case here. Listening to Eli right now made her want to take every gift available to her and draw it all down on the dumb bitch. If she wasn't smart enough to know when she had no chance, she deserved what she got.

Eli must have seen something in her face or picked up from her body language. As was his way, he sought to defuse the situation before her rage took hold. "Easy, Boss. I'm telling you, we'll get her to stop. I've already put it into motion. You can keep your focus on the plan."

"Put what into motion?" Lately it seemed to her that Eli was intent on showing her he could be a leader of sorts, and while under other circumstances she might appreciate his enthusiasm, this wasn't "other" circumstances. This was a normal run-of-the-mill, stop-her-in-her-tracks kind of situation. In fact, it wouldn't be the first time in the last twenty years or so that she'd had to take action against someone who was too nosy. In the good old days she could go many decades without a human causing her grief. Now she was lucky if she got five years before a gnat appeared. God, she hated this century. The more access to information people got, the more problems it created for her.

"You're going to like it." A small smile flirted at the corners of his mouth. He was an incredibly handsome man, and someone inclined toward his gender might be swayed.

Something in his expression made her wary. Sometimes he could be entirely too creative and she had to rein him in. "And you know we've got to be careful."

"It'll be fine, Boss. It always is. Have I ever let you down?"

"No, Eli. You're a good soldier." She got tired of always having to reassure him.

His smile grew bigger, and his eyes seemed to glitter with a look of satisfaction. "You have no idea."

He was wrong about that. She knew exactly how good a soldier he was. After all, she'd made him and then molded him into a man who would serve at her side without question. She didn't take on projects that would fail, so yes, she knew. With a sigh, she waved her hand in the air. Eli recognized the gesture and exited without another word. Good boy. He knew her moods, her signals, her unspoken commands. It was one of the reasons he was still at her right hand a hundred and twenty years after she'd noticed him harvesting in a Nebraska cornfield. Even then, with him in dirty work clothes and wearing that awful cap, she'd seen something in the young husband and father that had saved him. She'd realized he had potential, and in the intervening years she'd not been disappointed. He was a rare find, and that's why she'd brought him into the inner fold. At this point no one would ever guess his roots were common because she had trained him so well he could pass for royal born.

Only the best of the best became part of her group. It had to be that way if they were to achieve their ultimate goal. She had been dreaming of this since the day she'd been turned and was finally going to make it a reality, this latest little complication aside. The annoying writer would be handled as they all were, and then…

Well, then the world would be hers. She closed the folder on the naughty writer and folded her hands on top of it. She breathed in deeply and centered herself in preparation for the night. Serenity filled her, and as it did, a familiar sensation came over her. She was hungry, and from downstairs the hum of voices whispered on the air. That made her smile. God bless Eli. He had such a way with intimate little gatherings. He managed to find just the right people, and Katrina never went away hungry. She wouldn't now either. Tossing back her long, silky hair, she headed out of her office. She could deal with this latest pain in the ass later.

Tonight, she planned to party and to drink.

She intended to kill.

CHAPTER TWO

Sasha was restless, and it had less to do with celebrating yet another birthday and more to do with what she anticipated: a war. It had been coming for a long time, a very long time, but to know that it would soon be a reality made her buzz with excitement.

She'd been a smart girl right from the beginning, and her parents had nurtured her intelligence. Even given her mother's nearly all-consuming obsession with her brother, she'd nonetheless made certain Sasha and her sisters were afforded everything their wealth and position could provide. Sasha's natural intelligence was honed to a fine point by the time...well, by the time everything changed. That early foundation had been critical in the years that were to follow, and she silently thanked her parents every day.

Her mind turned back to the day that was seared into her memory so deeply every detail was as clear as if it had happened yesterday. The familiar fury rolled through her. She'd spent the first few decades after her change fixated on what-if scenarios. What if she hadn't fallen in love? What if she hadn't trusted the wrong person? What if she'd confided in at least one of her sisters? What if. What if. What if. It had nearly driven her insane. Finally, she let go of that way of thinking and focused instead on the one who had done this to her. It was the image of that face in her mind that continued to incite rage in her soul, and it kept her going year after year, decade after decade. That one would pay, and at long last, the time was nearly upon her. She knew exactly what she was going to do.

In her office, her computer pinged, and Sasha frowned. A glance at the clock and she shook her head. What human would be working at this time of the morning? Yet that ping told her that someone was searching names they shouldn't be. Someone was digging into a past that could very well lead them to the grave. She'd managed to save a couple of such inquirers through the years, but far more paid for their curiosity. The way things appeared to be going, she might not have the time or energy to help this unfortunate soul. Still, she was curious who had made it past the firewalls and into the inner sanctum.

At her desk, Sasha sank into the chair and opened up the screen. It was amazing what the techs could set up these days. No one could slide through anything without her knowing. It was helpful enough that her company was an international leader in security, both physical and cyber, but those she employed were also at the top of their game. It gave her a reach that was worldwide and infinitely detailed, not to mention fun.

Like now. She was looking at the search history of one Dee Arkin. The name rang vaguely familiar, and it took her a minute to figure out why. Then it hit her, and she shook her head. The author whose face was often on billboards and television commercials had just blown through a carefully constructed security screen. The treasured jewel of the thriller genre, where her strong, female detective hit just the right notes with the male and female reading public, was more than just a storyteller. No doubt that fine touch had made her a multimillionaire. These more-money-than-brains people often caused her problems and had been the same throughout the decades. These people had both time and enough cash to gather information, so that's what they did. Sometimes they got their hands on material they shouldn't. That's when Sasha had to step in and stop them before they were in too deep. The Consortium did not take kindly to humans who meddled in their business.

Most of the time she was successful in diverting the curious, and they went on their way without ever really knowing what had happened. Every once in a while, a person who was like a dog with a bone they wouldn't let go of had an ending that wasn't quite as ideal. If Sasha didn't reach them before the Consortium scouts did, she couldn't do anything to help. Timing was everything, and on occasion, hers sucked. The task of saving humans from themselves was a job that had no end date. She tried not to care. It didn't work.

Her search pulled up a photograph of a woman with a pretty face and a stylish short hairdo with bright-blue streaks. Sasha shook her head. Why anyone would want to look like that, she didn't know. It made her stand out and be noticed, and as she thought about it, she realized that was probably why. Dee Arkin obviously wanted to stand out and be noticed, which was one hundred and eighty degrees from what Sasha wanted. She liked to stay out of the spotlight. Actually, that wasn't quite correct. She needed to stay out of sight, period.

When someone lived as long as she had, it was imperative to play games of smoke and mirrors. No one could really know she was the same person who had started the company in 1923 and was still at the helm in the twenty-first century. As far as the outside world was aware, her great-grandfather had started it, and she, of course, had posed as him because no one in the early twentieth century would take a woman seriously. From her supposed great-grandfather, the company had been passed along until she became the most recent of the Rudin family to run the company. The "family's" skill in their trade was legendary, and no one else had ever been able to duplicate their results.

Of course, no one ever knew the true secret of her success and, by default, her company's. When a company was founded by a vampire, run by a vampire, and employed the services of other vampires, well, it was bound to be successful. Immortality had its distinct advantages. Through much patience it yielded success both in terms of finances and revenge. She'd been enjoying the financial side for nearly a century. Now it was time to revel in revenge. It was coming; she could feel it.

Sasha got up and left her computer. She began to pace as she thought through the best way to deal with the writer, stopping when she reached the glass cabinet displaying many wondrous things she'd collected over the years. She opened the door and picked up the birthday present she'd purchased for herself and which had arrived by armed escort an hour earlier.

Thoughts of the problem writer disappeared as tears filled her eyes. Memories flooded her mind as she recalled the day in 1902 when Papa had gifted the blue and gold Imperial Egg to Grandmama. He'd had it made especially for his mother as an Easter gift, and she'd been delighted. To hold it now after so many years was a miracle. She ran a finger across the delicate gold work and smiled. Papa would be proud of her persistence and focus. Since it had been listed as one of the lost eggs, it had taken decades to track it down and much persuasion before the private collector had been willing to part with it. She didn't mind twisting arms, literally and figuratively, when necessary. Much of what had belonged to her family had been stolen. Some had been recovered and was now on display in museums around the world. Her goal for years had been to find the rest, those pieces like this egg that were listed as lost. She was taking back what was rightfully hers. If those private collectors cared to be reasonable, fine. If not, then she did what she had to.

Her attention was drawn away from the egg as she noticed a change outside her window. Carefully she returned it to the cabinet and walked to the doors leading out to a balcony off her office. She stepped outside and studied what moments before had been a clear night. Now a cool mist rolled toward her like a storm coming off the ocean. However, she was hundreds of miles away from the Pacific Ocean and three stories off the ground.

Closing her eyes, Sasha breathed in deeply, willing the sudden tension in her body to ease. Memories of the family and life long past faded as she centered herself in this moment. Her senses tingled in a way she hadn't experienced in decades, and the alarm normally brought on by the sight of such a mist eased. It had been a very long time since she'd witnessed the mist or any of the visitors it heralded. "Why are you here?"

From the murky depths a woman floated out, her features coming into focus as she moved closer to Sasha. She was tall, with pale hair and sky-blue eyes, the blue so alluring it had broken more than one heart. She walked with the grace of a dancer, which wasn't surprising considering she had once commanded the stage as a prima ballerina. She had lost none of the magic of body movement that had made her a star throughout the world. "He sent me to bring you a message."

The rat bastard. He knew that now, of all times, they couldn't take the risk. "I don't need you."

"Really? That's how it's going to be?"

"I don't need you."

Celine Hauer stepped close. She still smelled of flowers and sunshine, just as she had the first time Sasha had seen her on a summer night in Paris where she'd been a dancing vision in toe shoes and chiffon. That had been more than fifty years ago, and many things had changed. Now Celine wore leather pants, heeled boots, and a form-fitting shirt. The softness that had appealed to Sasha when they'd met was no longer evident. Neither was the flicker of emotional attraction that had kept them together for a decade. It had died right along with the softness. It was the second time she'd been seduced by words of love, only to discover the words were as hollow as the woman who spoke them.

"They're going to come for you."

Not such big news there. She'd been waiting for them or others like them for pretty much her entire life. "Tell me something I don't know. Something, oh, I don't know, useful?"

Celine's eyes darkened. "You don't understand. You never did. They're more powerful than you can imagine, and they will kill you. They will kill anyone who doesn't go along. She's leading them, and she will not stop until everyone kneels in front of her. She wants you, more than anyone, on your knees."

Celine was wrong. She could imagine how powerful they were. Their mistake was going to be underestimating her. Her mistake was to think she was the same young woman she'd been a hundred years ago. "I'll never bow to them. I will never kneel to her."

"Then you'll die."

Sasha squared her shoulders and locked eyes with Celine. "So bring flowers to my grave. Try to push out a tear or two. Make it look like you care."

Celine closed her eyes and shook her head. "Why? Things could be so different if only you would listen. Why won't you do the right thing? I've never truly understood why."

"You don't need to understand. Please, Celine, just go."

"Let me help." She almost sounded sincere. Sasha wasn't fool enough to fall for it a second time.

It was her turn to shake her head. "I don't need the kind of help you bring, and as long as you stand with them, you can't do a damn thing for me."

"I…"

"Please, just go."

This time Celine dipped her head and backed away until the shadows swallowed her. She wasn't sorry to see her go.

Sasha stood watching as the mist that had accompanied Celine disappeared, replaced by a curtain of darkness and a fresh breeze. A chilling thought raced through her mind as she lingered there, and she pulled her phone out of her pocket. She had someone on the inside, and for him to approach Celine, he had to think things were going south in a hurry.

She hit Rodney's name on the contacts list and listened to the ring. He picked up on the third ring. "How close are they?"

❖

Dee stared at the words and felt ice slide down her back. Threats weren't all that unheard of in her line of business. One of the things she'd learned after becoming successful was how some people fixate on authors. Look at what happened to Stephen King. His wife found some weirdo fan standing in the kitchen of their home. Other big names had similar stories. She'd gotten some very disturbing mail herself, and it wasn't anything she'd care to call fan mail because it was too creepy. She didn't want that kind of fan, and she sure didn't want to find anyone standing in her kitchen.

Maybe that's all this was now, except she couldn't quite wrap her head around that idea. All along, this project had felt different, and at the moment even more so. Whoever had sent the message might think they knew her, but they didn't. If they thought they were going to scare her, they were mistaken. If they thought the note would make her stop, wrong again. She was more determined than ever to forge ahead.

The only thing she'd done different lately was to get into serious research on Katrina and Imre. Leave it alone? Not going to happen. She refused to quit until she figured out exactly what their story meant and why someone would try to scare her off. Something was buried beneath the pictures and the names, and she wanted to know what it was. Besides sating her curiosity, it was bound to give her tons of material for her new book. The answer to the reason behind the threat had to be there as well. Energy surged through her despite the late or, rather, early hour. Midnight was long gone, and she wasn't even remotely tired.

Kicked back in her office chair, she stared at the results from her latest search. The more she pondered where to take it next, the more she wanted to call her best friend, Prima Moon. She'd so dig this latest twist and could probably give her some great insight. Prima was a real-deal psychic. People could be as skeptical as they wanted, but it wouldn't change a damn thing. She'd seen it up close and personal since she was a kid, and Prima was as genuine as it got.

It would be very cool if Prima could put her hands on the computer right now and give her a feel for the message. She would likely say it wasn't really her thing, but Dee was so convinced of her super powers that she figured Prima could pick up something just from the printed words. Of course, she could see the look on Prima's face about the time she asked her to give her something otherworldly off the computer. She'd roll her eyes and tell Dee to get out. And then she'd tell her something amazing. She always did.

Dee picked up her cell phone and stared at it. The time on the display showed 3:15. No, she wouldn't call. That would be all kinds of rude. The polite thing to do would be to wait until morning. Nothing here was critical enough for her to pull Prima out of bed. Yes, she'd call her in the morning. Then she hit her speed dial and let it ring. Her fingers tapping on the desk, she listened and waited.

"Really? Three in the flipping morning."

"Quarter after three, actually." Dee smiled. Prima was the only person she knew who'd make a joke when she was awakened in the middle of the night. Most people would assume the worst, and maybe if it had been anybody but Dee, she might have. They'd known each other a long time, and it would take a lot to surprise either one of them. It also wasn't the first time she'd called her in the wee hours.

"What's up?" She could hear the resignation in her voice. Prima knew that she was going to tell her something that would banish sleep for her, just as it was doing for Dee.

"I need you."

"Nice to be needed, but better to be needed after eight."

"We night owls need you at all times, not just banker's hours."

Prima laughed. "You are such a weirdo."

"My fans would be shocked to hear you say that. I prefer to classify myself as an eccentric writer."

"Indeed. Well, let your fans be subjected to your insomnia for a few decades, and we'll see if they still think you're a cute, eccentric writer or if they side with me on weirdo."

"See. You think I'm cute."

"You're a pain."

"Details. Details. I'll make you a latte." She had a fancy-dancy machine in her kitchen that made killer espresso. The perks of making a nicer-than-average living were nicer-than-average toys.

"This better be good."

"The latte?"

"Well, yeah, that too. But whatever has you scared, it better be good."

"Who says I'm scared?"

"And who do you think you're trying to bullshit?"

It was kind of dumb on her part to think she could bluff a psychic. "Touché."

"I'll be there in forty-five. Make sure that latte is hot and ready."

Dee ended the call and headed to the kitchen, where the espresso machine waited to perform its magic on dark roast, water, and milk. She had her orders.

Eli looked up from his laptop and smiled. "One shot fired."

He was prone to barge forward on any project, and that's exactly what he'd done tonight. Katrina was far more methodical and would have preferred taking time to find out what level of threat this person was going to be and then develop a plan to neutralize her. Eli liked to shoot first and ask questions later. Sometimes that was great. Sometimes it made a huge mess. It remained to be seen how this one would turn out.

"What did you do?" She was almost afraid to ask. His glee at his own action was evident, and she was afraid he might have gone overboard. That could cause all kinds of mayhem she didn't want to deal with right now.

"No grand gesture yet. A little warning, that's all. If she's like most humans, she'll get the drift and back off. They're such cowards. Shout boo at them, and they crawl right back under the covers."

That he'd exercised restraint was surprising. Eli was young and idealistic. In some respect those qualities were very admirable. She would need his youth and vigor for the task ahead. They were heading into a war many centuries in the making. It was internal as well as external. Most of the old ones were entrenched in the ways of the past, and though she believed she had them all on board at this point, many were truly comfortable in the shadows they didn't want to abandon. They were going to need a push to get them into the light, so to speak.

Others, like Katrina, wanted much more, and the enthusiasm of the up-and-comers like Eli would give them the power they needed to make the long overdue move. However, the young were so enthralled with the strength of their new reality, they believed themselves invincible and thought it would take only the strength of a vampire to win this war.

They were wrong. Eli was wrong. Humans were persistent, and a great many were far from powerless. She had never underestimated them and didn't plan to now. It was one of the reasons she'd survived, thrived, for as long as she had. For everything to work as she'd designed would require perfect moves. All the chess pieces had to be in place. No surprises and no missteps.

"Tell me exactly what you did."

He did, and while it was fairly low-key, she wasn't convinced it would be effective. Sometimes Eli didn't think through the big picture, and some day that would get him into trouble and she wouldn't be there to save him.

"She won't stop." Katrina had come up against the type before. They were determined and, worse, fascinated. This Dee person would see a message like the one Eli had sent her as a challenge and keep right on digging. In fact, she'd probably dig even harder. Yes, she was going to be a problem.

"She's smart enough to realize it's in her best interest to back off. She'll take heed."

He was confident about his threat's effectiveness, and she did like that about him, even if at a fundamental level he was wrong. Confidence came in handy if placed correctly. Somehow she would teach him the path he'd need to take in order to survive. Later, once her plan was fully realized, she'd need someone like Eli at her side. So far, they made a good team, and he was the lead contender for the job. It would take too much time to train someone else to step into his place. "Email me everything you have on her, and we'll talk later."

"It'll be fine, Boss. Trust me."

She held up her hand and shook her head. "I trust you, Eli. I never would have turned you if I had any doubts about your loyalty. It is a two-way street, though, and you must trust me as well. I have a great deal more experience with the fickle nature of humans. I will be the one to make the call on your writer." In terms of loyalty, he was true. But his misplaced confidence in his abilities had her worried.

His face paled, which was a feat given how pale his normal complexion was. Sunned wasn't a look any of them sported. "Boss, I've never trusted anyone more than you."

She waved her hand. Of course he did, though she was pleased to see that her words hit home. "Go now. Send me what you have. We'll talk tomorrow."

He studied her and seemed satisfied with whatever he saw in her face. She surmised it was her superiority. Regardless of the power and strength he'd embraced when he was brought into her world, he also understood that he would never match her. It was more than respect; it was reality. The smart ones figured that out quickly. The not-so-smart ones? They weren't around to attest to what had happened to them.

When her computer popped on, reflecting that a message had been received, she sat down and opened the zip file Eli had sent. The first folder held a picture of a handsome woman with short, spiky hair and eyes that shone with deep intelligence. An interesting face and one she would remember. She opened the next three folders and read with growing fascination. She wasn't just a run-of-the-mill writer. Much more to this one, and Eli had read her right. As had she. This woman was going to be a problem. Katrina continued to stare at the picture on the screen and smiled. True, the timing was bad, but sometimes challenges could lend a little spice.

Chapter Three

Patience had certainly been Sasha's greatest virtue since that horrible day in 1918. Even before then she'd been the calming influence in the eye of any storm. She'd refined that trait in the years since, and it had stood her well, like now. She had waited and waited for the moment to be right. Finally it was all coming together. It was time to mobilize the troops, so to speak, and to be at the ready.

She sat at her computer and opened the files that only she had access to. The first one pulled up a picture that still filled her with ice even after all these years. It brought back so many unwanted memories, filled with sights, sounds, and smells that made her want to throw up. If she lived to be a thousand years old, she would always taste the blood, smell the scent of weapons fire, and hear the screams of her family. Most of all she'd remember the scent of *her.*

Thousands of baths and showers and she'd never been able to wash that smell away. It clung to her in the same way tree sap would stick to her hand after picking up a broken branch. When this was all done, would she finally be free of her and that smell? Would she be able to remember and not want to retch?

Leaning back in her chair she read through file after file on her screen, even though she didn't need to. She could recite the words from memory. Easy enough to do, considering she'd written every single one. She'd never forget, and painful as it was, she wanted to remember every detail. When it got really quiet, she could hear the screams of her sisters and her little brother, like right now, and it brought tears to her eyes and a fire to her heart. Olga had been holding her hand, and she could still feel her fingers as they slipped away from hers.

SHERI LEWIS WOHL

A sound outside caught her attention, and she raised her head, banishing the sights, sounds, and smells of a long-ago night. For a second she thought her guest had returned and then realized it was nature doing its thing. She wiped the tears from her cheeks and smiled. The rain on the balcony roof sounded like a hundred elves tap-dancing. She loved the sound of rain. It reminded her of home. Kind of silly to think about it like that, considering this had been her home for more than twenty years. It didn't matter how many years she lived in one city. The Winter Palace continued to hold a special spot in her heart and was the one place she would always think of as home. She closed her eyes, transported back to a different piece of her past, when she could hear another rainstorm as drops fell outside in the elaborate gardens where they had run and played as children. She continued to smile even as the memories filled her with sadness for that which was lost forever. Since the day they'd been taken away, she hadn't stepped foot again in the palace, and really, what would be the point? She wasn't the girl who'd been dragged away screaming anymore. That girl had died a long time ago, and she couldn't go back.

She shouldn't feel sorry for herself. She lived, not quite in the way she would have liked to, but lived nonetheless. In the intervening years, she'd done more than survive; she'd excelled. No one who'd known her in her previous life would have ever guessed she'd become the driving force behind an international business, yet here she was. It also gave her an advantage. The one who'd preyed on the pretty young woman when she'd been the most vulnerable would never see her coming.

Her computer beeped and her eyes opened. Big surprise. Rodney was sending her another file. For a guy who lived off the grid, he certainly was adept at lurking about in it, albeit undetected. It had been a very long time since she'd been around a man she liked and admired as much as Rodney. She wished he'd come to work for her, because she could appreciate both his kind of skill and his kind of crazy. It was a dynamic combination.

His message was typical in its brevity: *We have another problem.*

❖

Prima was already in the kitchen with the espresso machine rolling by the time Dee made it out of bed. She could smell the heady scent of the fresh-ground coffee as she walked down the hallway. In the big picture it had been a quick night. She'd managed a whopping three hours of sleep and Prima four. Or at least four after she'd arrived at Dee's house. Nobody was a better sport than her smart and free-spirited friend. It was that spirit that allowed her to be open to forces that others pooh-poohed.

Dee was, relatively speaking, a down-to-earth kind of person. She believed in what she could see and touch. Even given the kind of research she did for her novels where she dived into the minds of some very warped people, she still believed that what made some of them so very bad wasn't paranormal; it was simply a combination of biology and choice. Some were victims of physiological damage, and some just flat-out chose to be evil. Even her desire to write the vampire book was rooted in reality. The folk legends that gave rise to the belief that vampires existed fascinated her. Vampires didn't exist, but that didn't mean they weren't fun to write about.

Given her strong belief in the quite real, she also believed in what Prima possessed. There was no rational explanation for what she could do, yet Dee totally bought in. The why of it was simple: she'd seen it be true more than once in a way that no one could figure out, and plenty of very educated people had tried. It was completely awesome, and she trusted Prima like no one else. It was the only piece of what she considered to be paranormal that she bought into.

"Okay, sister, so I slept on it for a little bit."

"And?" Dee took the latte that Prima handed her and sipped. It was good. Very good. Amazing what a good espresso drink could do for the soul.

Prima stared at her over the rim of her own mug. "First of all, I'm taking this machine home with me when I leave today."

Dee raised an eyebrow. "Okay..." She'd give Prima anything she wanted, and that included her new espresso machine. Besides, she handled it better than Dee did. Clearly it was meant for her.

"No okay about it. It's the price you pay for getting me up in the middle of the night, and that thing," she pointed to it, "is awesome. Secondly, I think you've touched on something pretty freaking weird, and for me to say that, you know it is far out there."

She didn't have to explain that concept to her. Prima was open to everything, and if it was odd to her, then all she could say was whoa.

It was scary and exciting all at the same time. The stuff she'd come across in her research, at least in her mind, was fascinating. Prima had mentioned it too as she'd showed her what she'd been working on before the message came through.

"It's related, don't you think?"

Dee continued to sip on the latte, the fragrance of good coffee and steamed milk filling the kitchen with a heavenly scent. She hated to think she was addicted to the stuff, but it was kind of hard to deny. She was a stereotypical Washingtonian who loved their coffee at the level of a true snob. She'd order a replacement machine this morning.

"I do think, as a matter of fact."

She felt immensely relieved. Until this second she hadn't realized how important it was to have Prima see the situation like she did. Dee was smart enough to acknowledge she was a storyteller by trade and it was easy for her to see a story where perhaps none existed. This didn't feel that way to her, and she was glad she wasn't the only one. "It has to be. Too coincidental. I mean, how much research have I done over the years, and I've never come across anything quite like this before. It's freaky."

"Actually," Prima set her cup down, "I do more than think. I know it's all related."

The look on Prima's face earlier this morning when she'd sat down at Dee's computer was classic shock. In fact her face had gone so pale she'd been worried her friend might pass out. She hadn't, but her words had chilled Dee. "You're in danger." It wasn't cool to have a psychic declare danger.

Now she studied her friend over the rim of her mug. "What did you mean earlier about me being in danger? You didn't really give me a very good explanation, and I was too tired at the time to push it. Now that we're both all rested up, time to explain"

Prima snorted. "Rested up? Are you serious? Like you're not tired now? How long did you sleep? Two? Three hours?"

A mirror wasn't necessary to confirm she looked like crap. It would take more than three hours of sleep to banish the black circles under her eyes or put some color back into her face. Her normally spiky hair that she found so entertaining was flattened against her skull in a not-so-flattering way. Her cool blue streaks looked more like she'd been playing in finger paint and smeared some in her hair. In short, she was about as far from hot as she could get. "Okay, yes, I could use some sleep, and trust me, I'm not arguing that point. The thing is, I'll get it, later. There will be plenty of time to snooze tonight. Right now, I want to know who or what is threatening me and why they care about some writer doing research. Am I getting punked by some computer hacker who finds it fun to screw with people?" It seemed a reasonable assumption. Who else could or would be able to track her searches? Had to be somebody sitting in a dark basement with lots of skills and no friends.

Prima set her mug down and shook her head. Her face showed signs of fatigue as well. Maybe dragging her out in the middle of the night wasn't her best idea. No maybe about it. "Not even close."

"So who?" It had to be somebody who had mad computer skills because it was the only thing that made sense. Well, sense in a strange way. She'd researched all sorts of odd and unsavory things as she'd worked on her novels. This was the first time that background work had resulted in a threat. The many faces of Imre and Katrina floated through her mind.

"You won't believe me."

She looked over at Prima and tilted her head. It was an unusual statement, given the fact that Prima knew Dee had no misgivings about her skills. "I don't know how you can say that to me. Of course I'll believe you. I always have, and I've never doubted a single thing you've shared with me."

Prima shook her head slowly. "All that's true, and on top of that, you've been my best friend. This time is different. The truth of what's going on here is outside your wheelhouse."

Well, that was insulting. She created fiction for a living. They'd known each other ever since she'd moved here. In fact, she was the first person Dee had met in Spokane and they'd been fast friends ever since. "Wheelhouse, my ass. What in the world are you talking about? I'm writing a damn vampire novel. Nothing's outside of my imagination at the moment."

Prima wrapped her hands around her mug again. Her eyes were downcast as she seemed to study the drink as if she'd never seen it before. Finally she brought her gaze up to meet Dee's. Her eyes were hard to read, something in them she'd never seen before. "It came to me in crazy detail the moment my fingertips touched your screen."

Ha. So she'd been wrong about Prima not being able to get anything psychic from the computer. "What came to you? And since when can you read something from a monitor?" Prima wasn't usually this cryptic, but what she said next was nothing Dee could have ever imagined.

"I didn't get a psychic reading from your monitor. It's what you showed me that brought it all into focus. My psychic abilities have nothing to do with this."

"Have nothing to do with what came into focus? You're driving me crazy. Just spit it out."

"The vampires."

"Yeah, yeah." Dee nodded. She'd never known Prima to be so vague or mysterious, at least not with her. "No big surprise there. Like I said, I'm writing a vampire novel. Always wanted to do something in the paranormal genre, and now I am. That's how I discovered all this stuff."

"No, Dee." Prima's words were slow and steady. She put her a hand on Dee's shoulder. "I'm not talking about your imagination and the characters you're crafting. I'm talking real walking, talking, blood-drinking vampires."

❖

Katrina was sitting in her chair thinking when Eli came in again. "Yes?" She was not happy about the interruption.

He was shaking his head. "Things in this century certainly aren't as easy as before. In the good old days, you could make a threat and they would listen. Humans, the ones that knew of us, had a high regard for our superiority and what we could do to them. Or for them, if they behaved. They were respectful. Now they're bloody insufferable." A look of disgust crossed his handsome features. "It gets on my nerves."

Sometimes his refusal to assimilate into the world as it moved and changed got on her nerves. For her, each passing year brought something new and interesting. Yes, it was easier in some ways back when there were no phones, no cars, and definitely no internet. It had also been dirty, smelly, and far less comfortable. Hunting in those days was less complicated, as was controlling the curious. She'd take more difficult if it allowed for clean and comfortable. This century suited her in so many ways.

She narrowed her eyes as she studied him. His expression was too tight, his words too clipped. "Are you trying in your indirect way to tell me you've failed?"

He kept his chin high, though a spark of something showed in his eyes. "I wouldn't call it a failure as much as the target neglecting to take us seriously. She's still digging into things."

She looked down at her nails as if bored, even though inside she was boiling. She expected nothing short of success from him. "In any language, that is the definition of failure."

"Fine," he snapped. "Then I fucking failed. The dumb bitch is plunging forward as if nothing happened. And, if that's not bad enough, she's calling in for help from knowledgeable friends."

This did surprise her, and she snapped her head up. How could this information have slipped by her? "I didn't know she was in that loop."

"Come on, Katrina. You know as well as I do that everybody's in that loop if they press hard enough."

He had a point, and it was possible. Even though the human population knowledgeable of their existence was small, she might knowingly or unknowingly be acquainted with one of those humans. "Who?"

He tossed a printout onto her desk with the picture of an attractive woman. "A psychic named Prima Moon."

Staring down at the picture, she blew out a long breath. "Prima Moon. God, where do they come up with such silly names?" As long as she'd been around, those who possessed the second sight also seemed to possess a propensity to give themselves what she was certain they believed were mystic names. Prima. Astral. Moonbeam. She could recite at least a dozen more off the top of her head. To Katrina they were trite and ridiculous.

"No argument there, dumb name. The problem is she's the real thing, Boss. A true psychic."

Actually, questioning her validity had never entered Katrina's mind because it wasn't important. She didn't care if any of them were real, and living a long life had taught her that many who called themselves psychics were authentic. Just because most of the human population wrote them off as fakes didn't mean they were. If this Prima Moon psychic bitch knew of the existence of the preternaturals, it was a moot point. What did concern her was that she might be talking to the writer. They didn't need to be comparing notes, especially right now, when so much was at stake. "We need to find her."

"Already on it. I sent the boys to that writer's house and to track down the psychic she's been talking to."

That didn't make her feel any better. "It's daylight." They were inside and protected from the rays of the sun that could burn their skin and turn them to dust if they were exposed to it for too long. They couldn't risk going out.

He nodded. "Noted. I meant, I'm sending the boys in at sunset."

"A lot of damage can be done by then."

"We'll get them."

"And if we don't?"

"We will."

"You're so sure."

"I am."

"Why?"

He gave her a smile that was far from jovial. In fact it was the opposite and accurately mirrored the darkness that passed for Eli's soul. That was precisely why he was the perfect lieutenant for a leader like her. No questions. No hesitation. No remorse.

He slapped his hands together and then pulled them far apart as he said, "Kaboom!"

For a moment she couldn't decipher his meaning. When she did, her smile matched his.

Chapter Four

A s much as Sasha wanted to head directly to Rodney's bat cave, the ordeal it would require was more than she wanted to deal with, even if she was old enough to tolerate some daylight. Unlike the youngsters, she wouldn't burst into immediate flame, though it had taken nearly a hundred years to become tolerant.

It wasn't comfortable. There was a big difference between tolerance and comfort, and she felt the sun five minutes after exposing herself to its rays. In another hundred years she'd be as tough as those they referred to as the Elders. They had evaded wooden stakes, silver, and holy water, the things none of them could survive, long enough that they developed short-term immunity to the touch of the sun. It could still destroy them. It just took a little longer.

Even when she was able to move about more freely, she was smart enough to know that it didn't change what she was or when she was at her most powerful. The night was their natural environment and where they garnered the powers that gave them supernatural strength. Yes, they could endure the daylight for extended periods of time once they matured, but in that golden light, their strength was suppressed, as if the universe was reminding them that they ruled only the darkness. The folktales about vampires and sunlight weren't a complete exaggeration.

Though she hated what she'd been turned into, she had vowed on the night that truth had been revealed to her that she would embrace her new reality and use it to accomplish two goals: make sure vampires never took over the day and take her revenge on the one who had done this to her.

The former had been in the works for decades, and she was pleased with how much they'd been able to accomplish. It surprised her that in the darkness, she found light in other souls who shared her goal. Not every vampire was evil. That realization did come as a shock. Sasha had grown up listening to stories of the rulers of the night and how they could drain the blood from little girls who didn't say prayers and wear their crosses. To find out many were like her—unwilling victims whose lives were forever altered—was empowering.

The latter had also been in the works for decades but, despite her dedicated research, had lacked one piece to make it a reality. Until recently, that is. It was exciting to finally feel the surge of adrenaline that came with her long-awaited discovery and to know that soon she would be looking into the face that had haunted her rest for far too much of her life.

She now anticipated that rest rather than dreaded it. Anyone who thought vampires lay deathlike in coffins was quite mistaken. She'd never slept in a coffin and never planned to. No, she spent her daylight hours prone in a luxury bed with blackout blinds and dreaming just as she'd done when she was a child. Granted, the subjects of her current dreams were quite different, but she still dreamt. And one face came to her over and over and over again. Before the month was out, she planned to wipe that visage not only from her dreams but from the world.

She would do it once the sun set and the darkness gave her the strength she would need to go up against an elder. Stupid wasn't her natural habitat, and she would be smart in order to be successful.

She didn't feel dread as she lay down this morning. It was anticipation. She closed her eyes and let the deep slumber take her away. For once, she didn't dream, and when she rose it was well past seven, the sun dipping behind the mountains to the west. From the small refrigerator designed to look like a rich piece of bedroom furniture, she took a plastic packet of blood. It was nasty cold. At the moment she didn't care. She emptied the packet and appreciated the rush of energy it brought. The pleasure she felt from doing something so abhorrent never ceased to amaze. She didn't want it to make her feel invincible, but there it was.

In the beginning, she had resisted the need to nourish herself with human blood to the point it had nearly destroyed her. Then she'd had an epiphany: if she ended her existence, revenge would never be hers. The need for that trumped everything else, and she gave in to the urges that were inescapable if she wanted to go forward. Modern times had made feeding the beast within much easier and less distasteful. She was never into killing needlessly, particularly not those who were innocent. Those who were not…well, she'd made peace with her God about them.

Her trademark since the moment she'd realized her existence was forever altered had been to protect the innocent. It was part of the philosophy that had led her to found a successful enterprise that brought her everything she needed to survive: wealth, sustenance, and unlimited resources. Her security firm gave her eyes-on all over the world. It gave her the resources to uncover the evil that lurked in more souls than most of the population wanted to believe. And those evil souls gave her what she needed to survive, their demise making the world a better place. Her business allowed her to protect the innocent.

Wealth, on the other hand, wasn't new to her. She'd been born into it and had taken for granted growing up a daughter of privilege. Actually, that didn't even describe it. She had been born into royalty and had enjoyed more than mere privilege during her early years. When it was all gone and she was reduced to total poverty, first in captivity and then after she'd been turned, she'd had to dig deep to find a strength she'd been unaware she even possessed. Growing up, she'd believed she existed in the real world, while in reality she'd been clueless. She never forgot those lessons, and thus finding her own success was both novel and fulfilling. She'd done it, and her father would be immensely proud. Through the years, that assurance had been a great source of comfort.

Now it was time to start making final plans, and Rodney was waiting to assist her. She dressed, as she always did, in unremarkable casual wear. Gone were the cloud-like dresses, strings of pearls, and large-brimmed hats festooned with flowers and ribbons. It was hard to even remember the young woman who took such delight in frills and flounces. Tonight she sported black jeans, leather boots, and a button-down shirt with the Imperial Investigations logo. Her hair pulled back into a ponytail that hung down her back, she looked nothing like the young woman she used to be. Probably a good thing. She could never be that woman again even if she wanted to.

An hour later, with her car parked a good mile away in a grove of aspens and pines, she ran through the darkened woods until she stood next to a hillside and a large, unremarkable tree.

❖

At Prima's words, Dee's hand had begun to shake, causing her latte to spill over the rim and a wave of creamy liquid to flow over her hands. Without giving it much thought she tried to set it on the table and missed. It crashed to the floor. She hadn't given the mess a second thought or moved to get a rag. She'd let it puddle on the hardwood laminate. Prima's words were a bad joke, right? Prima was messing with her and setting up a good laugh at her expense.

Prima had put off her barrage of questions as she'd dropped her hand from Dee's shoulder and left the kitchen, waving on her way out the door. "I've got classes to teach, but tell you what. Pull out a bottle of that marvelous wine you keep stashed away, and I'll be back at sevenish to finish this conversation. I've got a lot to tell you, and we'll need more time than I have right now."

After Prima had left, Dee finally gathered enough energy to clean up her mess. She took the roll of paper towels off the rack and began soaking up the liquid. The whole time she worked she'd thought about how fucking crazy it was that Prima would even float something like real-life vampires. She'd always believed in her friend and never for a second thought Prima anything but legit. This morning she started questioning her solid belief. In fact, the rest of the day she kept mulling over the comment Prima had made about real walking, talking, blood-drinking vampires. She wanted to believe Prima was simply playing her, but then she'd recall what she'd discovered about Imre and Katrina, and a chill washed over her.

Now, she and Prima sat at the kitchen table staring across at each other. Instead of holding hot mugs of lattes, they held stemless wineglasses filled with a luscious merlot. She'd pulled out one of her best bottles. No soft and gentle wine for this conversation. No, it called for bold, strong, and biting. If they were going to crazy-town, she was going to do it with something that tasted really good.

She took a big sip and let the alcohol fuel her with a buzz all the way to her fingertips. Yeah, she was ready now. They picked up where they'd left off in the morning. "Vampires? I've been trying to figure out all day if you're screwing with me. You're messing with me, right?"

Prima shook her head. "No, my beautiful friend, I am not." She picked up her own glass to take a sip. Hers was a little more delicate than the swig Dee had taken a second ago. She slowly set the glass back on the table, and her eyes met Dee's. "Vampires are real." The eyes that held hers were clear and steady.

"Come on. That's insane. They don't exist." She really wanted to hold on to the idea that the world was as she always believed it to be. Sure, she was writing a book with paranormal elements, but it was fiction pure and simple. Her pages were going to be filled with fantasy and make-believe.

"Really? Look deep inside, Dee, really deep. Tell me what you find there, and be honest. You truly believe it's impossible for vampires to exist?"

Dee didn't even hesitate. "Of course I do. Anybody in their right mind believes it. Creatures like that are nothing more than folklore, a way for those who didn't have the scientific knowledge we possess today to make sense of the world."

Prima picked up her glass once more and took another sip. A slight smile crossed her lips, and tiny wrinkles appeared around her eyes. It might have been the wine, or it might have been something else that made her eyes shine. "You mean kind of like there's no such thing as a real psychic?"

Clearly it was the something else. "That's different." Lame but the best she had.

"How? And how exactly?" Prima turned her glass in her hands, making the ruby liquid swirl and move inside it. It sent a sweet scent floating into the air. "There are no rational explanations for what I can do. Scientists have been trying for centuries to explain people like me. So far, nada."

She did have to think about that for a second, and then it hit her. "What you do is more like enhanced senses. You're not some supernatural creature. Just because science can't explain it doesn't mean it's not real, unlike a vampire, which is a creature of folklore. The living dead are not possible. In this day and age everyone knows that, and any good history buff can explain how the legends came to be."

"I disagree. Not about the basis for the folk legends. On that I agree, and there's validity to it. It's the difference between me and vampires that defies explanation by science or history. Think about it, Dee. In many ways a vampire isn't very different from me. It's just degrees on a spectrum." She held her hands about two feet apart. "I happen to have what my grandma always called second sight. A vampire is simply farther along the spectrum."

She wasn't buying it. Not with her whole heart anyway. "Oh, come on. You can't possibly believe in vampires. What's next, werewolves?" Despite her protests, the names Imre and Katrina kept echoing in the back of her mind.

"They exist," Prima said in the same calm voice. It was like she was explaining a simple concept to a particularly dense student.

Dee found it surprising that her friend was this adamant. It was impossible, flat-out. No other way to explain it. She'd been a researcher since she started writing in middle school. While her most recent research had turned up a few anomalies in the life and lack of death in a few names, somewhere buried in there had to be a rational explanation. It certainly wasn't that those names belonged to vampires. All she had to do was dig in deeper, and she'd find the answer.

"Legend," she said simply as Prima said nothing while staring across the table at her. "What?" she finally asked.

Prima reached across the table and took her hands. "Look into my eyes and tell me if you think I'm not telling you the truth, if I'm trying to sell you a line of crap."

Regardless of what else she might think, Prima wasn't the kind to mess with her. It wasn't her style. She was gentle and kind and gifted. Lying wasn't in her DNA. She didn't play games. Dee pulled her hands free and put both of them around her glass. She turned it between her hands a dozen times before she looked back over at Prima. She sighed and said, "I believe you believe what you're telling me."

Prima patted her hand. "I can prove it to you."

She believed that Prima believed what she was saying. Prove it to her? Not likely. "Bullshit."

A smile turned up the corners of Prima's mouth, and a mischievous look glinted from her eyes. "Get ready for your world to be rocked."

❖

Katrina didn't like waiting, and so she didn't. Though she left the continuing problem of the psychic and the writer in Eli's capable hands, she opted to keep her own hand on the pulse of Sasha Rudin. She'd been waiting a very long time to pin her down, and now that she knew her name and where she was, things were going to be made right that should have been years ago.

Personal insult was not something Katrina tolerated, ever. Sasha—the name tasted like poison on her tongue—had delivered the one and only unanswered insult of her long life. Soon, she would be able to look that bitch in the face and make her pay.

At one level, it gave her a rush of excitement that even draining a gorgeous woman couldn't provide. This was going to be so much sweeter. Time and frustration were very effective stimulants. This was personal, and so too would be Sasha's death. She couldn't wait to grip her around the neck and stare into her eyes as she ended her life.

Closing her eyes, Katrina easily called up that face. She'd been enthralled by many women over the years. Beautiful, exotic, alluring women. No one had ever captured her heart except one, and she had been nothing like the others. She'd been quiet and gentle and lovely. She had made Katrina a believer in love.

That had been her mistake, for that lovely woman who stole her heart in turn had betrayed her. No one knew. No one ever would. She would carry that secret forever, and it would also fester year after year. She embraced that rage because it sustained her, almost.

She ran her hands over her face and on this rare occasion acknowledged the truth. As much as she wanted to hate Sasha completely, she never could. Even after all this time and heartache, she still longed to hold her and kiss her, and pass the night with passion as they had in the mansion's gardens at Tobolsk. Katrina shook off the moment. It had been a year of passion and love that would never come again. Betrayal had that effect. Now, death would come calling without a single kiss.

She shook out her hands as if that would banish any lingering memories and dropped them to the keyboard. Her fingers were flying across the keyboard when Eli burst through her door unannounced. As much as she appreciated his good work, at times she could cheerfully put a stake through his heart. She didn't only because the unshakable loyalty of those like Eli occurred rarely. Though she wouldn't tell him, she valued him.

"Closed doors mean knock before entering."

"Yeah, yeah." She wondered when he'd reverted to such sloppy speech. She had taken great pains to turn him into the model of a high-born assistant. Her education plan had taken him all over the world to mix with those of the highest pedigree. For the most part, her training had been highly successful, and the farm-boy beginnings had been shed like the skin of a snake. It struck her now that in recent years he sounded more like the kid from a public high school that he'd actually been. She didn't like it. They would talk about it once this was behind them. She'd worked too hard on making him over to have him revert to that boy on the tractor.

"The word is 'yes,' not 'yeah.'" She lifted her hands from the keyboard and leaned back in her chair, gazing at him. "Tell me."

He was frowning. "She's gone. The writer, she's gone."

She couldn't have heard him correctly. To have lost track of the woman already was unthinkable. "No."

"Yes." At least he paid attention to her rebuke and was once again speaking correctly. "By the time the boys arrived, the house was empty."

Fury roiled inside her. This wasn't good. The woman had stumbled onto information she had no business possessing, and it was imperative that they shut her down before she did damage with it. The "boys," as they all referred to them, were twin brothers turned about a hundred and fifty years ago. They'd been big, tough, and mean as humans. Dumb as rocks too. As vampires…well, the enhancements had made them two of her most prized possessions. They always acted as directed. They never questioned. They always delivered results. At least they did until tonight. "This is not acceptable."

"Before you go into crazy mode…"

She whirled on him. How dare he say such a thing to her! Her expression would chill even the hardiest, but it didn't seem to faze him, which made her even angrier. In fact, a smile played at the corners of his lips. His gall was unbelievable. Some day he was going to take it too far. Her fingers curled until they drew blood in her palms.

He held up a hand, and his smile disappeared as his expression turned serious. "I'm sorry. I didn't mean to say crazy. Let me explain.

We have a plan and it'll work. Trust me. Not only that..." He hurried on before she could say anything. "I have another surprise for you."

"I'm not in the mood for any more of your surprises. So far, I'm less than impressed. This night is turning into a disaster that we can ill afford."

This time the wattage of his smile was sunshine bright. "You're going to love this one."

"Impress me, then."

"We found her."

CHAPTER FIVE

S asha simply waited next to the massive tree with her hands folded in front of her. Soon enough, as she knew it would, the tree began to move. Well, not exactly the tree. More like the base of the tree began to shift until a door appeared beside it. Expertly set into the ground next to the pine, it opened to reveal a set of dimly lit descending steps. In all her long years, this was the most interesting abode she had ever seen, and every time she came here it made her smile. Who would even think of something like this? Even though she knew it was here, she was still amazed every time at how it blended into the landscape and kept its existence a secret.

If only they'd had something like this when it all went south in Russia, her family might have survived. And she might have died an old woman decades ago.

The wind blew, and drops of rain began to kiss her face. June in this area meant anything goes. It could be eighty with clear blue skies or fifty with pouring rain. Unpredictable was a fact of life, and one she didn't mind. It reminded her of home, where spring could be elusive and winter could be a real bitch, and she suspected it had a lot to do with why she'd stayed here longer than was her style. Today Mother Nature was flexing her muscles. Instead of encouraging the hope of sunny swims in the lake, it was suggesting light jackets and umbrellas.

For her, the gentle wind and the kiss of the raindrops were refreshing. She could remember frolicking in rainstorms with her sisters until their outerwear was soaked through and the servants herded them back inside. They'd sit in front of the fire drying out while sipping fragrant tea and eating sweet, buttery biscuits. Those had been magical, wonderful times. Tonight she was herding herself inside, but being alone didn't lessen the smile that the memories brought to her lips.

The secret door widened enough for her to step in, and as she moved downward, it closed silently behind her. The lights stayed bright enough for her to descend safely, not that she required the assistance. One of the perks of her altered state was that she could move easily in the most complete darkness. For one who'd been afraid of the dark as a child, it was a welcome skill.

At the bottom of the steps in a space big enough for three or four people stood yet another door—large and made of impenetrable gray steel. More than once she'd wondered how exactly the maker got this massive door down here. Then again, with the magic she'd seen Rodney wield, she shouldn't be surprised he could get a door this size in a hidden space.

As she'd done aboveground, she stood in front of the door and waited. The cameras, cleverly concealed both outside and here at the landing, made sure no one passed through uninvited. She had a standing invitation to this place, which was not to be confused with free access. No, each and every person who passed through this door did so only with specific permission every single time. So far it had never been denied. In a moment, she heard a faint click, and the door popped open. She stepped through, permission granted.

The room beyond the steel door was filled with light and warmth, in direct contrast to the severe outer vestibule. She took off her coat and hung it on the hook to the right of the door. Next she slipped off the shoulder holster the well-tailored coat hid and hung it on a second hook right next to her coat. In the truest sense of the word, this was a safe place where she didn't need handguns loaded with custom silver bullets.

"About time you got here, sister."

Rodney Cornell rounded a corner chomping on a carrot and looking as he always did—tall, lean, and hairy. The last part never failed to stop her, because with his waist-length brown hair and the shaggy beard that reached his chest, he reminded her of someone from another time and place. His personality, on the other hand, wasn't even close to that ghost of the past, and that's what made it easy to forget the uncanny resemblance. For a guy who made it his mission to be a phantom in every sense of the word, he was upbeat and caring. Well, to be more precise, he was upbeat and caring to those he allowed into his world, and to the best of her knowledge, those people, like herself, were quite small in number. Sasha was grateful to be one of them.

Her inclusion in his circle was entirely accidental. She'd saved his life, and their deep connection had been born from that moment in time. It was a strange partnership: one off-the-grid computer genius and one vampire. Yet, it worked for them, and no one in the world made her feel as safe as Rodney did. Any other human, that is. Most of the vampires in her particular orbit were relatively trustworthy, although she'd be hard-pressed to say they all were. She had her doubts about a few of them.

"Had some things to take care of. More stuff going on. I'm here now."

He chomped on the carrot for a second as he nodded. "Yeah, got that one, Sherlock. Was gonna reach out to you again, tell you to get your ass out here, but as usual, you beat me to it. Someday you're gonna have to teach me that trick. You know what I'm sayin'?"

That trick was something she would never share with him. Just as doctors lived by a "do no harm" rule, she lived by the "turn no human" rule. Not once in all her years had she turned a single soul. Had she killed anyone? Yes. She had no lingering guilt over most, and only a very few had left black marks on her soul.

"What else have you picked up since we talked?" She left the entryway and followed him back the way he'd come. This place was amazing, and from topside no one would have even the slightest hint of its existence. From the vestibule-type entry where the big steel door dominated, the bat-cave, as Rodney referred to it, opened up into a massive underground kingdom. He'd given her the grand tour on her first visit. She'd been impressed then and wasn't any less impressed now with its three bedrooms, a huge bathroom, a stainless-steel kitchen any chef would love, and a comfortable great room area. The shining jewel of the great room was the command center that NASA would covet. Rodney could rule the world from that place.

In many ways he did.

He plopped into the worn chair that squeaked in protest and whirled toward the wall of monitors. "Besides the powers-that-be mobilizing, there's unease everywhere, sister."

"It's starting."

His hands were flying over the keyboard, and pictures flitted across the multiple screens. His vision was almost vampiric, as she knew he was taking it all in as quickly as she was. She wouldn't ever need to turn him; he already possessed super powers. "The last week has been bubbling."

None of this really surprised her. It had been coming for decades, if not centuries. "They're getting themselves into position."

He leaned back in his chair and turned his face toward hers. "I think they're doing more than getting into position."

His words made the hair stand up on the back of her neck. "What do you mean?"

One eyebrow came up. "Don't tell me you missed the biggie? That's not like you, Sash."

Now her stomach dropped. "Missed what? Don't screw with me, Rodney."

"Weldon Kramer went down last week." Those words rendered her speechless. "You know what that means." He wasn't asking her a question.

She answered him anyway. "They're coming after me."

"You really think this is a good idea?" Dee was in the passenger's seat of Prima's compact all-wheel-drive car, staring out the window at the rain beginning to fall.

"What's a little rain?"

"Not the rain as much as the drinking wine and then driving halfway to Canada."

Prima laughed. "I'm pretty sure one small glass of wine two hours ago before we ate dinner won't send us crashing into a ditch, and we're not going anywhere close to Canada."

Perhaps she'd exaggerated a little, though they were heading north quite a ways. As for the wine? She had a point. Not only were the glasses of wine they'd had pretty small, but they'd both been hungry enough to plow through big plates of pasta, salad, and garlic bread. She didn't feel even a hint of the alcohol. Still, as she gazed at the rain and the rapidly disappearing lights of the city, unease fluttered in her stomach. Staying at the house would have been a far better idea than their current endeavor.

"I know. It's just…"

Prima patted her hand. "Trust me on this one. You're going to love this twist."

"I still think you're full of it."

"Really? I hear some doubt creeping into your voice."

"Vampires don't exist." She was holding onto that belief like a drowning woman clutching a life preserver. *Imre. Katrina.*

"You're kind of disappointing me here, Dee. You creative types are supposed to have big open minds. How come yours is suddenly closed like a steel trap?"

As a humanities torchbearer she had always considered herself very open-minded. When Prima threw out the V-word, she'd be lying if she said her mind hadn't closed. She liked folktales as much as the next person but kept circling back to the idea they were based on realities that people of the time didn't understand. Vampires didn't just rise from the grave. Vampires didn't rise at all because they simply didn't exist.

"I'm as open as they get," she said. Sounded a little hollow even to her.

"Not from where I'm sitting."

"Just keep your eyes on the road."

Prima laughed. "Rodney's going to love you."

"Rodney?"

"Our host for the night and one of my best friends. I met him the second day I moved here with my family, when I was in the third grade. We've been pals ever since."

Dee was a little jealous. Her family had moved constantly, as her father was a career diplomat. In many ways it had been exciting and cool to live all over the world and even graduate from the American high school in Venezuela. That early nomadic lifestyle experience had provided her with so much material for her novels, and she was certain it had helped propel her to success. It also played into her desire to write the very different vampire novel. Every culture they lived in had its own version of the vampire myth, and it gave her tons of material to work with.

At the same time, such a background had caused her to be very insular. She'd made friends and still had them, but she didn't have the tight connection of someone she'd gone through all stages of life with. Her friends were the ones she'd spend two or three years hanging with before moving to another place, another country, and another life. It would be amazing to have a friendship that spanned decades. It was also why she still lived in Spokane. She'd come here to attend Eastern Washington University and stayed after graduation. It was the longest she'd ever lived in one place, which made it feel like home. With enough money to live anywhere in the world, she'd chosen this eastern Washington city.

"Your friend Rodney's going to prove that vampires exist?"

"Oh, he so is."

"We'll see."

She doubted it, despite Prima's supreme confidence. For half an hour they rode in companionable silence. When Prima turned the car off the highway onto a tree-lined dirt road, her doubts about this adventure surged right back up. If they didn't get stuck on the rutted road that was turning into mud, she'd be surprised. Actually, what surprised her more was when Prima made another turn that took them to a sort of makeshift parking area where one vehicle already sat dark and empty.

"What are we doing here?" Her previous opinion of a crazy trip was now fully reinforced.

Prima was out of the car already and had opened the back door to retrieve her jacket. "We have to walk from here. Might want to pull up your hood, or your fancy do is going to get wet."

Dee got out and looked around. Raindrops kissed her face, and a cool breeze made her shiver. She couldn't see much. It was inky dark, with only a bit of moon to cut through the darkness and the light rain. "Are you nuts? We'll kill ourselves out here." The getting-wet part didn't much bother her. The tripping and falling on her face did.

"Now you know why I told you to wear your boots."

"Seriously, Prima, this is insane."

Prima came around the car, handing her the jacket she'd put in the back seat earlier. "Put this on, zip up, and let's go. Moonlight's wasting."

"We'll get lost." She pulled up the hood and was immediately grateful for the warmth and protection from the rain, which was picking up as they stood there talking.

"No, we won't."

"It's too dark."

"No, it's not." Prima held out a headlamp, and only then did she notice that Prima already wore one on her head.

"This is crazy," she muttered as she pulled the hood back so she could put the headlamp on.

"You're overusing that word, and for a writer…shame on you. Don't be a big baby. Now, suck it up, buttercup. Let's go." Prima took off at a jog.

Dee blew out a breath and followed her, the light on her head bouncing off the thick trees that swallowed them as they moved farther and farther away from the car.

"What did you just say?" Katrina didn't have to ask who *her* was and was certain she'd heard him wrong. She'd been searching for her for almost a century. The fact that she hadn't been able to track her created an angst that never got better. She had been sensing lately that they were closing in on her and had been optimistic they were going to find her, but to actually hear him say it was like a dream.

Eli's smile continued to grow. "We pinpointed her location."

"Where?" They already had plans in motion, and while she couldn't afford distractions, she would make an exception.

"Well, that's the interesting part. She's just across the mountains. Same place the boys are currently working."

Spokane. What would she be doing there? That didn't make sense. She would have sensed if they were that close to each other. After all, she was her maker, and that kind of bond was special. Besides, it was an unlikely place to live, unlike Katrina's choice of Seattle. That city made sense for many reasons. Its climate was nice, while frequently overcast, giving her more freedom to move about. It was a major city, providing every resource she could possibly need. The plan was to hit all the major cities, Seattle being the first because Katrina would lead the charge. Everyone in the Consortium followed her lead, even the old ones. She'd earned the right to be in charge and didn't plan to ever give it up.

If what Eli was telling her was true, it might call for a slight change in strategy. That move would be easy enough to justify for a couple of reasons. First, Spokane was the location for the home office of Imperial Investigations. That was important because Imperial was a front for a counteroffensive of vampires that had to be eliminated. No one had been able to get close to the head of the corporation for years. Every time they did, the company moved, forcing Katrina to start over. If they worked quickly now, Imperial wouldn't have time to evade them. She would be able to take them all down quick and easy.

Spokane would also be a good starting point because of the air force base. They already had some strategically placed operatives on their payroll, and it would provide her with access to a major military operation. The value a fleet of jets could provide was immeasurable.

The more she thought about it, the more perfect it seemed. They could make the first shot from the eastern Washington city, and it would definitely be a shot heard around the world. From there, they could begin to topple the humans once and for all, and she would take her rightful place as ruler. Best of all, she'd finally take her long-overdue revenge.

"Where in Spokane?"

"She's Imperial."

Katrina's head snapped up. She stared at him. "That can't be. We would have known before this if she was at the helm."

"Once we took Kramer out of the mix, we put all our resources on Imperial and hit pay dirt. I was able to turn two of her closest agents, and trust me," he laid two eight-by-ten photographs on the desk, "it's her."

Katrina felt like someone had punched her in the stomach. The face that stared back at her was the one from her dreams. She was as lovely as the first day she'd seen her, and the sight made her heart beat faster. How she wanted to hate her, and in so many ways she did. Why then couldn't she ever shake the longing? No one of her immense power should ever be brought to her knees by a little girl. No, that girl would be brought to her knees.

She picked up one of the photographs and stared at it. All these years and she had been hiding in plain sight the entire time. Her hand trembled. If Eli hadn't been here, she would have started screaming and breaking everything she could get her hands on. Instead, she looked up at him and said, "Send the boys to the Imperial headquarters for her and tell them not to kill her. She's mine."

Chapter Six

Sasha paced and thought about what Rodney had just shown her, irrefutable proof that her biggest competitor had been taken down—and without her knowing about it until now. It worried her for one really big reason: it signaled how close they were getting to her. She'd been watching for this since the day she started the firm. Kramer was very much human but a man with skills that verged on preternatural. He had to have help of the vampire variety to even come close to competing with Imperial. They'd been locked in a competitive battle for decades, and she liked to believe she'd been a step ahead of him, something that the very macho Kramer had to have hated. In the back of her mind, she'd always wondered if they'd use him to find her. If he was willing to make a deal with the devil, it made sense that the Consortium could seize control of a powerful company like Kramer's and then watch to see what her next move would be. He would make that kind of deal if it meant he could one-up her.

It concerned her too because her own staff had failed to alert her, which gave her a chill that was glacial. It wasn't because they weren't aware of Kramer's death. She had handpicked every person in her company and was well aware of their capabilities. His death would not go unnoticed. Maybe it could slide by one or two, but never all of them. That said, it meant that information had been willfully withheld from her.

The million-dollar question of course was why, and she was terribly afraid she knew the answer. It wasn't a good one.

"You okay?" Rodney's voice held a note of concern.

For a second she thought about lying. It was her problem, and an embarrassing one at that. No need to advertise her shortcoming at knowing her own organization. Then again, this was Rodney. "Not really."

He stared at her, his surprise clear in his face. "You didn't know."

She shook her head. "No."

"You realized this was a possibility. A probability really."

He was right. They'd discussed it many times over the years as they played out various scenarios. This was one of the most likely, and they had discussed all the different roads they would take if it did. "Of course."

He nodded. "Still sucks." He popped another carrot into his mouth. Rodney got that one right. "Indeed it does."

He crunched the carrot and swallowed. "So what next?"

It didn't take a lot of thought on her part. "First thing is to uncover the traitor in my own organization. Somebody knew about Kramer, probably even before he was hit. That same somebody…"

"Could be somebodies," Rodney threw in.

She nodded. "We have to uncover whoever's responsible for this gross lapse in my corporation and deal with them as soon as possible. Who knows what kind of intel has already been leaked."

Rodney was nodding with gusto. "Exactly my thought, and I started tracing before you even got here."

Sasha studied him. "You breached my security?"

A sheepish smile crossed his face. "Well, yeah, it's kinda what I do, you know?"

"Mine?" She raised a single eyebrow. Her networks should be foolproof. She paid a lot of money to the best and the brightest. If Rodney was able to get into her networks, she needed new people. Like the Rodney kind of people.

He leaned back in his chair and let the smile grow. He tossed a carrot into the air, let it fall into his mouth, and crunched loudly. If she lived with this guy, those carrots would have to go. "Think about all the lessons you've taught me since we met. You have given me a whole new way to look at the world. I learned to flex my muscles, and I'm not talking about the guns." He held up his arms in a classic weightlifter pose. "I flexed my sleuthing muscles, and that, my beautiful friend, is return on investment."

"By breaching my security?" It seemed like a messed-up way to return what he was making sound like a huge favor. Not to mention it pissed her off to discover someone could blow through her firewalls and nobody had noticed. Her highly paid techs should at least be on a par with Rodney.

"To quote you, indeed."

She lowered herself into a chair next to him and stared at the screens anchored to the wall. She wanted to be pissed off, but she was more intrigued. With her hands steepled beneath her chin, she turned her face to him. "Educate me."

The third time Dee stumbled over a downed pine, she swore loudly. This was the dumbest thing she'd ever done, and she couldn't believe she'd let Prima talk her into this fairy-dance traipse through the dark woods. She wasn't exactly a ballerina on flat ground. This uneven, brush-strewn terrain was impossible. As she muttered obscenities, Prima turned to look at her, and in the beam of Dee's headlight, she could see her getting ready to make a comment. She stopped her.

"If you say 'suck it up, buttercup' again, I swear to God I will take you out right here, right now."

Prima laughed. Actually laughed. Bitch. It was all she could do not to throttle her. Not that she actually would. Despite writing books filled with violence, Dee was pretty much a believer in peace at all costs. So, she wouldn't throttle her, but at the very least she wanted to stomp her feet and throw a tantrum.

"I wasn't going to say that at all. What I planned to say is that we're here."

Now that was a load of crap if she'd ever heard it. They'd been doing a sort of run/walk for at least thirty minutes and were now in the middle of what? Hell and gone? All that was around them were trees and more trees. It was clear to her Prima was having some fun at her expense.

"Right, and he lives in a tree house?" Her head went up as the light of her headlamp illuminated the massive trunk of the pine tree in front of them. Rain pelted her in the eyes, and she blinked to try to keep her vision clear. She didn't see anything remotely resembling a tree house. There was a pretty good-sized hill behind all the trees, and if Prima thought for one second she was climbing that thing, she was dead wrong.

Prima shrugged. "In a manner of speaking, yes, though I would say Rodney's abode is more bunker than tree house. In fact, I'd call it more a tree neighbor."

"What in the world are you talking about?" At this point, she wanted to go back to the car and return home, where a nice, warm sofa would feel fantastic on her aching legs. Hiking wasn't usually her gig, even in daylight. Definitely not her thing at night in a rainstorm that was picking up speed. It was cool, wet, and smelly.

This time Prima grinned. "Once more, I have to say suck…"

"Don't. You. Dare."

Prima made a zipping motion across her mouth. "Fine, but give it a minute, and I promise it'll be worth your while. Ready for a little magic?"

A big raindrop plopped right in the middle of her forehead. She swiped it away. "Sure, right along with your so-called vampires. Why not? Bring it on, big, bad psychic. Then maybe we can go home before we get soaked."

"Your wish is my command." Still smiling broadly, Prima touched the bark of the big tree and then stepped back.

"Retreating so quickly? Giving up so soon on showing me the magic? Or did you just get a splinter?" Dee was glad to see Prima was admitting defeat, although the thought of the trek back to the car didn't exactly thrill her despite how ready she was to go home. She had started to turn back when the ground next to the tree began to move. What the hell? Dee swung her head around and directed her light to the moving earth. She swore softly again. "Son of a bitch."

Prima waved a hand toward steps that appeared like the magic she'd promised. A moment before there had been nothing but wild grass and brush in the same spot. "I told you I had some surprises in store."

"Who in their right mind builds a staircase in a place like this? What's the tree, a doorbell?" It was hard to believe even though she was seeing it.

"Oh, sister, this is just the beginning, and yes, the tree is a doorbell of sorts. A little sensor's hidden beneath the part. You just have to know where to touch."

She was done. Prima had her, as the saying went, hook, line, and sinker. All thoughts of returning to the car vanished, and she didn't hesitate to follow Prima down the rabbit hole that, as it turned out, wasn't a rabbit hole at all, but a cleverly disguised entry into some kind of underground bunker. It was simply the most interesting thing she had ever seen. Prima might be screwing with her over the vampire thing, but even if she was, this made up for it.

Resting his back against a closed steel door, a man, a very large man, was waiting for them at the base of the stairs. His long hair and beard made him look like one of those reality-television personalities. He was pale, though more of a shade that seemed to suggest he spent the majority of his time down here as opposed to being a creature of the night. Then again, perhaps this is what Prima meant when she said she was going to introduce her to vampires.

"If it isn't the magnificent Prima, finally gracing me with her presence. I was beginning to think you were never going to come back for a visit. I was getting very sad."

"Oh, Rodney, you know I'd never snub you." Prima's voice held a hint of a smile, and Dee sensed there was something special about this man. Interesting indeed. As long as she'd known Prima, she'd never heard her use that tone before.

"Who's your most intriguing pal? Someone special, I presume." His gaze only briefly swept over Dee before settling back on Prima. She usually had a pretty good read on people, and it was telling her these two were drawn to each other. Interesting that Prima had never mentioned him before.

Prima nodded and smiled. "This is Dee Arkin, the one and only *New York Times* best-selling author. I've told you about her." His face took on a darkened expression that told Dee he wasn't happy with this particular introduction. It was a little insulting, and his next words brought that feeling home. "Why would you bring her here? You know—"

Prima held up her hand. "She's not like that."

"If she's an *NYT* bestseller, she's most certainly like that."

"Like what?" She was already insulted by his clear objection to her presence. It was equally irritating to be talked about like she wasn't even there.

His eyes swept over her again, only this time with clear disdain. "Establishment."

Prima put a hand on his arm, and he didn't shrug it off. "Laughing all the way to the bank, you mean. She's not establishment. She's creative and brave and a powerful voice. Don't lump her in with the assholes. And listen up, Mr. R. She's got some mad skills, and that's why we're here. She needs to know."

Prima didn't elaborate on that last point.

"Why?" He wasn't giving any ground. Usually people loved to meet her, which could be a bit overwhelming for someone who wasn't that social. She was beginning to get pissed off that he was treating her like she was a carrier for the plague.

"Trust me, she needs to know."

"You swear on your life she's okay?" Dee had the distinct impression he wasn't making a theoretical statement.

"I do." Prima's response was laser fast.

He studied her face and she didn't blink. Finally, he nodded. "Okay."

"Okay." She smiled. "Let's do this."

"You picked the perfect night to open a mind."

"What do you mean?" Prima tilted her head as she looked at him.

Rodney winked and then clicked a button on a small device that until now Dee hadn't even noticed he was holding. The steel door behind slid open to reveal yet another surprise.

Katrina settled into the fine leather seat and held out her hand. A young woman dressed in a short skirt, a tight blouse, and four-inch heels lowered a silver tray that held a single crystal glass. As she leaned into Katrina, her cleavage was on full display, just as she liked. On longer trips, she would enjoy more than just the view, but not now. Not quite enough time between takeoff and landing to make it worthwhile.

She picked up the glass from the tray and studied the deep-crimson blood inside. It was fresh and warm, and exactly what she needed at this moment. It was always better when blood was taken directly from the source, although it wasn't always possible. This was the next best thing. Besides time being an issue, she didn't want to soil her clothing. She wanted nothing to slow down this journey, including the need to clean up.

The plane took off smoothly, and she smiled as she sipped from the glass and inhaled the heady scent. An excellent choice. There was much to be said about modern conveniences like private planes. In the past this trip would have taken many hours to accomplish. Not any longer. Her plane was comfortable and fast, with no TSA security to slow her down. They would be on the ground in Spokane in less than an hour.

Eli sat at a small table, his fingers flying across his laptop. It was almost as if he and the machine were one. Wherever one saw Eli, they also saw a laptop, as well as the requisite smartphone and watch. Since the moment they left he'd been in constant communication with the boys. When he frowned, an uncomfortable feeling assailed her. "What is it now?"

"The boys went to Imperial."

"They have her, correct?" How she would have liked to have been there with the boys to see her shock and surprise.

"No. They do not. They said she was walking out of the building, took a call, and cleared out fast."

"Tell me the idiots followed her."

Again he frowned. "No, they believe they might have been compromised and didn't want to follow on the off chance she didn't see them."

"Then take care of it, you imbecile." These continual failures, however small, were problematic. Was she going to have to take care of everything herself?

His eyes glittered, as they always did when she insulted him. He also stayed quiet, as he always did. Smart on his part. He knew better than to respond. After a brief silence, he asked, "The boys?"

She thought about that for a moment. Perhaps they were correct and had indeed been compromised. Then again, if they hadn't, they could still be useful. "Tell them to get out of there for now. They can go back when no one's around."

Another nice thing about an assistant who'd been by her side for decades—she didn't have to go into great detail. He would know what she wanted him to do and how to accomplish it.

He looked at her and nodded. "Got it." His attention returned to the array of electronics spread out on the table.

Leaning back in her chair, she put her feet up on another of the plush leather seats and finished off the glass of blood as she contemplated what their next move would be. Flushing her out would be the fun part. Taking her down would be pure ecstasy. Talk about timing. She'd nailed this one. Everything was coming together with perfection.

CHAPTER SEVEN

Sasha was so pissed off by the time Rodney finished briefing her on his research that she was ready to kill and probably would. She barely glanced up at the monitor when it gave off a signal that alerted him to the presence of a new visitor. He gave a short laugh and muttered, "I'll be damned," but they barely registered. After he went to greet this same visitor in the vestibule area, she didn't move. Her mind was whirling with the new knowledge she'd gained and what to do about it.

Granted, she'd been expecting this surge for power from the Consortium for a long time. The handwriting had been on the wall for years, which is why they'd been preparing, and now the time had arrived. She was ready for whatever they came with. What she hadn't been expecting was the knife plunged into her own back. Damn it, but she'd treated those two like her own family, and they did this to her? She'd played this game before, been the victim one time too many, and she'd vowed to keep her circle free of treachery. So much for her skill at reading the hearts and souls of her people. But now she could do something about it. Heads were going to roll, literally.

The issue more pressing than cleaning her own house was being in the right place at the right time in order to stop the machinery from going into motion. If she'd learned anything over the last century, it was that the vampires had no business running the world. By and large they were greedy and egotistical. Immortality had a way of nurturing those qualities in a soul, even if a person started out as very good. She would like to believe she was different, but sometimes even she felt the pull of ego, which, when she gave in to it, made her a total ass. Her father had always liked those moments when she displayed a little edginess and a bit less Goody Two-shoes, yet if she indulged in it wholeheartedly, he would not be proud of her. Even after all this time, she wanted to make him proud. She supposed that part of her would never fade, and she didn't want it to. It kept her connected to the woman she once was and the family taken from her in the worst way possible.

She couldn't stick around here because she couldn't think. Particularly if Rodney was bringing in a couple of strangers. Her eyes drifted to the monitors. It was actually a little odd, given that he was a confirmed hermit. Today it seemed like the few he did allow into his shadowy world were all showing up at the same time. A little tight for her comfort, and she would solve the claustrophobia problem by leaving. She would go home and make a few battle plans. By this time tomorrow, she'd have her own mess cleaned up, and hopefully by then, the Consortium would tip their hand so she could stop what she thought of as the spread of the red tide.

While it was true she'd been preparing for this confrontation for a long time, she still had a lingering fear that she hadn't done enough. Rodney's faith that they were well prepared for the encounters to come was encouraging. Then again, he hadn't dealt with these creatures as long as she had, and his success at living off the grid made him overly optimistic. What she needed was some quiet time to think it all through.

As the door slid open on its silent glides, she moved toward it, stopping before she made it more than a couple of feet. Rodney came through the door first, followed by two women: one petite beauty with a mass of long red hair and eyes so green they looked like emeralds and one tall, with dark, spiky hair and intense eyes. From her ears, tiny red stones dangled and caught the light. Her gaze flicked over the redhead and lingered on the second woman, who was captivating and vaguely familiar. It took her a moment to figure out why. Then it hit her—the writer from Spokane who was making millions of dollars on a series of books. Those photographs on the back of her novels or in the newspapers didn't do her justice. She was stunning in person, and as their eyes met, a thrill raced through her. As intent as she'd been about leaving a minute ago, her drive to get going had suddenly dropped to somewhere around zero.

Good lord, how shallow was she? A pretty face and she backslid at a time like this? Wasn't that part of what had gotten her in this mess to begin with? She'd fallen for another dark-haired beauty, and it had cost her everything. It would serve her well to remember that fact. Doing a full-out skid now because a woman was beautiful and fascinating? No. She refused to trip herself up again.

She began once more to walk toward the door. "I have to go." She knew she sounded abrupt. Couldn't help it. She was pissed at herself for falling back on timeworn ways, even only for a second. As the saying went, she was old enough to know better.

"Okay." Rodney wasn't the kind who would stop to dissect a decision or take it personally. Undoubtedly, he would have preferred she stay for a while so they could talk strategy. His excitement at the coming war was easy to see, even though he tried to come off as cool and calm. She saw through him just as he knew her well enough to realize that what he'd told her would spur her into immediate action.

"I'll be in touch."

"Copy that." Rodney closed the steel door behind her, and as he did the small lights along the steps appeared. She ran up them and out into the night, rain hitting her in the face.

She crossed the woods in half the time it would take her human counterparts. Darkness has been her friend for so long now, it was a welcome respite from the intensity of her confab with Rodney and the jolt she'd felt when looking into the woman's dark eyes. The light rain felt cool on her skin, and the fresh air energized her. Every nerve in her body buzzed, gearing her up to take action and keeping the vision of a beautiful face in her mind.

At the car, she stood and stared into the cloud-covered sky, so dark it was a giant black abyss. "Shake it off," she whispered as she shook out her hands and her arms. Better. She was focused again. Good to go. She got in, turned the key, and was on the highway headed toward town, mulling over everything Rodney had shared with her. All thoughts of the beautiful writer were pushed to the far recesses.

After she pondered the undeniable truth that she'd been betrayed, Sasha was more than hot by the time she arrived back at her office. It had been decades since she'd longed to feel blood slide over her teeth, and tonight she wanted more than blood. She wanted souls, two in particular, and by the time daylight came calling, she'd have them. Some things could be forgiven. Some things couldn't. She was amped up with emotion, making her slam the car door, the sound echoing in the night.

When she first got back to her apartment, she changed her clothes. She'd left for Rodney's in what for years had been her normal attire. By design she strove to maintain a neutral appearance, catch no one's attention by standing out. It was easier to move in the world undetected that way. She was an attractive woman, had been since she was a child. How often had her parents described her as the angel of the family? Father worried she was too good, and on those rare occasions when she acted out, he'd celebrated. During those long-ago days she'd dreamed of being nothing more than a wife and a mother. She'd have a marriage arranged by her parents with a prince that she would learn to accept though knew she would never, could never, love. Even as a child, she'd realized she was different, but duty meant that her truth would always be her secret. In the end, none of it mattered. All of what could have been had been denied her, and in the subsequent years, her desire for love, marriage, and motherhood had waned and then vanished. She wasn't an angel anymore.

She was a survivor and, more important, a warrior. When she'd realized what had happened to her, she could think of nothing but destroying the one who had denied her the only thing that would reunite her with her family: death. Her desire for revenge had made her stronger than even the superior powers her preternatural status granted her.

In the intervening years, more than a desire for revenge had come to drive her. Justice also came into play. When she was strong enough to truly survive on her own, she'd come to understand the undercurrent that rippled through society. There were others like her, and they wanted to rule everyone. That could not be allowed to happen. They didn't want simple dominance but absolute power. She had seen what that kind of drive brought, and she would not allow it to happen as long as she walked this earth. Her entire family had been destroyed all in the name of power, and it had been human power. Multiply that by one hundred, and that's what those of the night desired. What vampires could do could never be allowed. On the surface, she played their game. Behind the façade, she prepared to stop them. She had been powerless to save her family. Things had changed, and she was far from that now.

Her apartment was on the top floor above the business, and a back entrance allowed her to come and go discreetly. In every location where she'd brought the business, she'd set it up the same way. Few saw her, which was the way it had to be. Her face could not be a public image. Like now, she could enter and leave without anyone seeing her. In her bedroom, she discarded neutrality and instead pulled on black leather pants, a figure-hugging black shirt, and her custom-made leather coat. Inside the hidden pockets were the tools of another trade but one she'd been waiting to embrace for decades: everything she needed to kill another vampire. She was ready to face the traitors.

A private elevator took her down to the executive level, where she could finish preparing for the battle to come. She didn't expect a great deal of action once she arrived, as her human staff worked normal daytime hours. But with a large vampire staff, she expected activity in some of the office. Here she was not afraid to show her face, for like her, most had seen many decades, if not centuries, of existence. Until tonight, she'd thought she had nothing to fear from any of them.

The dead silence when she stepped in the reception area made her nerves tingle. One of her company's greatest strengths, which had allowed her to crush so many competitors through the years, was the ability to function twenty-four seven. She and her crew were at the ready whenever they needed to be, any day and any hour. Tonight it was as if the building had been abandoned. That was not just unusual; it was unheard of and unacceptable. If the Consortium had gotten their hands on Weldon's company, she was going to have to work double time to keep her edge.

No lights shone out of open doors or from beneath closed ones. Slowly she walked toward her own office at the end of the corridor, looking into offices as she went. Crystal and Rory should have been inside two of the windowless eight-by-ten workspaces. They were the two she'd come down here to destroy, but they weren't here. No one was here. Not just anger boiled within her. Fear gripped her. Something was very wrong here.

As she stepped into the doorway to her office, her hand faltered before she could turn on the overhead light. She didn't need light to see what hadn't been there when she'd left earlier. A digital reader in the middle of her desk, its lights glowing ominously red, was counting down. Two minutes and thirty-seven seconds. Two minutes and thirty-six seconds. She cut her gaze to the shelf where earlier she'd set the egg. Without stopping to think about it, she grabbed it without regard to its delicate antique nature and shoved it into the messenger bag she'd picked up from a side chair and slung across her shoulders. Then she ran for the stairs. She made it down three flights of stairs in less than two minutes. She was almost to her car when the blast hit her in the back.

❖

"I'm waiting to be dazzled." Well, that wasn't exactly true. Dee was already impressed with the cleverly concealed entrance to this place as well as what she was seeing now that she'd been invited in. It was amazing, way beyond what her imagination could come up with, and this was real. What was the old saying? Truth was stranger than fiction. Case in point.

After seeing the beautiful woman on her way, Rodney returned and, at Dee's words, smiled. "I don't dazzle," he said with a bow. "I blow your mind." His earlier reluctance to invite her in seemed to have faded away. She had the sense that he trusted Prima.

"He's already done it too," Prima declared as she looked at Dee with a smug expression. Her smile was as broad as Rodney's. Prima did know her well, didn't she?

Dee went ahead and made a concession. She waved a hand as if to encompass the entire space. "Yes, mind officially blown. This place is incredible. I can't believe what you've done here. That hidden entrance outside is brilliant."

Prima shook her head. "That's not what I'm talking about. It's not this place that's done the impossible."

No, that wasn't right. It was this bunker that had her reeling. "I don't know what you're talking about."

The smile wasn't fading in wattage from Prima's face. "Let me enlighten you. It's your belief that vampires are simply folklore that has been blown heavenward." Prima and Rodney exchanged knowing smiles.

Dee turned her gaze to Rodney. He was big and solid, and, more important, healthy looking. No pointy teeth dripping with blood. Prima was just messing with her now. "You're a vampire?" She couldn't keep the skepticism out of her words.

This time Rodney laughed hard, and his cheeks turned a pale pink. "Oh God, no. I may live underground and forgo the pleasures of daylight most of the time, but it's not because I'm a night creature. I have other reasons for all this." He waved his hand to encompass the bunker. "Don't need Big Brother watching me while I work."

"Then I don't understand. If you're not a vampire, then nothing's been blown. I mean, I'm not one and neither are you." She looked at Prima.

Prima smiled and raised a single eyebrow. "Au contraire, my friend. You came face-to-face with one. You just didn't realize it."

She opened her mouth to argue and then stopped. "Wait...you're saying that woman who raced out of here is a vampire?"

This time Prima nodded, and her smile grew even more smug. "That's exactly what I'm saying. Five minutes ago you met Sasha Rudin, and she's very much one of those folklores you're so very certain don't exist."

"Bullshit." She didn't believe them. The one who'd just left was very much a flesh-and-blood woman. She'd know the difference, right? And she wouldn't be thinking about how beautiful she was if she was a vampire. No one in their right mind could be attracted to the undead. The whole idea was creepy.

"Oh, Dee, Dee, Dee. How wrong you are." Prima slung an arm around Rodney's shoulders. "Show her, my friend."

"You're sure?" As happy as he'd appeared a minute earlier about enlightening her to the so-called vampire meeting, he seemed hesitant to take it any further. His fingers tapped the sides of his legs.

She hugged him a little tighter. "Very. I told you, she's trustworthy."

"All right then. I'm going to trust you know what you're doing." He kissed the side of Prima's head. "Come on." He turned away from her and walked to a bank of monitors, where he sat in a well-worn rolling task chair. Immediately, his hands began to fly over the keyboard, and images popped up on the screens.

To Dee's eyes they all seemed random and disconnected. At first anyway. After a minute a pattern began to emerge. Dee's knees got weak, and she gratefully sank into the chair Prima had pulled close for her. Everything she believed about the world she lived in had just gone up in flames.

"Holy crap," she muttered. "How in the fucking world?"

❖

Their plane was nearing the airport when Katrina saw the first explosion. It lit up the night sky in a way she found quite pleasurable. She glanced over at Eli, who smiled and shrugged. "The handiwork of the boys, I presume."

He glanced at his laptop and then nodded. "Imperial Investigations. They wired it and gave themselves plenty of time to be gone before it blew. Their report to me was that our spies were out of there when it happened, and those who happened to be around when the boys first went in…" He shrugged again.

"Was she there?" As much as she enjoyed the light show, it had to be done right. If those boys blew her up too, she'd rip them apart.

"No."

"Do they know where she is?" They better have a location.

"No."

"Find her," she snapped. She was pleased to know she was still alive. Her dismay that the boys didn't know her whereabouts was deep.

"I've sent in the best."

"You better hope. So far the boys aren't getting it done, and my patience with them is gone."

"They're good at what they do and can follow directions like none I've ever worked with before. But their work with her is over, and now I have better trackers. They're on it. I'm expecting their report shortly."

"Excellent. What about the writer? Have they taken care of her yet?"

"The boys have orchestrated a doubleheader for your entertainment tonight. Their second stop was the writer's house." He glanced down at the Blancpain on his wrist. "It's set to blow in another fifteen minutes. I give them kudos, as they've done an admirable job of timing everything to keep the emergency services scrambling. When the boys are on a roll with their C-4, they can create quite a show. We'll get Arkin before she can cause any lasting damage."

"So they have the writer?" At least they could stop one pain in the ass.

His gaze slid away. "Well, no, but they're going to force her to stop. She'll heed this message."

"You're telling me they haven't found her or the writer?" Her moment of serenity fled as anger flashed through her.

"No one was in the Imperial building, including Sasha Rudin, when they left. Or more accurately, no one was alive in the Imperial building. The way that thing went up, they'll spend years trying to identify what's left of the bodies. The writer's house was empty. The boys said that it was clear she lives alone. The surprise they left for her was the only occupant of the house."

"How do we know she'll return in time to go up in the explosion?"

"We don't."

"Then what good is all this?" God, it was like talking to a child. What was wrong with Eli? He knew these were horrible results. She demanded more from him. From all her soldiers. This was a poor time to be producing sloppy work.

He was nonplussed by her rising agitation. "Even if we don't get her, think about it. We destroy whatever information she's compiled. It's worth something, and these events will flush both of them out. We will have them both, and soon."

His plan had some validity, even if it wasn't at all what she wanted to hear. "We better."

Her attention rolled back to the name Eli had tossed out a moment before. Sasha Rudin. The unlikely name made her want to laugh. She knew exactly why she'd taken on that persona. It irritated her to realize she hadn't caught on sooner. That name held meaning for both of them, and it was like a red cape being waved in front of a bull's angry face. All these years and that's exactly what she'd been doing to Katrina. Taunting her and daring her. If her intent had been to send the bull into hoof-stomping fury, well done, Sasha.

She turned her gaze back out to the night and the city lights that spread out below them as they began their descent into the airport. "Talk to the pilot and have him circle until it's time. I don't want to miss the show. I do love how the boys embrace a flair for the dramatic."

"They might be dumb as a box of rocks, but I've always maintained the boys have skills."

"Yes, they do." And so do I, she thought. Two were down there somewhere in the darkness who were about to find out in an up-close-and-personal way what happened when they defied a vampire as powerful as Katrina. They would make that mistake only once. She allowed no second chances, and she'd waited a long time to impart that lesson to one of them.

The world was going to learn as well. Yes, she had a personal agenda that she fully intended to see through to the end. At the same time, the bigger picture was finally going to come into view. No longer would she or her kind hide in the shadows. No longer would they pretend to be less than the humans who thought the universe was rightfully theirs. She intended to take what should have been hers all along: the world.

CHAPTER EIGHT

L aughter exploded in Sasha's head as she pushed herself to her feet. It sent chills down her spine. It had been years since something like this had happened, and in her heart, she'd hoped it never would again. It had taken her a very long time to sever the ties with her maker and keep her mind her own. It rarely happened in her world, and it had taken every ounce of drive and determination she'd ever possessed.

Her heart might have hoped for the same disconnection, except it didn't work that way. She was always intelligent, and that's why this came as no surprise. Despite her confidence that she'd done it, she supposed she'd never truly severed the ties that were part of what made her preternatural. The connection between a maker and a vampire were always there, beginning to end. Her thoughts were her own, but her heart would always sense the one who had taken her to the dark side.

The blast had stunned her, and it took a couple of minutes to climb back to her feet. Dirt and debris were stuck in her hair and sprinkled all over her car. Staring at what had been an impressive piece of architecture that now had blown-out windows and flames shooting from the roof, she felt her heart sink. So much for keeping a foot in both camps. It had begun, and the message sent to her was loud and clear. She was no longer part of the family, and as such, they would be out for more than just the destruction of her business.

Given her beginnings in life as the pampered daughter of royalty, it would have been easy to fall back on the attitude of privilege. She'd learned what false security that birthright was before her twentieth birthday. Still, despite hard-won knowledge and experience, she'd always possessed a bit of arrogance, and she knew it. She'd believed that the world she'd created was safe and impenetrable. Believed she could play both sides in order to secure a win. That bit of arrogance had just bitten her in the ass.

Blowing out a long breath, she shook her head to clear the cobwebs, as well as the bits of debris from her hair, and patted the bag that remained on her body despite the force of the blast. At least she'd had one bit of good fortune. She hadn't landed on the bag; it had landed on her. If nothing else went well from here on forward, and she suspected it would not, the egg was safe. She slipped her hand inside the bag and stroked it. The simple gesture gave her strength, for she felt as though her family were reaching out to her through the small, beautiful work of art that had once made them all smile. How could she fail with their spirits holding her up?

But where to go from here? Walking into that empty office told her the betrayal of those around her appeared to be far deeper than the two Rodney had uncovered. If that weren't the case, the building that was burning to the ground would have had more people—correction—vampires in it at the time of the explosion. The fact that it appeared to be completely empty was frightening on several fronts. If others were in there, something had happened to them. If they weren't? It meant she was in this alone.

The train had left the station, and now she had to stop it. She couldn't achieve her goals by herself, even with the power and might she'd developed over the last century. She had Rodney, but he was only a human. Brains and ingenuity he possessed. The might of a preternatural, not a drop. There were too many of them, and they were determined. Nothing new. They had been as long as she'd known of them.

Like everything, it was a matter of timing. She'd learned this lesson from her father, and while he'd been defeated in the most horrible way possible, he had possessed great knowledge that he'd shared with her. Publicly he'd talked of his sadness that his progeny consisted mostly of girls. What might not have been as publicly known was that he had still loved and cherished his daughters. He had not neglected their education, either traditional or political. Sadly, in the years since, she'd realized that having knowledge and using it wisely were two different things. She hoped to do better than her father.

At least her car was undamaged. Small favors and all that. The last thing she wanted was to be here when the fire department and law enforcement arrived. What would she be able to tell them? That a coup was in the making and a cadre of vampires was orchestrating it? She could almost feel the cold steel of the handcuffs around her wrists. So few humans knew about the existence of vampires that the reality of making them believe her or marshaling any kind of meaningful help from them in any significant number was low. With the exception of Rodney and Prima, that is.

First things first. She had to get out of here. She despised handcuffs. Her tires squealed as she turned the car around and drove away from the building. The debris littering the parking lot was dangerous, and she swerved like a drunk as she made her way to the highway. She also didn't need a flat tire. In less than five minutes she was clear and on her way in the opposite direction of the lights and sirens coming from all the nearby fire stations. That wasn't a big surprise, considering the size of her building. The colonial-looking structure had in its former life been a large real-estate operation. The subsequent arrest and imprisonment of its original owners for fraud had put it on the market for a price she couldn't say no to. All of that coincided perfectly with her timing. Every decade or so, she moved the corporate headquarters to a new city in a new state. Easier to move undetected when she didn't put down permanent roots. That strategy had been working for years.

Still, she was a little sad. The building and the home she'd created on the top floor were one of the best. From both her office and her apartment she had a fantastic view of Mt. Spokane and could often watch small planes take off and land at the regional airport a mile or so away. She had a Cessna Skycatcher there and a pilot on call twenty-four seven. Easy access in and out was perfect for her needs. There was nothing about the place to dislike. Now, it was all gone.

After taking the back roads to avoid the emergency and police response to the explosion, she cut over to Highway 2 and pulled into a big-box-store parking lot right off the highway. Before she got out of the car, she punched in the number of her oldest and most trusted friend. The phone rang and rang. No one answered. A little concerning, although it could just mean that she was out or her cell phone was dead. She tried another number. Another friend. By the fourth call, a terrible truth settled into the pit of her stomach. She stared down at the phone in her hands and wanted to scream. One vampire friend not answering wasn't a concern. All of them unavailable was a disaster. It meant only one thing. They were after her and anyone who affiliated themselves with her. The unanswered calls meant she truly was alone, and for a second, she allowed the panic to rip at her. It truly had begun.

Only for a moment, and then sitting up in her seat, she punched in a joint text message to two she knew would receive it before tossing the phone onto the passenger seat. The way it looked right now, she was alone except for a human who had been her ally for years, and another who had been her friend. Both were worth their weight in gold. Sounded corny. Was true nonetheless. As she turned the key in the ignition, the car roared to life. She maneuvered a one-eighty with her car and retraced her earlier journey to that place deep in the woods.

❖

Before either of them could delve into explanations of how these creatures lived among unsuspecting humans like Dee, something large and bright flashed across one of the screens.

Rodney's head snapped up and to the right. "Motherfucker. What was that?"

"What just happened?' Prima was leaning over him, one hand on his shoulder while staring at the same screen.

Dee took up her post on the other side of Rodney. It appeared that a building was engulfed in a massive fire. "I don't recognize the area," she said as she peered closely at the screen. A shadowy figure was rising from the ground and after a moment ran to a car.

"Son of a bitch. I do. Imperial Investigations just blew to the moon, and that looks like Sasha who just got up. Somebody's got a death wish."

Still didn't resonate with her. She'd never heard of Imperial. "Okay, so you recognize the place, but why would that mean a death wish?"

Prima straightened and looked at her with eyes wide. "It's messed up because Imperial Investigations is the company that Sasha runs, and I for one don't believe it was an accident. She must have just gotten out of there or she'd be in pieces right now."

"The so-called vampire?"

"No so-called about it. She's a vampire, and her world-class business just blew to the moon." Prima looked down at Rodney. "You think it was an accident?"

"No fucking way. They were trying to kill her."

"See, we're both on the same page. Somebody is working hard to get to Sasha." She turned and looked at Dee. "You caught on to something, and from what I'm seeing here, it's the tip of the iceberg. If they're going after Sasha, something is happening out there."

Rodney sat up and whirled in his chair. "What are you talking about? What has Dee uncovered?"

It occurred to Dee then that Prima had been so caught up in proving to her that vampires existed that neither of them had yet told Rodney what she'd uncovered. She explained about her research and then told him about the threat that had come in last night.

"What are the names you came up with?"

"Imre Thurzo and Katrina Petrin."

"Holy shit, girl. You latched on to pretty much the king and the queen of the vampire empire. Well, if the king and queen hated each other, that is."

"I can't be the only one who figured out the two have been around forever."

"No. But you're probably the only one still alive. Besides me, that is, and that's only because Sasha's had my back on that front. They don't know that I know."

Chills raced down her arms, and her gaze flicked back to the burning building on Rodney's monitor. "Are they going to blow me up too?"

He shrugged. "Either that or kill you. The kill thing is pretty much their standard MO."

Prima lightly swatted the back of Rodney's head. "Way to scare the crap out of her."

"Sorry, but honestly those two are dangerous, and if one of them sent you that message, you're gonna want to watch your back. They kinda have a take-no-prisoners philosophy when it comes to the human race."

As much as what he was saying scared her, a thought occurred to her that brought her back around to the vampire. She pointed to the screen. "Why are you monitoring Sasha's business? Why would you have cameras out there?"

He was shaking his head. "I don't have special equipment anywhere other than on my own property. I don't have to. It's easy for me to hack into what's already out there. Hence, this big brother is watching everything the other big brother is doing. I'm pretty proud of the irony of it."

"Again, why monitor Sasha? If she's a world-class investigations firm like you say, she wouldn't need a babysitter, right?"

"No." He laughed. "If anyone does not need a keeper, it's Sasha. The thing is, I keep eyes on my friends when I can. It's not babysitting. It's caring. Besides, we've been expecting some kind of move. We just didn't know when or where. Apparently, it's tonight, and clearly it's her home base."

Before Dee could ask, Prima jumped in. "Who're *we*? They? Sounds like some kind of conspiracy."

Rodney leaned back in his chair and sighed. "Sasha and I are the *we*. We've been watching and waiting for this clear movement. *They* are what beyond the mist is known as the Consortium, a group of elder, powerful vampires whose entire mission is take over the world. They're tired of living in the shadows, and they want everything the humans possess. Not just their blood. Everything. We knew they'd make a stand somehow, somewhere. I wasn't really anticipating they'd go right for Sasha. That's a pretty bold move."

Dee was intrigued now. "Why would anyone be after her? I mean, she's one woman. Correction, vampire." She felt silly saying the word.

"Oh, she's one vampire all right, and one with some pretty powerful secrets. There are some out there who don't like that. Not to mention, she's not a fan of the Consortium. She believes they're arrogant and dangerous."

Now that made sense. Blowing up a building to make a point was ballsy, to say the least. "Given what she does for a living, I would think she holds a whole lot of secrets. It's kind of the nature of the beast, wouldn't you agree?"

"True enough," Rodney said. "And that kind of information would absolutely make her a target. It's not what really put the bull's-eye on her back, though."

"So what did?"

He looked at her and in apparent seriousness declared, "I'd tell you, but then I'd have to kill you."

"Are you serious?"

His expression didn't lighten. "Serious as a heart attack, baby. Serious as a heart attack." He spun his chair back around, and his fingers resumed their lightning-fast movement across the keyboard.

Prima was quiet as she studied the screens that were once again alive with various images. Her intake of breath was loud and her face pale as she turned to look at Dee.

"Prima, what is it?" The sudden tension that seemed to flow over her friend was as strong as an incoming ocean tide.

"Look," she said as she pointed to another of Rodney's screens. "It's not only Imperial that blew up."

Dee stared over her shoulder, expecting to see the image of another business going up in flames. "Oh, hell, no." The local news station was airing a bit of video clearly taken by someone's smartphone. She recognized the neighborhood.

Prima was standing close and staring at the same broadcast. "You get it now?"

"Yeah, I get it."

Prima put an arm around her waist. "Did you notice that was your house burning down?"

"Yeah, I noticed."

❖

After the second explosion lit up the night sky, Katrina ordered the pilot to set down. A car was waiting, and they were away from the airport in a matter of minutes. She didn't care to spend any more time than necessary on the west plains of the city, where it was flat and the wind always seemed to blow. She preferred the heart of the city, with lovely hotels, mountain views, and nourishment at every corner. It wasn't hard to stay sated in this city.

She was bothered by the knowledge that the one she sought had been here and undetected for longer than should have been possible. What kind of people did she employ? Imbeciles, obviously. Except perhaps for Eli. His quick mind had come up with the idea to infiltrate Imperial Investigations, and that, as it turned out, was a genius move. With the combination of his spies and taking over Imperial's rival, she finally had her after all these years.

Unfortunately, that wasn't exactly true. They had narrowed down the search area but failed to corner their prey, despite the massive blow delivered less than an hour ago. The boys had been able to aptly deliver a physical blow to property, but the woman she sought wasn't in her hands. Neither was the pesky writer. Someone needed to pay for those failures.

The car pulled into the covered entrance to the Davenport Hotel. It was the best and most prestigious hotel in the area, which is why her rooms were waiting for her here. The sharply dressed doorman held open her car door. She ignored him as she got out, intent on getting to her room so she could begin work on the next phase of their attack. Sometimes relying on others wasn't effective. Sometimes, she had to do the work herself.

Behind her, the attractive flight attendant murmured a thank you to the doorman. Katrina frowned. She didn't like the woman's drawing attention to herself. "Come," she spat out, and the woman hurried away from the uniformed man. "Don't bother with the help." Apparently she needed to school the woman on how to behave while in her company. Whoever had hired this one had dropped the ball when it came to instructions. She would deal with that as well.

"I'm sorry." She had her head down as she hurried to keep up with Katrina.

Katrina didn't look back. "Just keep your mouth shut unless I tell you differently."

"Yes, ma'am."

When they arrived in the suite, she sent the bellman away with a healthy tip. Not that she wanted to tip him. It was a matter of critical thinking. In other words, it made less of an impression if she followed local custom. She threw her jacket on the sofa and whirled to face the woman. "Take off your clothes."

A startled look crossed her pretty face. "What?"

She raised a single eyebrow and said quietly, "I don't believe I'm hard to understand. Take off your clothes." Any accent she'd had from her beginnings in the motherland had been erased a long time ago. These days she sounded like any other West Coast American.

Wisely, the woman didn't question again. When Katrina used that low, slow voice, only the very unwise dared to challenge her. Though she took the time to lay her uniform neatly over the back of the chair, presumably because she thought she would be putting it back on again, it was only a minute or two before the woman was standing naked in the entryway of the spacious suite. She was stunning in the nude, just as Katrina had envisioned all the way from Seattle. Eli knew her tastes and planned accordingly.

"A drink?" Katrina turned to the sideboard that was fully stocked with a wide variety of excellent alcoholic beverages. "Whiskey, wine… beer?" God, she hoped this one wasn't a beer drinker. The beverage always seemed to take them down a common path that she didn't care for and removed the luster from an otherwise shiny toy. Not to mention that the smell of it made her gag.

"Wine." The woman's voice trembled. "Please."

"Excellent choice. Wine it is." She poured from an open and waiting bottle of merlot, then handed the woman the glass. No white wine in her world. Only bold and red. She noticed that her hand shook a little as she took the glass Katrina offered. She smiled and let her gaze wander over her full breasts and flat stomach. Oh yes, she was going to do just fine. *Kudos, Eli.*

"Drink up," she encouraged her. If the woman noticed that Katrina didn't join her in a drink, she didn't say anything. That was good, for it signaled she was catching on to the rules of the game.

Her hands were shaking even harder as she brought the wine to her lips. "It's very good," she murmured.

Katrina smiled. "Yes, it is. A favorite of mine from a local winery. It's a special stock they bring in for me."

She sipped again, and this time, the shaking seemed to lessen. Good. She liked it better when they were relaxed. Not that she minded a bit of spunk now and again. A little fear to add flavor to the game.

Katrina gave her a warm smile. It was less about the woman and more about anticipation. "Why don't we take this to the bedroom? Bring your wine."

CHAPTER NINE

This time, Sasha left her vehicle in an area even farther away from the entrance to Rodney's bunker than she had last time. She wasn't going to risk anyone following her, or at least following her easily. She'd pulled off on a rough service road that didn't appear to have been used for some time and drove down it for about a quarter of a mile until she spotted a stand of trees with a gap just big enough for her to tuck in. No one would be able to see it without also driving in all the way. She also left no identification in it, so without serious digging no one would be able to trace the vehicle to her company.

She stood outside and thought about what had happened. It was surreal that after all this time, it was finally here. All their preparation and planning would be put to the test. She hoped they'd done enough. Her body buzzed, and her thoughts were fast though focused. She'd been preparing both physically and mentally since the day she'd been turned. One always wished for more time, yet she knew she was truly ready.

The forest was quiet and, at the same time, not. Subtle sounds wafted through the air—the tiny feet of a rabbit scurrying through the underbrush and an owl alighting on a strong overhead branch. Like her world, behind the veil of darkness it was alive and vivid. Deep shadows embraced the forest, broken only by slivers of moonlight through the boughs of the pines. Her step was light, almost silent, as she moved through the trees. Despite having left her vehicle a significant distance away, she covered the ground from her car to the entrance as quickly as a deer fleeing from a cougar. She had no time to waste and feared that, despite all her precautions, she would be detected.

Once again she found herself at the tree. She was about to reach out and touch the bark when she paused. A slight rustle to her left, so slight most would never have noticed, made her pull back behind a massive nearby pine. It occurred to her as she stood motionless that she'd made a critical error. Though she'd been certain no one was behind her when she'd sped away from the remains of her building, she'd made that drive in an Imperial Investigations vehicle. If someone was very clever, they would be able to pick her up and tail her to these woods. Another quiet snap of a twig told her someone was, indeed, very clever. She waited, but not long.

His young face was framed by long blond hair and eyes so blue they glowed even in the darkness. She gave him credit for being good because she hadn't detected either his tail on her vehicle or his presence in the dark woods until now. His bad luck was that he just wasn't good enough. From here it was hard to tell if he was old or new. Though he moved with the grace of an old one, the glee clearly visible from where she studied him behind the tree made her believe he was newly turned. Too often the youngsters were so enamored by the enhanced abilities their preternatural senses gave them that they lacked control. They couldn't embrace constraint, and this inability cost a great many of them their chance at immortality.

Old or new, this vampire was soon to discover that very lesson. Her breath was light enough that he would never hear her, while his was heavy and filled the air around her with the acrid scent of excitement. He was obviously anticipating not just killing her but also feeding on the humans he must know she'd come here to meet. She was angry at herself for allowing a tail. How long had he been tracking her? That he had been able to do that at all made her ill. She was better than that.

She couldn't do much about her misstep now. All she could do was stop this one before he did any damage. Or was it really a misstep? It might, in fact, work to her advantage. She just had to take care of this vampire, and the next one, and each one after that until she found herself face-to-face with the one she'd been searching for all these years. She liked that she was seen as a threat, and she liked that her new situation was going to open a door that had been closed to her for a century.

Every dark cloud had a silver lining.

The subtle hiss of his breath brought an unmistakable new wave of stench on the night air. Yes, her suspicions were accurate. He was but a child and, judging by the smell on his breath, had recently fed. Undoubtedly, he'd killed someone on the way here because his urges had been too great to control. Now he was filled with something akin to adrenaline, the rush any vampire got when blood was warm, fresh, and human. It was why so many couldn't break free of the desire to feed on people.

His footsteps had slowed, and she knew he was sniffing the air himself, searching for his prize. What was the bounty on her head? Or was he someone's soldier sent for her? Either way, it was a major mistake on their part because now she knew they were looking for her. Why her own traitorous people hadn't taken her head was a mystery. They had most certainly turned on her, their betrayal something she'd never recover from, but they had let her live, and she seriously wondered why. This one, however, didn't intend to; she could sense that truth in every step he took.

The stench grew so strong it made her gag. He was getting very close, even though he moved in silence. She was ready when he stepped past. His mistake, as his eyes were on a spot in the distance and his back was to her. He was tall, with broad shoulders and hair that hung down nearly to his waist. A pretty boy, but not for long. Had he been older, more experienced, he'd have known where she waited for him. He would have quieted in order to feel her spirit and catch her scent. Instead, he was too caught up in the game to use all that was available to him as a vampire.

By the time he was close, Sasha had already slipped her hand into an inside pocket of her jacket where her fingers curled around the handle of a weapon. Silently she said a "thank God" for taking extra minutes to change before her home was blown apart. It had seemed important at the time to arm herself, and now she understood why. She was prepared for a fight with more than her wits.

She stepped into her swing, her movement silent, save for the whoosh of her tantō as she separated his head from his neck. Blond hair fluttered through the air like a beautiful scarf catching on the wind.

❖

"We got company." Rodney jumped up and headed to the security door. "Ain't this a night?" he muttered as he went. "It's like I have a neon Vacancy sign hanging up out there."

"This can't be good." Prima looked over at the monitor that showed the tree and the hidden entrance.

Dee saw her for only a few minutes, yet she recognized the figure in the monitor. "It's her."

"It is, and I repeat, it's not good."

Rodney came back a moment later with the woman—correction—vampire who'd left earlier. Sasha. Once more Dee was struck by how lovely she was. Staring at her was rude, and she knew it, but she couldn't help her intense focus on her intriguing face. It didn't seem possible that she was anything different from Dee. She was beautiful and her eyes captivating, and if she wasn't covered in blood splatter, she'd be a real vision. It was as if someone had dipped a paint brush in red paint and then flung it at her. Only this paint was the kind that came right out of someone's veins. Not good. Not good at all.

"What is going on?" She couldn't help her outburst. Really, it was bad enough that Prima had dragged her out to prove her point that vampires were real and lived among them. Point made, and then some.

Now the world she thought she knew was falling to pieces right before her eyes. Or rather right before her eyes on the monitors of a guy who lived underground like a mole, a really smart mole with a whole lot of impressive technology. This was taking proving a point way above and beyond.

Sasha's eyes met Dee's. They were dark and intense, sending a shiver through her. "Nothing that concerns you, writer."

The effect of those eyes was momentary. Dee's shoulders came up. "Sort of does when you're standing right in front of me. And the name's Dee, not *writer*."

"Drop it, Sasha and Dee." Rodney pulled the door shut with a loud snap. "If you're here, you're all friends. Period. If you can't be civil, get out."

Dee got it and zipped it. He was right, especially about her, given this was the first time she'd even met the man or the vampire. "Sorry," she said quietly, and she meant it. She was not fond of those who used their power and success as an excuse to be assholes.

Sasha gave her a slight nod. "As am I." The intensity in her eyes dulled a fraction. "It does concern you. It concerns us all."

Prima rushed to Sasha and took her by the shoulders. "Are you all right? What happened? What can I do?"

Sasha waved a hand. "It's not my blood."

"There's an awful lot of it." Dee was looking at her too, searching for a wound. With that much blood, she'd been hurt somewhere. Had to be.

Sasha's eyes met hers and the stare shook her once again. No one had ever given her such an intense look. "It's not mine and I'm not hurt. I was followed. I handled it."

Rodney, who'd dropped back into his chair, whirled around. "Damn it, they followed you? They know I'm here? I can't afford the breach, Sasha. None of us can afford that kind of thing."

"Not they. Him. I told you, Rodney, it's handled. No trace, and you're not compromised."

"You're sure?"

Her voice was sharp. "Do you think I'd come down here if I wasn't?"

He didn't appear to take offense. If she used that voice on Dee, she'd probably start crying, and she didn't consider herself an overly sensitive woman. He looked at her, shrugged, and whirled back to his monitors. "Good point."

Dee studied Sasha more closely this time and noticed some subtle things she hadn't earlier. All she'd focused on before in their brief encounter was how pretty the woman was. Now she caught the paleness of her skin that looked as though sunlight hadn't whispered over it for a very long time. She caught the haunted look in her intense eyes that couldn't quite be covered up by intensity. She felt the strength that she possessed wash over her. So many layers to this woman, and yes, she realized she was more than that, but the female part of her called to Dee.

"They blew up my house." The words seemed to fall out of Dee's mouth. Well, now wasn't that lame? What on earth had possessed her to pop off like that? Sasha was really going to think that she was a certifiable loser. So much for being a cool best-selling author. She was, and always would be, that gawky, uncool kid from middle school with an unrequited crush on Sue Ford. Some things never changed.

Sasha gave her a curt nod. Funny, though, that it seemed to her more like an acknowledgment than a dismissal. Made Dee feel a little better. Maybe she wasn't still quite as gawky as she'd been back in middle school.

Pointing to various screens on Rodney's impressive control panel, Sasha directed her comment to Dee. "You, me, and who knows how many others. The bastards have hidden for years, waiting and planning for their chance to strike. Tonight is their night and they're going for it. Only God knows what all they have in store for us. They're beginning to tear down our city, and they started with me."

"Why here?" It didn't make sense that Spokane would be a hotbed of activity. Why not Seattle? Portland? San Francisco?

"Three good reasons that I can come up with, and I'm pretty sure Rodney will agree." Sasha kept her gaze on the monitors. "Spokane is a big enough city to have impact, and it has a military base…"

They all watched her for a moment. Dee could see something was going on inside her, and it was personal. She waited, thinking Sasha would continue. When she didn't, Dee asked, "What's the third reason?"

At first Dee didn't think she intended to answer. Slowly Sasha turned, and her deep, dark eyes met hers once more. "Me."

❖

Even after all these years, Katrina still loved that ever-so-energizing feeling that came from rough sex and fresh blood. The combination was explosive and irresistible. Showered and changed, she was ready for the rest of the night's activities. So much had already taken place it was like one of those epic vacations that humans seemed to be quite fond of. She'd been charged up before they arrived in the city, but now she was, as the old saying went, on fire.

As were the headquarters of Imperial Investigations and a certain successful writer's home. The boys had done an excellent job on those two fronts, and the smile she couldn't suppress matched the glow in her eyes. Her earlier annoyance with the boys was fading. Anyone who saw her now would think something wonderful had just happened to her. They'd be right too, and there was more to come.

Eli knocked once and entered her room. She should be angry at his impertinence, but she wasn't. His timing was perfect and it wasn't an accident. He knew her habits well, her likes and dislikes. Besides being an assistant extraordinaire, he was the A-team when it came to cleanup. In no more than an hour, the room would be as pristine as the moment they'd stepped inside. If he was a superhero, this would be his super power.

He glanced at the bed, and only a tiny twitch at the corner of one eye gave a clue as to his real thoughts. Those he would keep to himself. Kudos again. She didn't need to know what he thought and would never care. The only opinions that held value were hers, and he knew it.

"You have a call." He handed her a sleek black smartphone. "Mix."

Her smile disappeared. Jared Mixell, Mix for short, was one of her best scouts. He'd been with her for about sixty years, and like Eli, he was incredibly reliable. He was part of the reason they were in their current, most excellent position. The thing was, he worked with an independence that didn't require checking in unless there was an issue.

She put the phone to her ear. "Talk to me." Behind her she could hear Eli moving about. It wasn't necessary to turn around to see what he was doing. He'd be doing what he did best. Problem solving.

When Mix finished, she was smiling. The bad news she feared he'd be relaying didn't come. On the contrary, it was excellent information. "Everything is in motion, then?"

"Of course. We've been getting ready for the offensive long enough. The results are beginning to show. By this time tomorrow, we'll have this stupid city under our total control. Same in the other major cities."

"Very good." She'd say excellent, but it wouldn't do to give them too much praise. It went to their heads, and she didn't need that.

"Thank you."

"And what about *her*?"

He didn't hesitate before answering. "I've got one of my best on her."

"Don't screw this up."

"Not my first rodeo."

"Others have failed me. Don't be another one."

"I don't do failure."

"Good. Call me the second you have her." She ended the call and walked into the other room. She didn't care to be around when Eli was tidying up. Her role was to have fun and make the mess. She didn't do cleanup. As one grew older, the benefits became greater. Once, when she was very young, that would have been her job. Not for a very long time. It was up to the Elis of the world now.

Eli had set her laptop on the desk, and now she pulled a chair in front of it. Once it was powered up and connected to the hotel's network, she logged onto a secure site. Her fingers zipped over the keys. She loved technology and appreciated how much easier communication was these days. It was hard to even imagine what she used to have to do before the era of instant messaging.

She had a dozen incoming messages and was pleased by what was being sent. All the years of planning were bearing fruit. There were occasional moments over the years when she wondered if it would actually come to pass or if, like the others of the preternatural fraternity, she would be relegated to second-class-citizen status for her entire existence. It wasn't right and never had been. They were the true torchbearers of power and intelligence, and to always have to hide in the shadows was wrong in too many ways.

Well, that was about to end. There would be second-class citizens, and they would be called humans. That alone was worth everything. That she would eliminate the problem writer was a bonus. That she would destroy the one who had betrayed her was priceless.

She grabbed the remote control and clicked on the massive television mounted on the wall over the fireplace. As she expected, the channels were all broadcasting special news reports. No one could quite figure out what was happening on the streets of major cities, Spokane included. People were collapsing everywhere, many displaying puncture marks on their necks. Panic was taking hold. Emergency crews were unable to keep up with the calls.

Katrina tilted her head back and laughed. Yes, this was turning out to be a very good night indeed.

Chapter Ten

Sasha had covered the head and the body with branches and pine needles enough to make it hard to distinguish in the darkness. There was little moonlight, and the chance of discovery was minute. On a rainy night like this, despite it being June, the chance of a random hiker coming through the area was slim. Once daylight came, the sun would take care of the rest. The scent of fresh blood that had wafted into the air, fused with that of moldy pine needles and disturbed earth, had made her nerves roar, but she'd ignored it even though in the back of her mind a hunger pressed. Her supply of sustenance had gone up in the explosion, and she couldn't think about the alternative to that catastrophe at this moment. Particularly as she stood in the same space with three humans, their veins flowing with the very thing that kept her alive.

As she'd waited for the staircase to be revealed, she'd been surprised when Rodney had met her at the top steps rather than at the steel door. He'd grabbed her arm and dragged her down, saying as he did, "Get your ass in here." Shocked as she'd been, she hadn't argued and had followed him quickly down the steps and into the bunker. It made her uneasy, and not because she was afraid of him. He wasn't that kind of guy. Brilliant but more assuredly nonviolent.

Looking into their faces now, she was pretty sure she'd made them understand and reassured Rodney his bunker hadn't been compromised. There was more to be done. She had to explain the rest of it. "They're after me. I thought I was safe and working beneath the Consortium's radar, and now I realize I was quite wrong."

"It's your two employees." Rodney sounded certain, and she agreed with him, at least partly.

She'd been thinking about them as she was driving back out here, and she had a theory. "Yes and no. The traitors in my organization are minor players in this thing. They're being used for what they can provide and nothing more. The reality is, I'm certain I've always been on the Consortium's hit list. I never played nice, and the Elders don't take kindly to those of us who don't operate by their rules. I've seen them strike down more than one for failing to play the game their way. What's more, I defied someone quite powerful a long time ago, and it was a slight that won't ever be forgiven. I've spent my entire existence as a vampire hiding from that one."

Rodney stared at her through narrowed eyes. "You've never told me this."

He was right; in their many conversations she'd left out that little part. It was an episode in her life she wasn't proud of and thus something she never shared. "I wanted to take care of that piece myself. Nobody needs to be involved in my private war because it's going to get very bloody." That was the other part of it. Anyone caught up in her personal vendetta could easily end up dead.

"I'm your friend. I can help."

"So am I," Prima added. "I'm with Rodney, and we help you. We might be human, but don't forget we have unique skills."

She nodded in a silent acknowledgment of their friendship and their offer, but they really didn't have a good idea of what they were up against. She'd started this alone, and she'd end it alone. "For a little while, all I need is a safe place to think."

Safe. Interesting how that word had popped into her head. Earlier when she'd started coming back here, she had felt like she was heading to sanctuary. Now that she was here, it struck her that it felt more like coming home. Strange that she would feel that way about a bunker far below the ground and a quasi brother and sister. Yet, there it was. She'd leave it be for now. Too many things more important than psychoanalyzing herself.

Sasha looked down at her bloody hands and shuddered. She'd seen a lot of blood over the last century, and usually it didn't bother her. It did now for many reasons, not the least of which was the way it reminded her of a night in a basement standing next to her family and her body jerking as the bullets hit her. On that night too she'd looked down at the blood on her hands.

"I need to clean up." She held her hands up in the air, not wanting to think about that other time. Not how her own blood had run through her fingers or how her sister's had spotted her face like raindrops. No, she definitely didn't want to think about that. She went to the sink and lowered her hands only to turn on the tap and position them beneath the running water.

She pulled her thoughts away from the bitter past, and with her head down, she focused on scrubbing away all remnants of the creature that had tried so hard to dispose of her. The more she scrubbed, the more her sad memories turned to anger. How dare they do this to her? Everything had been taken from her. Every last person and possession. Worst of all, her life had been stolen, and now they come and do this? Once upon a time, she was powerless. Not any longer. This time they would be the ones to lose everything. Or to be more precise...*she* was going to lose it all. She'd put this whole thing in motion because it was exactly what she would do. Payback was a bitch.

"She's going to regret this," Sasha said quietly as she scrubbed, the water flowing into the sink fading from red to pink. "She's going to regret ever laying eyes on me."

Dee had been shocked at Sasha's appearance when she'd come through the door. Earlier she'd been beautiful in her jeans, boots, and shirt. Casual and yet strong, a great combination. One woman had left and another had walked back in. She'd returned looking like a warrior in black leather. If not for the blood splattered across her jacket and the red stain on her hands, she'd have made Dee's breath catch. Actually, that wasn't quite true. Blood and all, Dee had felt a thrill of excitement run through her as Sasha had stepped into the room. Her breath did catch, albeit quietly. Maybe she had a thing for so-called vampires and didn't know it. Considering she'd only accepted the existence of vampires over the course of a couple hours, that wasn't surprising.

Wait, yes, it was surprising. She liked women. Simple and

uncomplicated. She also liked her women human because that's what she'd believed them all to be. It was too mind-boggling to think otherwise, regardless of how hot the vampire standing near her was. Yes, human women, that was her preference.

Now she stepped closer as Sasha scrubbed her hands in the sink. Even though she was a writer who could create scenes of death and destruction, in real life, it was a bit harder to wrap her mind around not only the sight of violence but the smell and the emotion it evoked. She didn't think she'd ever be able to accurately capture it all with words, though she knew herself well enough to know she'd try. Later, that is, after the rawness faded a little.

"Who's going to pay?" Sasha had clearly meant to murmur the words to only herself, yet Dee had heard them without trying to eavesdrop.

Sasha spun, water spraying as she did and making wet drops appear on the front of Dee's shirt. Her eyes were deep, dark, and terrifying, her fangs clearly visible as she pulled back her lips. Dee took a step back as Sasha spat out something in Russian, and it was definitely not an apology for the water on her shirt. Or at least she was pretty sure that's the language she spoke. There was a large Russian population in the Spokane area, so hearing the language wasn't all that unusual. If she had any lingering doubts about her being a vampire, they'd just been laid to rest.

Dee didn't know if it was her expression or the step back, but in a flash, the fangs disappeared and her eyes softened. Sasha picked up a towel from the counter and began to dry her hands. When she laid the towel back on the counter, her hands were once more pale and free of the crimson splatter. A lemony scent from the dish soap wafted up in the air.

"Katrina," she said softly as she raised her eyes from her hands to once more meet Dee's. "Katrina will pay."

"Katrina?"

"You know who I mean."

Dee was shocked. The implication was pretty darned clear. "You know what I was doing?" It wasn't possible that Sasha could know of her work unless... Good grief, had everybody hacked her computer? A long talk with the guy who did her security was first thing on her agenda after leaving here. She'd thought she was protected way better than she apparently was.

Sasha threw the towel on the counter. "Yes, and it was foolish of you to dig there."

She didn't appreciate the schoolteacher-style scolding, and her voice telegraphed her sentiment. "I was curious, and if she didn't want to be found, maybe she shouldn't have stuff out there for God and everybody to see."

Sasha didn't seem to take offense at the snap in her words. "Have you ever heard about curiosity and a cat?"

Oh, for heaven's sake. She didn't even bother to answer. No sense in arguing. It was clear that she'd never convince her she had every right to research whatever and whomever she wanted. A change in topic was appropriate. "Did Katrina destroy your place?"

She nodded slightly, making the shift with Dee easily. "I must assume so, among her many other sins."

"I'm sorry." Now what was that about? A second ago she was somewhat offended when Sasha seemed to be attacking her personally. Now it sounded like they were pals. She didn't even know her, so why on earth would she feel compelled to apologize? Why should she care about the relationship between Sasha and this enigma named Katrina? What a strange journey this was turning out to be. Prima had brought her here to make her a believer. Mission accomplished. Massive amounts of blood and fangs had a way of doing that. She'd say it was surreal, but that didn't even come close to describing this.

"For what?" It was a snap, and once more Dee took a step back.

"I'm...I'm...just..." God, this woman, this vampire, kept her off balance. She didn't like it. She didn't dislike it.

Rodney stepped in and defused what was rapidly returning to the tension of a moment before. "Give it a rest, Sasha. Leave Dee in peace. We have bigger problems. We need to come up with our strategy, and quickly."

His intervention worked. Her body relaxed, and she nodded in his direction. "Yes, we do. They need to go." This time her nod was in the direction of Dee and Prima.

"Yeah, well, that's a problem," Dee muttered under her breath, or so she thought. She wanted to say "fuck off," but she didn't.

"No, it's not. This isn't your fight. The only problem we'll have is if you don't leave. Go." She directed the last word to Dee. "You need to get out of here. Now."

This time Dee stood up straight and defensive. No one had the right to push her around, and that included the vampire staring at her with eyes so dark they looked black. "Like the man said, we all have bigger problems tonight. Me included."

"And that would concern me how exactly?"

"How quickly you forget." Eyes filled with fire met hers, but Dee didn't budge. "Remember what you saw on the screens a few minutes ago? They blew up my house right after they blew up yours." *Take that, you beautiful, haughty vamp.*

It was easier to concentrate now that she'd sated herself in all ways possible. Katrina sat at her laptop, studied the files coming in, and listened to the continuing news reports on the suite's television that had been turned low enough to be heard but not be intrusive. Ignoring Eli as he scurried around the bedroom, talking on his phone with the earpieces pressed into his ears, wasn't all that difficult. She even ignored the cleanup team, one man and one woman, who showed up shortly after Eli had slipped his phone back into his pocket. They did their work in a quiet, efficient manner. They weren't new to their duties, and it showed. By the time they left, the bedroom looked just as it had when they first unlocked the suite's door. Just as it should be. It always paid to engage the best help available for all jobs, high or low.

Her beginnings might have been quite humble, but the power that had been bestowed upon her by the ultimate gift had transformed her into the woman that had been inside her all along. She loved it and everything that went along with it. She was beautiful, alluring, and feared. She had risen within the Consortium like the most brilliant night star and stayed seated at the apex of power. It had been gratifying, but now, as everything came together, it was beyond intoxicating.

Eli came into the room sipping from a glass. His nourishment undoubtedly came from a bag, as his privileges weren't as broad as hers. If he wanted something more, he had to hunt outside in the night like those more common than she. Given his many duties, he didn't have the time. He rarely did, and she couldn't recall when she'd last seen him actually hunt. Or, as she thought about it, if she'd ever seen him hunt. Minor detail. How her staff sustained themselves was of little importance. She cared only about the level of service they provided her. The rest was their problem.

"I'm not seeing any reports from the man Mix sent after her." She'd been scouring her messages for the last hour, and so far nothing had come through their secure server. She expected more from her hunters, this one in particular. Mix had assured her he had a capable tracker on the job. Young but highly skilled. It should be done by now, and the vampire on the way back to drop her at Katrina's feet. If she was a little bruised and beaten in the process, no matter, as long as she was alive.

Eli shook his head. "I've tried calling him three times. It's going to voice mail. That's not like him. I talked to Mix again, and he isn't getting an answer from him either."

The solution seemed obvious to her. For Eli and Mix it was apparently necessary to spell it out. "Track his phone."

His response troubled her. "Already tried it. The phone appears to be off, which also explains why he's not answering." Her initial impression was wrong. He wasn't as clueless about this as she first thought.

This was not the outcome she expected, and one she could ill afford right now. The element of surprise was on their side, and failure, as the saying went, was not an option. Her mind rolled over scenarios as quick as a supercomputer. "It explains nothing. That phone should never be off. Find him."

"I'm on it. I've sent out two more."

She slapped the laptop shut. "The B-team. That's just great. I expect better of you."

"They're not a B-team. They're excellent."

"If they're so excellent, why weren't they sent in first?"

"He was better."

"Apparently not."

His head was down, something he never did. "We made a mistake. These two will not fail."

"Make sure they don't, or I will hold you personally responsible. I want her before the sun comes up, and you're running out of time."

He brought his gaze up to meet hers. "You'll have her."

Slowly Katrina folded her hands on top of the closed laptop. "If I don't..."

It was the first time she'd ever seen a shadow of fear cross Eli's face. He'd been at her right hand for decades. He had her ear and her trust. At least until tonight. She didn't have a good feeling about this, and someone had to be held responsible. The position fell to Eli by default.

He glanced at the clock, the look of fear intensifying. She understood why. Time was growing short. The sun would be coming up soon.

Chapter Eleven

Sasha really didn't need a crowd, but this wasn't a time to be choosy. Besides, if the writer, correction, Dee, was telling the truth, the Consortium was after her too, and she had no real reason to doubt the truth of her words. Despite everything that had happened tonight, she was curious. Was her research into Imre and Katrina really severe enough to piss them off? These were strange times, and perhaps her intrusion at this particular moment might have been enough to worry them in a way they never had before.

Then again, maybe Dee was powerful in her own right. As a best-selling author, she had to be wealthy. That alone gave her power over many. Not enough to go up against those who had been planning for centuries, but perhaps enough to make trouble. By default, Dee was now a member of the partnership she and Rodney had formed years ago. It changed the game, and it struck her that she wasn't as opposed to the idea as she'd been a few minutes before.

She studied her now as she leaned against the counter. Dee was much taller than Sasha, although more than height set them apart. Her style was completely different. Dee was bold and modern and fascinating. Leather attire aside, Sasha had never completely let go of her early twentieth-century roots. That had been the time for her to come into her own, and she'd been doing it when everything changed. What should have been never came to pass, and perhaps that was why she clung to the familiar. The pearls were gone, as were the dresses and hats. It was her signature long hair that she'd never been able to part with, except for those few years early in the twentieth century when she had to pretend to be a man.

"Why would they destroy your home?" It was a legitimate question. She wanted to make sense of why they'd bother to blow up her home instead of taking the easiest path, which was to kill her outright. Sasha needed to understand why she'd become a threat in order to know how to use the knowledge.

"She's a little too smart for her own good." It was Prima who responded.

Sasha glanced over at her. She seemed an unlikely ally for Dee. One was a polished and successful literary name, while the other was a free-spirited woman with almost preternatural skills. Almost was the operative word, for though Prima could see beyond the veil separating the worlds, she wasn't one of them. She was very much human, which could very easily get her killed. Sasha had liked her the very first time they met, and she still did. She worried that Prima would put herself in the middle of the fight and it would cost her everything.

"I have a theory," Rodney added.

"Spit it out." She was in a hurry, though she didn't really want to share why. To blurt out that she needed to find sustenance would be akin to a fox jumping into a pen of rabbits. For the time being, she would keep that secret to herself.

"Dee was getting too close to uncovering information they didn't want exposed. Something in her research triggered an alarm, and voilà. She was on their radar."

"A trigger." It was actually a great theory, something she or her techs would think to do if on a case. In fact, they had.

"It's what I would do," Rodney said. "Put in a tracker. Make sure I know what's going on at all times. Somebody gets too close"—he snapped his fingers—"bye-bye."

Sasha turned back to Dee. "What did you uncover? Tell me exactly what you did and quickly."

"Well, if some asshat hadn't destroyed my home, I could show you."

"Asshat. I like that phrase. You don't seem all that upset about losing your home. I'm as angry as I've ever been about my business. Of course it was more than my business. It was also my home. The whole thing has me seeing red."

A shadow crossed Dee's face. "Oh, don't get me wrong. I'm angry, but I'm more scared. I mean, I'm not used to people who go to that kind of extreme just because I hit a nerve. I've dealt with lots of people in my career, and plenty of them were just horrible human beings. But horrible enough to try to destroy me, not so much, and that scares the daylights out of me."

It had been a long time since Sasha had felt anything even remotely like fear, so it was hard for her to relate. She wanted to tear someone's throat out, not hide from them. "We should go to your home and see if anything is viable."

Dee shook her head. "No."

"Don't you want to see what was done?" She knew exactly what they'd done to her, was there when it happened, and that personal look gave her more motive to do it right back. She wanted to find each and every one responsible and rip their heads off.

Dee nodded slowly. "I do, and at some point I'm going to have to see it with my own eyes to make it real. Right at the moment, I'm clinging to a bit of denial. I've had too many surprises tonight, you included. I don't want to stand in front of what used to be my life and see a big, charred pile of ash."

Sasha finally smiled. She liked that she was a surprise to this beautiful woman. It hit her as she looked into her deep, dark eyes that in another time and place, she'd like to be a lot more than a surprise to her.

It was still hard for Dee to really grasp that the woman in front of her was a vampire. Seriously, she looked like any attractive woman she might meet through mutual friends. Maybe a little paler than some, but some folks just weren't sun worshippers. What struck her the most: how beautiful she was. Despite the depiction of them in popular culture, vampires weren't beautiful, were they? They were mean and ugly and evil. A creature one wanted to stay a great distance away from.

Nothing about Sasha screamed mean or evil, blood-soaked clothing aside, and she sure as heck wasn't ugly. Far from it. She looked like she could hold her own in about any fight yet had a softness about her that the hard shell didn't quite hide. Or the black leather. My, oh, my, was that enticing. She reminded her of someone from a kick-ass vampire ninja movie…Wait, was that even a thing? If it wasn't, it should be, because Sasha could totally pull it off. If she ever got back to that vampire book she was planning to write, her protagonist would definitely be a kickass ninja vampire dressed all in leather with long, thick hair and mesmerizing eyes.

Dee's breath caught in her throat as the thought of pulling off all that leather jumped unbidden into her mind. With a ferocity that came out of nowhere, she suddenly wanted to see what was beneath all that toughness. Like right now.

"Knock it off" went through her mind just as quickly. Bigger fish to fry than satisfying a sudden hormonal itch, and honestly, that's what it had to be. The biggest fish in that frying pan was where she was going to live now that her house appeared to be a giant mound of torched kindling. If not for the genius of the cloud, she'd be wiped out. A fan of new and fancy technology, she'd been quick to establish her cloud backups. Plus, they allowed her to work anywhere, anytime. Sure, she heard all the naysayers and their predictions of theft via the cloud, but it was worth the risk. It made her life much easier.

Now it made her loss less damaging. Her works were safe, and even though she'd lost personal possessions, she still had what was most important: her stories. Too bad she'd failed to back up her most recent research on the vampires. She'd meant to but got so caught up in what she was finding, combined with Prima's promise to show her how it was all real, that she'd neglected that one final step. Everything she'd found had been saved in a nicely labeled folder on her hard drive. Now it was all gone.

Her eyes met Sasha's, and she was struck again by their depth. This woman—and it was difficult to think of her as anything else—was like a river. Smooth as glass on top, while deep and full of currents below. She would love to know what she was thinking about right now, because she was certain it was far more than the simple loss of her own property. She could almost see the wheels turning in her head, and she suspected plans were being made, organized, and a timetable for deployment established.

"I don't like that someone destroyed my home. I really don't. At the same time, it's just stuff. I can replace stuff."

Sparks appeared to flash in Sasha's dark eyes. Now that was a trick she was sure had to be all vampire. "It is more than that, and no one has the right to take away another's possessions."

Boy, she detected a whole lot of bitterness under her words.

There was a story there, and nobody had to tell her the ending wasn't a good one. Dee simply shrugged. Possessions were great and all, and yes, Sasha was right that no one had the right to take them away. Dee rationalized the loss a little differently. There were more important things in the world than a sofa or a jewelry box or even a treasured computer. She could make a life again without worrying about trinkets.

She didn't try to press the point with Sasha because Dee had the distinct impression this wasn't the first time something enormous had happened to her. Even though to her this all felt like a blitz attack, Sasha's take was clearly different, and with it came a personal affront. What had happened in her life that had her so attached to her belongings? That attachment didn't make sense. If she truly was a vampire, then she had forever to replace anything she lost.

Dee and Prima had become such good friends partially because they both valued the metaphysical over the physical. Though she might be reading it wrong, that didn't appear to be the case with the beautiful vampire. What an interesting layer to an already interesting woman.

Before either of them could go down that path, Rodney interrupted them. "Ladies, you might want to see this."

As she walked over to where Rodney sat in front of his bank of screens, Dee glanced at her fitness tracker, surprised to see that the night was almost gone. It was a quarter to four in the morning. How in the world had the night slipped by so quickly? And why wasn't she even remotely tired? She was, after all, a woman who loved her sleep, and she hadn't gotten a lot of it during the last twenty-four hours. There was going to be hell to pay later.

Rodney leaned back in his chair. "Take a look. As my favorite uncle used to say, shit's hitting the fan out there. It's looking like a *War of the Worlds* movie."

"Book," both Dee and Sasha said at the same time. A little flutter danced in Dee's heart as they echoed each other. She adored a woman who knew her literature, or genre fiction if talking to a true bibliophile snob. Bottom line, if she knew the works of H.G. Wells, she was okay as far as Dee was concerned. This vampire thing was getting stranger and more interesting. Did they read novels? Had she read her novels? She liked the idea.

A sudden thought stopped her. Was it more than simply knowing or reading the novel? She was a vampire, right? That's what Prima had told her and Rodney had confirmed. She had totally accepted it as the truth probably before Sasha came back. So, was it possible that she'd done more than read the book? Had she actually known H.G. Wells? The idea fascinated her, and Dee wasn't above asking. Well, perhaps not right now, but when the moment was right. How cool would it be if she could talk to someone who knew him?

She shifted her gaze from Sasha's profile to the bank of monitors. It took her a second before what she was seeing made sense. One monitor was still on her neighborhood, though now it had moved away from its focus on her house to the length of the street. Rodney appeared to be manipulating the cameras to try to get as much of a three-sixty view as possible.

"I thought the cameras weren't yours?"

He didn't look up. "Nope. But baby, I got skills. They try to outsmart me. They fail!"

"You hacked them."

"Damn straight. Big Brother wants to watch all of us, I'm gonna watch right back."

This man was hard to dislike. He was handsome, smart, and funny. Yeah, his off-the-grid mentality had the flavor of an eccentric, but then again, didn't they all have a touch of eccentricity? Returning her gaze to the screen, she studied the scene that filled it. Half a dozen unmoving forms lay stretched out on that familiar ribbon of asphalt. Her mind didn't want to process what she was seeing, yet her strong character did.

"This is live?" She didn't want to believe it was. She knew it was.

"It's live."

Her stomach turned. Bodies, many of them, lay this way and that. Some in the street and some half on the sidewalk, half in the road. One shape in particular caught her attention, and after a second, it hit her why. Patrice Self, her neighbor two doors down and sometimes running partner, was on her back, her open eyes pointing toward the sky. Even if she'd been facedown, Dee would have known her. She'd recognize the spandex tights and yellow jacket anywhere. If she'd seen that outfit once, she'd seen it twenty times. Now her neighbor, her friend, was splayed on the asphalt, a dark stain on her chin. She didn't want to consider what the stain might be.

On another monitor, Rodney had pulled up the massive park in downtown Spokane. It was beautiful and had something for everyone. Art, nature, ice-skating, and a stunning view of the falls. Like her street, it was cluttered with bodies. The sick feeling in her stomach intensified. It took a lot of effort not to throw up.

How could this be happening? What could take down Patrice and all the others? Rodney clicked through a series of screens, presumably all the cameras he'd hacked into, and each one displayed a similar picture. Place after place. Body after body. And, as they watched, the darkness punctuated by the tall streetlamps began to fade, and the true horror of what they were seeing came into clearer focus.

"Was there some kind of dirty bomb?" It was the only thing she could think of to make sense out of what she was seeing. Not that she really understood what a dirty bomb was or what it could do.

Rodney shook his head, and beside her she could feel the tension in Sasha's body. It was like she was filled with electricity about to burst forth like lightning. Prima was standing next to her on her other side and holding her arm so tight Dee was pretty sure she'd have bruises in the exact shape of fingers once she let go.

"No," Rodney said, his voice thick and dark. He used his mouse to move the focus of one of the cameras in for a close-up of one of the unmoving bodies. "It's something much worse."

Katrina felt the weight of fatigue bearing down on her shoulders. It was always like this. The higher the sun climbed in the sky, the harder the weariness pushed on her. When she was first turned, she had suffered as the newly turned often did. Hunger made her more animal than woman, and even a brush of sunlight on her skin caused excruciating pain. Her maker hadn't taught her the ways of a vampire, so she'd had to discover them on her own.

It still made her angry, even after all this time. She had been treated like trash, the whisper of death always in her ear. Many times it had been very close. Misery had been her closest companion. The nights of scratching and clawing to survive. The days of hiding so she could rest in peace. She'd done what she'd needed to, and her maker had gotten what she deserved. Katrina had been young and angry back then, and had acted rashly. It would have been better if she'd gone about it differently. Then again, it was a different time and place, and she'd acted the only way she felt she could. In the end, it had actually made her stronger and hungrier. That hunger had gotten her to where she was today, and that made it all worthwhile.

Now, as she let the fatigue settle over her, she allowed her mind to wander back to that predawn morning when she'd been summoned to the great study where so many momentous decisions were made. Once more a familiar demand was made. For the first time ever, Katrina had refused. She smiled, remembering how it all went down. She did not offer her wrist for the slice of the knife that would leave yet another scar. She did not allow her blood to flow into the crystal goblet. Instead, she pulled her hair back and offered her neck.

Invitation extended. Invitation accepted. Ninety minutes later, she was the only one left standing. She'd believed she'd won and was on top of the world.

In some ways, as they say in these times, the joke was on her. She'd raced into the night, free at last and full of blood lust. Such wild abandon had nearly undone her. She had quickly discovered she had a great deal to learn and that bridges burned could never be rebuilt. Out on the streets, finding her way, she was alone and, though she would never admit it to anyone, lonely. Then it all changed. One time, one single time in all these years, she'd found another who filled her heart. She had believed she would no longer be alone, and this time, rather than turning away, she had made the ultimate decision to bestow upon her love the most precious of gifts. She expected gratitude. She didn't get it.

Her one true love had turned on her after she had shared with her the most precious thing she had. Worse than that, she'd abandoned Katrina. She'd been looking for her ever since. Now, she'd found her.

In a way it was a fitting time for it to all come full circle. The Consortium that she now headed had been working for a very long time to make the world theirs. For thousands of years the vampires had been forced to hide in the shadows, to be something less than they were, and that was wrong. They were far superior to humans, and their rightful place was at the top of the hierarchy, not hiding in dark corners, not pretending.

It was a beautiful thing to be in her seat right now, for their time had finally come, and it had begun this night. That it started with the one she had been seeking for nearly a century was the most fitting piece of all. She could hardly wait to see her face and the look in her eyes when she finally understood what was to happen to her. What Katrina was about to accomplish would make previous world conquests look like schoolyard reenactments. She was going to be the one they talked about and revered for thousands of years.

Eli came into the room. "Katrina, you must rest."

He was right, of course. If her face looked anywhere close to his, it was true. His eyes were dim and his features tired. She shut the laptop and stood. "Everyone is in position." She'd finally received communications from all the key players. The plans they'd made were falling into place like a complicated and beautiful thousand-piece puzzle. By the end of the week, she would no longer have to hide in a luxury hotel room. All would bow to her.

She would bow to her.

CHAPTER TWELVE

Sasha fought against the physical weight of the drowsiness pushing at the back of her eyes and making her want to lie down and sleep right here. It didn't matter that she was belowground and far away from the rays of the dawning sun. It didn't matter that she still craved sustenance. Her body instinctively sensed that it was time to power down like a laptop. Even the oldest and most experienced of the vampires couldn't indefinitely resist the draw. It became easier as they got older, but it never went away. Two things were inescapable: their need to rest during daylight hours and their need for human blood.

The former had never really bothered Sasha. But the latter had taken her far more time to come to grips with. Once her new reality had sunk in, she'd attempted to make peace with it in her own way. She'd tried hard to sustain herself on animal blood. It was a colossal failure. Just the thought of what she'd gone through in those early days still made her shudder. She never wanted to be that sick again or to feel as though a thousand needles pierced her skin hour after hour. Even the gunshots ordered to end her mortal existence were less painful than the unsated hunger.

The gunshots. It had been a very long time since she let herself think of that night in the dark basement with her family. She could still vividly recall the searing pain of the shots piercing her body. They should have killed her as they'd done to Mama, Papa, Olga, Tatiana, Anastasia, and Alexei. The entire Russian royal family rendered bloody and lifeless on a dirty basement floor. All except her. She'd wanted them to kill her, had begged to join them because going on alone was worse than the agony of the wounds caused by the bullets. Her fingers drifted to her shoulder where one of the scars was hidden beneath her shirt. The smell of her blood as it had dripped to the floor while the one she trusted as no other carried her from the room and away from everything she'd ever known was still with her. Her wishes had counted for squat. Her pleas for release unanswered. She shook her head and let go of the memories. She returned her focus to the present.

Trickles of unease rippled through her, her body telling her it was not to be denied. Forgoing human blood was three times worse than the wounds that had bloodied the basement floor. Nothing had prepared her for what had happened when she attempted to deny what she had become. No amount of willpower could topple the hunger. Right now, she didn't have a choice.

Back then, she'd believed she did. When Dagmar had found her curled up in a ball, deep in a cave, she was almost gone, and her unintelligible mumbles were prayers for release. Her body was a shadow of what it had been, and if she'd had a mirror, she had no doubt a monster's face would have stared back at her. The beautiful daughter of a tsar had been erased. She'd been a skeleton with large eyes and a dying soul.

Fortunately for Sasha, Dagmar wasn't afraid or put off by the feral creature she discovered. Sasha smiled now, thinking of the kindly woman who had brought her back. It had surprised her to discover that Dagmar knew not only who she was but what she was, or rather what she'd become. Neither had put her off. In fact, Dagmar had taught her everything she needed to know to survive without becoming a cold-blooded killer. How to feed and sustain herself without leaving a trail. How to move and hunt and protect herself against those who sought to destroy her and her kind. Dagmar had become more of a mother to Sasha than the woman who had given birth to her.

That was one reason she so strongly identified as Sasha Rudin. Dagmar had bestowed the name upon her at her second birth day, the one where her past disappeared and she became what she was still.

If Dagmar were here now, she'd admonish Sasha for being stupid. Only a foolish vampire would push beyond rational limits. Everything that was happening outside the sanctuary where she now found herself would still be there when the sun set. Only a foolish vampire would forgo the rest and nourishment that would make her strong and ready for battle.

"I'm not foolish," she whispered and felt that somewhere in the great beyond, Dagmar could still hear her and was shaking a bony finger in her face, her black eyes fierce and her long silver braid swaying.

"What?" Dee turned and looked at her. A tiny thrill coursed through Sasha as those eyes met hers. What about this human was so appealing? When the world above them was no longer falling apart, perhaps she'd take time to figure it out. If, that is, the world survived.

Sasha shook her head slightly. "Nothing. Just thinking out loud." She turned to Rodney and opened her mouth. Before she could speak, he stood up.

"Come on. You need to lie down before you fall down." Good old Rodney. He reminded her of Dagmar. They'd have liked each other. In fact, she could almost hear Dagmar telling her he'd be a good man for her to marry. Even though Dagmar had accepted Sasha for the vampire she was, she'd always harbored a hope that she'd be like other women and find a soul mate. It was hard for her to accept that Sasha's soul mate would never be a man. Sasha didn't love her any less for that misguided hope.

Rodney put an arm around her shoulders and led her to a room in a back corner, where he flipped a switch to turn on the overhead light. It wasn't a big room, though large enough for the double bed pushed up against one wall. It wasn't her beautiful bedroom with the king-sized bed, plush bedding, and custom window blinds that blocked out all light. She'd never see that room again.

"This do it for you?"

"Yes." Her eyelids were growing very droopy, and her arms felt heavy. At the moment, a slab of plywood would work. This was more than marginally better.

Rodney nodded and left her. "I'll see you at sundown."

She nodded. "Thank you."

Her fingers found the wall switch, and she turned out the light before taking the few steps to the bed. It was soft and the room cool. Perfect. It was all she needed for now.

She'd worry about the blood part later.

❖

Dee watched Rodney and Sasha as they left the great room. She looked as good retreating as she did from the front. *Stop it.* What was with her? She didn't get puppy-dog eyes when a good-looking woman walked into a room. She was the cool, professional novelist who sat at the celebrity table at writers' conferences and signed autographs. People did that to her, not the other way around.

Until she met her first vampire. Or maybe it had just been so long since she'd had a date that she was susceptible to a pretty face. Except Sasha wasn't simply a pretty face. She had never met anyone this deep before, and it was like an addictive drug. She wanted more. She wanted it all.

"What's going on in that head of yours?" Prima handed her a cup of tea. "Herbal," she added.

"She's interesting."

Prima sipped her tea. "She's a lot more than interesting. That woman has some stories to tell. Not that you'd get her to spill a single one."

"Why didn't you ever spill to me about her?"

"Easy. Not my place."

"Lame excuse. I'm one of your best friends. How could you not let me in on this incredible secret?"

Prima put a hand on her shoulder. "I love you like a sister, you know that."

"I do." And she did. Prima was always there for her, good times and bad. When Dee became a hit, Prima didn't treat her any different, for which she was incredibly grateful. That wasn't the case with more than a few people she'd known her whole life, and it had made it difficult to maintain those relationships.

"Sasha is special, and her secret was always safe with me, just as yours are."

"Then why introduce us now?"

"Sasha has told me at least a dozen times since I met her that sometimes humans need to know. She can pick those she can trust, and she told me I'd know too. Not just the who but also the when. She was right. You opened that door, and I knew it was time for you to be brought into the fold."

"My research?"

"It was more than the research. It was the threat. That screamed to me it was time to bring you in, and most important, I knew you could be trusted."

Strange as it all sounded, it made sense to her. "Did you know about this?" She waved her hand toward the computer monitors, where chaos was still evident across the various sections of the city.

"No, but I get the feeling Rodney and Sasha suspected."

"Suspected what?" Rodney came back into the room and dropped into his chair. He had six or seven baby carrots in his hand. Instead of tossing them into his mouth, he set them on the desktop.

"What's happening out there?" Dee was looking at the monitor showing her street.

He nodded slowly. "It was more than suspicion. We knew they planned to do something and were waiting for them to play their hand."

"Now what?" Dee was lost. She wanted to go home, except she didn't have a home to go to, and frankly, she was scared what she'd find even if she did. If they were willing to blow up her home just because she'd uncovered their identities through her research, she was pretty sure they wouldn't stop at mere destruction of her property. She shivered as another thought struck. Perhaps they thought she was inside her home when it went skyward.

"Now, we rest."

Both Prima and Dee looked at him. "What?"

"Has anybody gotten any sleep? You realize we've been up all night."

At his words, fatigue hit her like a baseball bat. "You're right." She looked down at her hands. The tell was there. They were shaking, which told her one of two things: not enough sleep or too much coffee. She hadn't had coffee for hours.

"Pick a bed and I'll hit the sofa. Let's sleep for a few hours and then…"

Dee yawned. "And then what?"

Rodney whirled back around to face the monitors. "We're going out there."

❖

Katrina sensed the daylight dawning outside the blackout drapes of the hotel suite. It weighed on her heavily, yet she still resisted the pull. A great many things were going through her mind. A myriad of tasks to accomplish in the coming hours, and she didn't want to waste time by resting. The urge to resist was as powerful as the urge to lie down.

The biggest problem wasn't all that she needed to do to accomplish her coup. No. She couldn't get *her* out of her mind. She wanted to see her face sooner rather than later. Now. She wanted to stand before her this very moment. Not tomorrow. Not the next day. Now.

Even as a child she'd been this way—impatient and demanding. It was a survival mechanism. She'd embraced it as a human, gloried in it as the superior being she had become. She didn't have to wait for satisfaction or the obedience of those who surrounded her. She demanded and received it.

Only one had been contrary enough to defy her. In any other circumstance she would say strong enough to defy her and live. Not just live but also evade her and thrive as if throwing that very success in her face. She refused to think of this person as possessing the necessary strength and intelligence to become a ghost. Strength hadn't put her out of her reach for so long; it was dumb luck.

Like others who foolishly thought fortune was on their side, her luck had finally run out. The ghost had been found. She would bow before Katrina before another twenty-four hours elapsed. That's why Katrina was fighting so hard against the darkness that demanded her acquiescence. Her racing mind was warring with her bodily needs. Slumber was getting in the way of her glorious victory. She didn't want to waste precious time.

It didn't matter what she wanted. Ultimately she would lose only one fight, and it was the battle against rest. Her strength was legendary, her determination the envy of all, but she wasn't immune to the whims of the universe that set the rules for her kind.

She'd been railing against this complication for a very long time. It didn't make sense to her. How could the most powerful beings on the planet be brought to their knees by something as stupid as daylight? It wasn't right, and to her way of thinking there had to be a way around it. She'd been trying to find it for centuries and was close.

Clearly not close enough, or she'd be out there right now watching the waves of change flow over the city. When the sun set and she was able to rise, things would be different everywhere. Once she had her empire established, her research project to counteract the effects of daylight would go into overdrive. She'd put the best and the brightest on task to solve this particular quirk.

A plan formulating, she relaxed into the comfortable bed, her mind calming as well, and as it did, her thoughts returned to another time.

Katrina couldn't help but notice her as she sat on the low wall staring out into the night sky. She should have been inside by now, but the lively young woman couldn't be contained. At least that's what the others had warned her of when she agreed to take the watch. She wasn't like any royal she had ever encountered before. She was kind and gentle, and everyone liked her, which was why she was allowed to do what no one else could.

For Katrina, it was a fluke, a game. She didn't need to be here, certainly didn't need to pretend to be something she wasn't, yet the thrill of playing the game was irresistible. This was history in the making, even if the majority of those involved didn't realize the import of what was occurring. Katrina did and had decided it would be fun to see it up close and personal. Hence the demeaning job and horrible uniform. It gave her a ringside seat to witness what was to come.

Now as she stood by the corner of the building and watched the beauty in the unflattering skirt and blouse, something inside her blossomed. The feeling was as surprising as it was shocking. Her world no longer had room for attraction and emotion. Lust, yes. Desire, yes. The kind of attraction that was a precursor to love, never. Yet there it was. Strong and undeniable. She wanted to sit next to her on that low wall, hold her hand, and gaze into her eyes. She wanted to kiss her lips and hold her in her arms. She wanted to strip away the awful clothes and gaze on her perfect body.

As if sensing she was being watched, the young woman turned her head her way. A slight smile turned up the corners of her mouth. It was the smile of an angel. She was lost.

A tear slipped from the corner of Katrina's eye before the darkness she'd been fighting finally won the battle.

CHAPTER THIRTEEN

Sasha came back to consciousness with a start and snapped into full alert mode. She tensed at the unfamiliar darkness and strange sounds. Not at home. Then it returned in a flash. She didn't have a home to be in, and all of her trusted vampire friends were gone. Her home and business were destroyed. Those she thought were her allies were traitors. All she had was one off-the-grid survivalist and a gentle-soul psychic. Well, and perhaps one beautiful, smart, and headed-for-trouble writer.

She pushed up to a sitting position and thought about Dee. She smiled, which was surprising, given the state of her life at the moment. She couldn't help it. Dee wasn't just attractive, she was smart as they came, and from everything she'd seen so far, fearless. Seriously, she was the first one in decades to even get a sniff of the preternatural forces that had been working behind the mist for at least a thousand years. That was impressive. Dangerous, but impressive.

As she swung her feet around to the floor, she wished she'd had time to pack a bag of clothes. Her shirt was stiff with dried blood and not what she really wanted to wear. Since she didn't have anything clean, she was stuck with what she had, at least for now. On the upside, Rodney's hideaway possessed all the comforts of home, which included a shower. It was bound to be a long night, and she wanted to be fresh and ready for whatever was going to happen, even if she had to put blood-stained clothes back on.

Before she hit the shower, she walked out to the main living area. Empty. Rodney's command center was alive with images flashing across the screens but void of human monitoring. He wasn't in his chair, and neither Prima nor Dee was anywhere in sight. She stopped in front of the multiple monitors and watched for at least five minutes. The scenes that played out across them were something out of a futuristic movie. It was as if toxic poison had rained down upon the area, and in a twisted way that's what had happened.

Sasha possessed a great deal of information about toxins the Consortium was working on, designed not to kill all the humans but to destroy the weak and render the survivors powerless. In short, they intended to create a worldwide herd of cattle—strong, powerful, and full of nourishment but lacking the will or intelligence to do anything except as their new masters directed. The mist would clear, their masters would step out, and for the first time ever, the vampires would assume their rightful place.

She'd heard the story long before the rumors became persistent enough for her to realize they were more reality than rumor. The one who made her had bragged about the time to come when vampires would no longer have to hide. Sasha had been horrified then and had told her maker how she felt. It hadn't gone over well. It had gone over even worse when Sasha refused to become what her maker had intended her to be: a lover and a partner in the ultimate takeover. Fury didn't even begin to describe the emotion that had rained down on Sasha as she'd run for her life. She continued to feel the heat of that fury like a hot breath on the back of her neck.

Right now, she didn't want to remember any of that. Instead, she wanted to concentrate on how to reverse this situation before it was too late. For some, it already was, which was clear from the bodies shown on the many screens. Nothing more could be done for those tragic souls, but she could concentrate on helping everyone else. That and finding her maker. It was time for old debts to be paid in full.

After wandering through the rest of the bunker, she was surprised to discover it empty. Getting Rodney out of here was no small feat. The man was set up to be self-sufficient for years. He could be Social Security eligible before he would have to step out into the sunshine. Dee and Prima must have used some serious persuasion, and she would have loved to hear what they'd said to get him to agree to leave. At the same time, it was nice to have a little silence. She'd known this day would come and had plans at the ready. The problem was, some of her *trusted* colleagues were in on those plans, and right now, beyond the three she was holed up with, she didn't know who to trust. She checked her cell phone on the off chance the friends she'd tried to reach last night might have gotten back to her. Not a single call or message in the hours she'd been out. Just as she'd feared last night, instinct told her she'd never hear from any of them again.

Instead of dwelling on that depressing thought, she decided to take care of her immediate needs, and that meant the shower. She went back to her small room and undressed, leaving her clothes on the bed. She looked at the bag she'd taken when she left Imperial and wished it had more in it instead of just the egg, her cell phone, some folders, and a tablet. No clothes. No toothbrush. No packets of blood. She tried not to focus on the last missing item.

Naked, she walked the short distance to the compact but well-designed bathroom. She smiled as a vision of her mother popped into her head. How shocked she would be at the thought of her little princess walking around naked. *Times have changed, Mama.* The water was hot and felt nice against her cool skin. Surprisingly, Rodney stocked his shower with vanilla shampoo and a lovely lavender-scented soap. Who would have guessed the mountain man had a taste for sweet and floral. It was an unexpected and appreciated luxury.

After stepping out of the shower, she dried off and was walking back toward her room while rubbing the towel over her long hair when she heard a noise. Her head snapped up, and she stopped as she came face-to-face with Dee. She smiled as a flush colored Dee's neck.

❖

Dee didn't know what to say. Almost walking into a beautiful, naked vampire was absolutely the last thing on her mind when she'd started toward the bathroom. She couldn't pinpoint if it was nerves or the very large coffee she'd downed just before they made their way back here, but in any event, a trip to the bathroom was first on her agenda. The urge was so great she didn't even bother to drop the bag she gripped in her right hand.

Now, she stood with her mouth open, all thoughts of needing to use the bathroom gone. Her whole focus shifted in a millisecond from her own bodily needs to Sasha's incredible body. Her breathing seemed to have stopped as well, and the only word that came to her was "damn." She quickly shoved her left hand into the pocket of her jeans to keep herself from reaching out to touch the skin that was so smooth it looked like silk. Wasn't really her style to go around touching anyone without their permission, but for the first time ever, she was tempted. Shame on her.

Shame on Sasha for looking that gorgeous. Did all vampires look this incredible? If they did, it wasn't hard to understand how they could prey easily on humans.

Lordy, what was wrong with her? Okay, she could blame it on stress. After all, someone had blown up her house like it was nothing more than fuel for a campfire. All her things were gone—her clothes, her computers, her memories. Well, maybe not her memories. The photos, yes, what they represented, no. All of that still lived bright and clear in her mind.

Still, it was stressful, and that had become as clear as a summer sky when she, Prima, and Rodney had ventured out a few hours ago. They'd taken Sasha's lead and slept for a few hours, but by noon, they were awake and wanting to take measure of what was happening outside the bunker. Even Rodney, who preferred to spend the vast majority of his time inside his sanctuary, was up for the adventure to the surface. For Dee it was more about getting clean clothes, a toothbrush, and a few other essential items that had gone skyward when her house blew up. Once they made it back to the city, what on any other day might have been an easy errand turned into something out of a futuristic movie.

Chaos was everywhere. Death was everywhere, and no one quite understood why yet. CDC trailers were parked on streets. Armed national guard drove in those imposing green vehicles that made her want to run for cover. Stores were closed, and no one appeared to be out and about. Was anyone left to be out and about?

Fortunately, Prima had clothes and sundry items that fulfilled what she needed. She packed a couple of bags, as did Prima, and after driving around for an hour, they decided their best course of action was to get back to the bunker. Perhaps Sasha would have an idea about what was going on.

"You're back." Sasha's words, deep and sultry, brought her back to the moment.

"Ah, yeah." *Smooth, Dee, smooth.*

"Where were you?" She dropped the hand holding the towel she'd been drying her hair with to her side, seemingly quite comfortable with her back-to-nature look.

Dee liked that look a great deal but tried to keep her gaze on Sasha's eyes. Nothing good could come from acting like a lovesick puppy. "We went to get supplies."

"Supplies?"

"Yeah, like clean clothes, a toothbrush, and deodorant. Important stuff I didn't have any reason to bring with me yesterday because I thought I'd be going back home."

Sasha's eyes narrowed and then she nodded. "Yes, I understand. You must tell me what you found outside."

She'd be happy to share, in a few minutes. "You want to get dressed first?" Sasha came across as perfectly happy to trot out to the main room in the buff and go directly into a debrief session with her three bunker mates. If she did that, Dee would find it very hard to concentrate. It was taking an effort now not to lick her lips.

A flash of a smile flew across her face. Here and gone in an instant. Somehow she had the feeling that Sasha knew exactly what was going through Dee's mind. "Perhaps that would be a good idea."

"Here." Dee held out the second of the bags she'd filled at Prima's house. "I thought maybe you could use some things as well."

Again an expression flashed across her face. This time it seemed more like gratitude, and Dee was very glad she'd taken time to put the bag together for her.

"Thank you." Sasha took it from Dee's outstretched hand and then moved quickly down the short hallway and into the small bedroom, leaving Dee staring after her.

"Wow," she muttered softly. Just when she thought things couldn't get more interesting, they did. Twenty-four hours ago she didn't believe vampires existed, and now here she was not only lusting after one but bringing her clothes and a toothbrush. Did vampires need to brush their fangs? Her world was growing stranger by the moment.

All of a sudden she remembered why she'd come this way in the first place, and she raced to the bathroom, laughing as she went. It was official; her world had flipped upside down. Everything outside was going crazy in a way that made absolutely no sense, her home was gone, and she was laughing. Not in a hysterical, need-medication kind of way. Nope, it was a "hot damn, this is gonna be quite the ride" kind of way.

World apocalypse or not, Dee liked it.

❖

Katrina looked at herself in the mirror and smiled. As much as she hated losing time, it was time well spent. She looked incredible. A good meal and hours of rest did wonders for even the strongest of her kind. For her in particular, it was even better. She was the most beautiful vampire in the world, even if she did say so. And she did. So did everyone else, if they valued their existence, that is. No one could resist her.

That thought brought the ghost of a frown to her face. That statement was technically incorrect. One was able to resist her. In concert with the changes she'd put into motion, the single dark spot on her reputation would be wiped away as if it had never existed. Then she'd be able to sit back and enjoy her new status as was rightfully her due.

She smiled at herself again in the mirror. Everything thus far was going along swimmingly. She was quite happy with the reports that had come in so far, and she'd been up less than an hour. In the other room she could hear Eli moving around. He had beat her awake, as he always did, but then again, he didn't need the beauty sleep. He was handsome and efficient, just no prince. It wasn't important, considering she didn't need a prince at her side. She had no practical use for one unless he was as skilled at doing her bidding as Eli was. The very last thing she wanted in her bed, however, was a prince, or a duke, or even a king. That sort of companionship left her cold and disgusted. She never understood the desire and, even after centuries of existence, still couldn't fathom the appeal.

Now a princess, that was a whole other story. Women could warm her bed any time as long as they were beautiful and obedient. Willing wasn't a necessary element, and at this time in her life, she didn't care if they possessed an ounce of royal blood. There had once been a time when that had been a very concrete goal.

The last instance when she'd set her sights on royalty and even found herself unexpectedly falling in love, the end result was less than desirable. A defining characteristic for her was that she never made the same mistake twice. From then on she focused on straight-up sex and physical satisfaction. So much easier and cleaner, and who needed love anyway? She had everything without the necessity of touchy-feely emotions. Those sorts of things simply got in the way.

With one last pat to her hair, which didn't need it because it was already perfect, she turned away from the mirror. "What have you got for me?" She walked into the main room, toward the desk where Eli sat at his laptop. Outside, the big window that provided them a perfect view of the city and the river beyond sundown was complete, and the lights of the city were glowing. Eli had his head down and his fingers flying across the laptop keyboard.

He looked up and smiled. She had to admit, for a man, he was attractive, and he probably had his fair share of woman with a mere flash of that smile. It was mysterious and appealing. He did seem perpetually satisfied, so she suspected she was spot-on. "It's all coming together." He leaned back in the chair and nodded. "Everywhere from New York to LA, the Consortium is making their move, and it is incredible."

In many ways she wished they could be back in Seattle, where she could watch their carefully planned coup roll like a wave across the city. Spokane was big and urban, and it was dropping as it should. Still, it wasn't Seattle by any stretch, and that's where she wanted to be as her empire came into being. She loved the tall buildings, the Space Needle, the ocean—all things that were lacking from this place.

Seattle was missing only one thing, and that's what kept her here when she wanted to be on the other side of the state. *She* was somewhere out there in the darkness that spread across this falling city, and Katrina needed to be here when they finally flushed her out. She'd waited for this too long to be denied now. Even in the face of everything that was coming down on the humans who had selfishly clung to a world that should never have been theirs in the first place, she couldn't leave this city. Once the deed was done, she would fly back across the mountains and to the place that she preferred to call home.

"Have you located her yet?"

Now a frown darkened his face. "I don't know how she's doing it, but it's like she was never here. She should have surfaced after we blew her building, but nothing so far. It doesn't make sense. She should pop up somewhere."

"Have any of her people heard from her?"

He shook his head. "Nothing. Again, it's like she knows they've turned on her, although I can't figure out how. We were more than careful, and not a single one of them would have given us up. They all have an interest in what's coming down, and they aren't going to jeopardize it for her. She was good to them, just not as good as we've been. Their loyalty is to us."

Anger flowed over her and washed away all the good feelings she'd awakened with. Just like so many years ago, she was gone like the stars on a cloudy night. To say it pissed Katrina off was putting it politely. She calmed as she reminded herself that she couldn't hide forever. At some point she would be forced to surface if she wanted to survive.

One thing she was counting on was that her penchant to avoid human blood taken directly from the source would bring her out of hiding. Unlike Katrina, who had no such reservations, it made survival more complicated. Katrina liked simple and always had. Besides, taking it directly from the human source was infinitely more pleasurable, and she did prefer pleasure. In the little bit of time they'd had together, she'd tried to teach her that, but she'd resisted, and then she was gone.

"You have eyes on all sources of stored blood?" Unless she had changed in the last century, and Katrina doubted that was the case, she would have to make a run for one of the outlets that stored donated blood. If she refused to take it directly, it was the only logical choice.

"Indeed." Eli sounded a little offended that she would ask him such a question. He was thorough, and she supposed she'd be annoyed too if in his shoes.

"Don't get your panties in a twist."

"I know what I'm doing."

She nodded. "I'm aware of that. What about the writer? Surely you've tracked down Miss Snoop?" That one she was going to take great pleasure in drinking dry. How dare the busybody stick her nose in vampire business. They had a way of dealing with people like her when they got too close, and it was what one might term a permanent solution. She smiled again, her good humor returning.

This time Eli ran his fingers through his hair. "Funny thing is, she's gone missing in action too. I've never had this much trouble tracking down anyone before. I figured as soon as she heard about her house she'd come racing back. I put some of our best human soldiers on the watch, and according to what they're telling me, she hasn't stepped a single toe in the neighborhood."

That news bothered Katrina, though she couldn't quite nail down why. Someone as curious and smart as this woman would have to see the destruction for herself. She was sure of it. A tingling at the back of her neck made her think that perhaps this time she'd encountered a human that might cause more trouble than she was worth. Eliminating her intrusion should have been done and over with many hours ago. "Does she have any family in the city?"

He shook his head. "Way ahead of you there. The closest family she has is in Portland."

"She could have driven there. It's not that far."

"She could have, but she didn't. Her car was parked at her house when the boys did their handiwork. No rentals in her name. Unless she rode a bicycle, she's still in the city somewhere."

Katrina slammed her hand on the desk next to the laptop. "I don't care what you do or how you do it, but you will find her before sunrise."

CHAPTER FOURTEEN

Sasha almost laughed at Dee's expression when she encountered her outside the bathroom in all her natural glory. Sasha had gotten over her prim and conservative ways as the years rolled by. She'd been raised to be quite the proper princess. Nothing that could ever be considered revealing was ever to be worn. Never would she have considered walking into a common space with nothing on. Time had wiped away all those early lessons, and she said good riddance. Frankly, she didn't have time to worry about things like that. So she didn't.

The look on Dee's face had been endearing, and ego-building. Behind the shock that had been evident had been something else, and Sasha would be lying if she tried to say she hadn't liked it, a lot. Usually she didn't care what anyone else thought about her or her habits, her looks, or her body. Too much to do to worry about offending someone's puritan sensibilities.

By this time she would have thought those tendencies in an enlightened society would have faded. It wasn't the case. A certain segment of the population still clung to the antiquated beliefs, as if nothing else in the world was more important than modesty and propriety. She supposed that, to them, nothing was more precious, and that was fine with her as long as they kept their beliefs to themselves. She didn't need or want their piety.

What she did want, and maybe even needed, was to see that raw desire on another woman's face. She'd kept to herself for enough years now that the last time she'd been with a woman was more like a dream that fades in the morning upon awakening, a sort of shadowy memory with no form or definition. She'd decided that keeping everyone at arm's length was the best way to focus on the war that had been building for what seemed like forever. That was the only way she'd be prepared and ready when the day hit, and she'd been okay with that course of single-minded concentration.

By the gods, how wrong she'd been. She'd been so blindsided it was embarrassing. Traitors in her midst. Total destruction of her business and home. It was a wonder she ever became a successful businesswoman. Hopefully none of her clients would ever get wind of this colossal failure. But enough of that worry. It was for another day, considering she didn't even have a business to go back to at the moment. At least not the main office anyway. Surely a couple of divisional offices were still standing, she hoped.

Right now, neither business nor betrayal was foremost on her mind. She wanted to take a moment to simply bask in the enjoyment a woman's appreciation could bring her. It was something that let her feel good again, even if it was for a mere minute or two. Perhaps then she'd regain some feeling of control, because everything that had happened in the past twenty-four hours had pretty well stripped her of any whisper of power. She didn't care for the feeling. It had taken her far too long to capture and retain a sense of control, and to feel it slip away was abhorrent.

To see the admiring look in Dee's eyes gave her back some of what she'd lost in the last few hours, and she'd love to stand here and soak it in. If only she could. Good sense told her that Dee's suggestion she get dressed was a solid one. She'd love to take it further, to see where it might go. Maybe, if they lived through this, she would have time enough to see if what was behind the shock was worth exploring. She was fairly certain it was. She was quite literally not born yesterday and knew raw desire when she saw it, also when she felt the same strong raw desire in herself. That shouldn't be wasted.

First things first. She had to get dressed, make a plan, and go take down those bastards who had destroyed her life and were now trying to do the same to the humans as well as any vampire, like her, who didn't bow to their master plan. They were coming for her, but she was ready, and what they didn't know was definitely going to hurt them.

Sasha opened the bag Dee had handed her and smiled first at the toothbrush. The long-sleeved T-shirt with the single word "Namaste" on it seemed appropriate. She slipped it on before pulling on the tight leather pants that would serve as her armor. The jeans that Dee had put in the bag weren't going to cut it, and she left them in the bag. While she appreciated the clean shirt, she'd stick with her own pants. She laced up her boots and stood. Now that she was dressed and ready to face the night, her mind turned to the one thing this hideaway couldn't provide: nourishment. She was old enough to have discipline and restraint, and she was drawing on that now. The need that pushed at her before she rested hadn't disappeared. It was still there, tapping at her, reminding her it wouldn't be denied indefinitely. For the moment it would have to.

Not, however, all night. Sooner or later, the hunger would take hold like a giant conflagration, and she'd have to feed. It wouldn't be here, where three humans out in the other room trusted her. She refused to hurt her friends, and she didn't want Dee to have to witness the reality of what she really was. Despite depictions in popular culture, it wasn't pretty, or neat, or clean. Dee didn't need to be exposed to that.

Funny how the same concern didn't extend to Rodney and Prima. Of course, they'd known her for some time and understood what she was, not that either of them had ever witnessed a feeding. She hadn't wanted or needed to put them in that position. With Dee she absolutely didn't want to expose her to the ugly reality. My, oh, my, how things could change in an instant.

Why should she be surprised? Wasn't that exactly how she had become what she was right now? One moment she was a young woman dying of multiple bullet wounds and in the next, a creature of the night. One instant. That's all it took to change everything.

Enough! She didn't plan to take the time to analyze herself. No, she was going to leave this room, check on the state of the world outside their shelter, and then step out into that world, kick ass, and take names. She didn't intend to allow those bastards to destroy what she held dear. They had taken everything away from her once, but not again. Never again.

She picked up the egg from the nightstand where she'd set it before she dropped off into twilight slumber. It was surprising that she hadn't broken it when the blast hit her in the back and threw her to the ground. The universe gave her a gift by protecting it, and here it was, blue and gold, and just as beautiful as the first time she'd seen it. A single tear trickled from her right eye, and she wiped it away with the back of her free hand. She set the egg back on the small table next to the bed, staring at it, and said very softly, "I will avenge you." She wasn't talking about the egg.

❖

Dee finished up in the bathroom and walked back to the main room. On the way she passed the door to Sasha's room. It was wide open, which made her smile. The woman was immodest, but she'd be hard-pressed to admit that she didn't like that. Actually, she was tempted to stop and stare. Good manners prevailed, and she pushed herself on until she stood in the small kitchen area. Rodney lay stretched out on the sofa in the living-room area, one arm across his eyes. Soft snores whispered on the air. He was sound asleep. Probably a good idea. She'd managed a few hours earlier this morning, as had Prima and Rodney, but nobody had captured more than a couple hours. Except, of course, Sasha, who had dropped as soon as the sun had come up and then seemed to have popped awake fully refreshed as soon as it went down. At least she was assuming Sasha had popped up when the sun went down, given she'd had enough time to get showered and beautifully naked.

For Dee it had been hard to fall sleep after what had happened to her and what she'd seen on the monitors. Every time she closed her eyes, she'd envisioned those images of her street, people she'd known, neighbors she'd both liked and disliked, dead and bleeding in the road and on their lawns. Even her eventual sleep had been restless and uneasy. She'd dreamed of death and destruction, only to awaken covered in a cold sweat and consumed by a fear she couldn't name.

The journey out into the daylight hadn't made any of it better. In fact, it made her feel worse. The imaginations of those who wrote those novels or directed those films that prophesied what it would be like in the event of an end-of-days catastrophe had been close, but nothing they'd come up with captured what it felt like to really have it happen. The chaos, the military presence, the fear—all of it was suffocating and terrifying. The three of them had quickly discovered that they had to be stealthy in order to avoid the military that, from all appearances, was rounding up survivors "for their own safety" and taking them God knows where. No way was she going with them. A tiny whisper in the back of her mind told her not to trust them, and she intended to listen.

Besides, she felt far safer with Rodney than with the men and women wearing green and riding around in giant military vehicles. They might have had the best of intentions, except it sure didn't feel that way. So, they stuck to leapfrogging from cover to cover, a pretty good feat in a bright-red car, and finally managed to make it to Prima's house, where they had piled clothes and sundries into four bags and all the food and drinks they could into two others.

It was a much slower journey back to the car they'd parked down at the end of Prima's street. Despite having made it to her neighborhood undetected, Rodney's suggestion they not pull into the driveway was most likely a wise one. He didn't want to risk drawing any unwanted attention to their little group, and so they had pulled to a curb behind a large hedge, where they were essentially hidden from view.

She needed to see her own house and pleaded until she talked them into driving there since it was on their way. At least until they turned onto her street where all the houses sat on parcels of one to two acres. Help hadn't made it yet, and the carnage was on full display.

"Nope." The single word Rodney spoke echoed what she was thinking.

"We need to go." She confirmed.

The remainder of the journey out of the city had seemed to take forever, as once more they had to employ a stop-and-go strategy to keep from being discovered. It had been a successful mission, and they'd made it back to his bunker with their booty.

Her arms and shoulders were screaming by the time they trekked from the car to the bunker. The bags of clothing and food got really heavy within minutes of leaving the car. She didn't complain, out loud anyway. Instead she focused on covering the ground as fast as she could. Rodney's bunker was beginning to feel like home—a really safe, undetectable home, and she wanted to get there as soon as possible.

Sasha came out of the bedroom at last, fully dressed and looking more like a warrior than she had when she'd made her return to the bunker. A different vibe was also surrounding her tonight. She was clearly more focused, more beautiful. Just standing next to her brought a rush of excitement like she'd never felt before. Maybe all vampires had this effect on humans because they were exotic and powerful. Yet somehow she doubted that very unscientific theory. Deep in her heart, she was pretty sure that only one vampire had this effect on her. Dee closed her eyes and could visualize Sasha somewhere down the hall pulling on leather pants. The downside of having a vivid imagination was wanting to pull those leather pants right back off Sasha.

Her eyes snapped open and she banished the erotic vision. Not the direction she needed to be going right now. Survival was just a touch more important, and by the look of what they'd seen outside, holding on to their lives would be touch-and-go. In what she was beginning to think about as life before, she'd been quick to watch those movies about plagues and contagions that put the world in jeopardy. She'd always envied writers who could come up with such rich tales of the human condition and the will to survive even in the bleakest of times. Now that such a scenario appeared to be reality, she didn't think it great at all. She wanted normal, boring daily life. She wanted her house back and neighbors alive, even the ones she couldn't stand. She wanted a do-over. A mulligan.

Unfortunately, she wasn't going to get what she wished for. Or at least that's the way it appeared. What was going on outside the bunker was like the destructive force of an impending tsunami, a forecast rife with bleakness and hopelessness. Yet as she settled her gaze on Sasha, she didn't see fear or despair in her face. Instead, Sasha seemed determined and confident, unconcerned about the world crumbling despite having lost her home and business. Dee wanted to know what was driving Sasha, partly because she was curious and partly because she would like to bottle it and drink it. Right now she could use that internal power because she would most likely need all the help she could get before this was done.

Katrina put down the phone, excitement buzzing through her. Things were going incredibly well. Better than she expected, actually. As much as she'd like to be in Seattle, supervising the events there, she was delighting in witnessing how the takedown of the military base here was progressing. All the years of preparation and stockpiling what they'd need was paying off. All the sacrifice it had taken to put both vampires and humans in strategic positions was worth it. The success proved that it had been lives and money well spent. It wouldn't be long now before she had everything she wanted.

Eli was still working away at the laptop, a grin on his face as he clicked the keys. "We're making good progress. We're going to bring the state to its knees by dawn." He sat back in the chair and gave Katrina a look of triumph. "They're killing it everywhere."

"What are the others reporting?" She might be the top of the hierarchy, but she couldn't make this happen by herself, much as she'd like to. To pull this off required many hands and many minds, and she had personally turned some of the best to the dark side so they would assist in the cause. If she'd allowed them to stay human they might turn against her. As her children, they would be perpetually loyal. She loved—more like thrived—on that unquestioning obedience. It was intoxicating and, as far as she was concerned, her due.

Eli's smile broadened. "All reports are excellent. Our plan is rolling out just as we predicted. We'll have all of Washington and Oregon tonight. California might take a little longer because of its size, but in another twenty-four hours, it will be ours."

She nodded. Her calculations had predicted the total domination of the United States within a week. By current accounts all was progressing exactly as she'd laid out to the Consortium. If any of the rest of the pompous old ones were hanging on to their doubts about her prowess and power, they were making a huge mistake. She was steamrolling now and would flatten anyone who got in her path, human or vampire.

"Excellent. Have you heard from the council?" She was the top dog, so to speak, yet history and tradition called for the rule of the council. Its members had been around for all time, at least according to the existing written records, and could not be circumvented even for one as powerful as Katrina. For a little while longer she had to pretend to play their game.

"The council has proffered some support of your plan. They like what you're doing, although they are withholding anything that smells of full support. I believe they're waiting to see what your success rate looks like, and if it's good, they'll jump on the bandwagon and hit the rest of the world."

"Fools," she spat out. This was why she'd been working essentially by herself for decades. Those cowards wouldn't have the balls to take on the human world. They'd lived in the shadows successfully for so long they didn't want to make any changes. They were rich and lived lives of conspicuous consumption that suited their antiquated ideas. She, on the other hand, was sick of the shadows. She'd been human once, and though it was a long time ago, she remembered what it was like. Since the day she'd been turned, she'd resented losing part of her life's choices. When one was as strong and powerful as she was, how was it possible that she couldn't exercise that power both in the dark and the light?

"Are they coming in?"

"They asked that you come to them."

She laughed heartily. They never changed. So damn predictable. "I presume you told them to fuck off?"

"Well." He laughed too. "Not quite that bluntly, but yes. I explained that it would be necessary for them to meet you here. I gave them a really good song and dance about why it was critical they come here rather than the other way around. Some resisted at first. I won them over with my charm and persuasion. They'll start arriving soon."

"Good." He could be persuasive, a skill that had come in useful many times throughout the years. Perhaps she would have him groom some of her soldiers when things settled in. She could use a cadre of beautiful, useful men. They ought to be good for something.

Eli glanced down at the laptop and tapped a finger against the screen. "You're going to like this, Boss. The first plane just landed, and number two is right behind it."

"You have all the necessary supplies at the ready?"

He gave her a suffering look. "Really? After all this time you'd ask me that? When are you going to trust me?"

He had a point. Eli was nothing if not efficient, and in that magnificent way that didn't require her telling him what to do. He always knew exactly what was needed in any given situation. He had done enough to earn her trust. The problem was, she didn't trust anyone except herself.

Katrina nodded to him. "Of course you're prepared. You've done a good job, Eli. I will remember this." She didn't believe in compliments. They put too many grandiose notions into the heads of subordinates. Tonight, she felt generous.

"Do you want some time to get ready?"

Her previous moment of generosity vanished, and irritation flamed through her. What was he trying to say? She didn't look presentable?

She had studied herself in the big mirrors before stepping out of her bedroom, and not only did she look good, she looked incredible. Her skin was glowing, her long hair shining, and this outfit was worth more than most people earned in several months. Her makeup was flawless and made her eyes look fantastic. There was no getting ready. She was ready.

"I do not." Her words were knife-edged.

He held up his hands as if he'd been cut. "Sorry, Boss. Didn't mean to offend. Just wanted to give you some time if you wanted it before the big push begins."

Her irritation didn't lessen, both because of his reference to her looks and his use of the word "boss." The fool should think before he spoke. "I couldn't look better if I tried. Besides, I've been ready since the storm-filled day when I was turned. She thought I was going to be her little plaything, at her beck and call forever. I disabused her of that notion quickly, just as I will do to the arrogant asses on their way here. Things are about to change."

Eli laughed. "I really want to be here to see that."

"And so you shall."

CHAPTER FIFTEEN

Sasha was spurred forward by the rest, the shower, and the feelings stirred up by the look in Dee's eyes. She hadn't felt a surge of energy like that for a very long time. She was ready to take on the forces outside the doors of this shelter and destroy them and was focusing more and more with each passing minute. By the time she walked into the main room, she was charged up and ready for battle.

Possibilities and strategies on how to defeat the Consortium and their ill-advised plan were tearing through Sasha's mind. Despite the clear indication that her vampire allies were MIA, she knew others of the human variety that she could pressure to help. She needed to make those calls and then realized she had no way to charge her dying phone, her one and only piece of equipment. She had turned it off, hoping to save what little battery it had left. "Rodney."

His head snapped around and a look of concern filled his face. It was only then she realized that she'd barked his name. "What?" The edge of fear that whispered through that single word made her feel bad. She hadn't meant to scare one of her few true friends.

She gentled her tone as she held out her small smartphone. "Do you have anything that can charge this?"

He looked at it and nodded, his face softening and a little smile flirting at his mouth. "Does a bear shit in the woods?"

She smiled back. His joke told her what she needed to know: all was forgiven. "I take it that's a yes."

"You take it correctly. Ask and thou shall receive." Rodney got up and went to a metal cabinet with two doors, swung open one of the doors, studied the contents, and then reached in to pull out a cord. "This should do it." How he could make out one cord from another she had no clue. The cabinet was stuffed full, and it appeared to be shelves of thrown-together electronics and cables that all looked alike to her.

Gratefully, she took the charger from his outstretched hand and attached it to her phone. The battery icon on her phone was now showing a charge of seven percent and glowing red to make sure she understood it was nearing the end of its life. She spotted a power strip next to Rodney's command center and plugged it in. A little lightning bolt appeared next to the flashing-red battery icon. The phone was charging. Good, it was working A few seconds after plugging it in, pings began to alert her to incoming text messages. She hit the green text-bubble icon and started to read.

She wanted to be furious, yet curiously she wasn't. Sometimes transgressions were so egregious, nothing could be done to make things okay again. Other times people simply made bad decisions, and their regret was genuine enough to give them the right to make amends. The text she was reading right now was the latter. One of her trusted cum traitorous employees, Crystal, was reaching out. She had information that she was sorry she hadn't brought to Sasha sooner, but in light of everything that had happened yesterday, she was anxious to meet with her now. That was definitely going to happen.

A second set of messages made her blood run cold. They were from Rory, traitor number two. Apparently he believed her to be clueless and wanted to continue his Academy Award–winning acting. He too wanted to meet. She too planned to meet him. After she got what she needed from Rory, she'd make sure it was the last meeting he ever held.

A thousand thoughts raced through her mind as she studied the phone, still plugged in and charging. Her back-door plan might have been compromised. As pissed as she was at Rory and Crystal, it was a bit like the pot calling the kettle black, as their governess used to like to say. She had been employing the same strategy for at least fifty years. Her intel on the Consortium was extensive because she also had an insider feeding her information on power struggles, plans, and battles. The arrangement had given her the opportunity to prepare, and all she'd had to do was keep her head down and wait for them to play a hand so she would know exactly how to proceed. Others were ready as well. It was a question of survival for most of them. It was for her too.

It was also about revenge.

That motive seemed petty in light of everything, yet there it was. She could protest all she wanted, and it wouldn't change a thing. A piece of her heart had been torn away, and the only thing that would come close to healing would be to take karma into her own two hands. She'd been waiting for the chance since the day the bullets had ripped through her body.

There were two things she didn't understand, despite having an insider. First was why the traitors in her own camp were not revealed to her, and second, the identity of the vampire leading the charge. Not once had that information come her way, and she wanted to press but couldn't risk losing what inside edge she had. Instead, she used what was shared with her to ready the resistance.

In a way none of that mattered. All would pay in the end, and that's what she cared about. Now, she stared at the battery symbol on her phone and willed it to hit a hundred percent. Sixty-five and counting. "Can you make this go faster?"

Rodney glanced over at the phone and shook his head. "Nope, but I have another solution if you're in a hurry to get on the road."

She thought that, despite what teachers liked to say, there really were stupid questions. "I'm in a hurry."

"Where are you going?" Dee asked, concern etched across her face. "It's pretty messed up out there. You have no idea what we found when we were in Spokane."

"Explain." Sasha was being snippy again, but she didn't have time to be polite. Dee wasn't wrong either. She didn't have a good grasp on what was happening in the city. That was the problem with having to check out from sunup to sundown. At this particular time, it was far more than inconvenient.

Before she spoke, Dee appeared to gather her thoughts. She liked that trait, as she'd always been drawn to thinkers. "I wish I could explain what I saw, but I really can't because I don't get it. People are dying everywhere, and nothing I can see or put my finger on explains why. I don't know if something's in the air or in the water or what, but they're dropping like flies. The city is being overrun by military, trying to get a handle on it, or at least that's what it looks like. Honestly, I can't tell if they're trying to help us or help whatever is trying to kill us. We got back here before sunset, both to avoid having the military scoop us up and to make sure we weren't out there in the dark. I know you get why that was important. The thing is, I'm pretty sure your kind are out there now having some kind of banquet. It's totally fucked up."

As Dee delivered her last few words, an expression that made Sasha feel sad crossed her face. It was unfiltered fear. Sasha was certain that *her kind* were doing the same thing out there that she would have to soon, if she wanted to be ready for battle. She couldn't deny her hunger much longer, or there would be tragic consequences. She refused to let that happen.

"You're safe." That was the only reassurance she could offer. It bothered her a great deal that her presence made Dee afraid. The last thing she ever wanted to be was a monster.

Dee shook her head. "I'm sorry. I wasn't trying to insult you. It's the storyteller in me. We observe and then call it like we see it. I never intended to throw shade on you by lumping you in with those outside."

"You didn't."

"I didn't..." Dee was looking at her with a confused expression.

"You didn't insult me."

"I did." Dee's protest sounded sincere. "I could see it on your face, and I'm truly sorry. I just wanted you to understand what's out there and what's happened since you went to sleep. I'm trying in a very bad way to provide you with as much information as I can so if you do go out there, you go well-armed."

A ripple of something went through her at Dee's apology. For many valid reasons, she allowed few humans into her world. Most couldn't take her raw bluntness, though Rodney and Prima were exceptions. Now it appeared there was a third.

"Thank you," Sasha told her, and Dee nodded. She was pretty sure they understood each other, and for that she was grateful.

"I don't think you should go out there." Prima stood with her hands on her hips, adding her thoughts to the mix. It was the first time Sasha had actually noticed her, and she looked quite different tonight. A free spirit, Prima embraced that philosophy in everything, including her clothing. Typically, she came across as bright and flowing and upbeat. Sasha had never seen the Prima in front of her before, and she wasn't sure she liked this version. It was off. Tonight, she was serious and wearing jeans and a sweatshirt. Sasha would never have guessed that Prima even owned a pair of jeans, let alone a bulky sweatshirt. Apparently she did, and now she was presenting as a woman getting ready for something, which concerned Sasha more than she would have imagined. Prima was not a warrior, and out there was most certainly a war zone.

"I don't think you should go either." Dee's eyes met hers. What she saw there shook Sasha. Dee was deeply concerned for her well-being, which hit her hard because it had been a very long time since anyone had cared whether she returned once she walked out a door. Well, her employees had a vested interest in her survival, but that was a completely different dynamic that screamed impersonal. She was the signature on their paychecks, and that was it. This woman cared about her.

Rodney stood up and handed Sasha a heavy black object about three inches wide by five inches long and half an inch thick. "Portable battery. You can power that baby on the go." He nodded toward her still-charging cell phone. "You really need to go out there? I'm leaning in the same direction as Prima and Dee. It's insane in the city. We can do what we need to from here, so is it all that critical that you leave? We have everything we need down here for months. By the time we run out, the insanity up there will be over. I vote we stay here and stay safe."

"It is more than important. I have to see it for myself in order to grasp what we're up against. Intel aside, I'm not working in the dark." There was no substitute for firsthand information.

"Then I'm going too." Dee was reaching for a jacket.

"You need to stay here." Dee would slow her down. It was important to get out there, take the temperature of the assault, and return with a solid plan to shut the Consortium down.

"Oh, hell no." Dee continued to slip her arms into her jacket. "You go, I go. We've already decided nobody goes out there alone, and that includes you."

"That's fine for you. I don't need a partner. I'm a bit more capable of taking care of myself." She didn't need to explain further. They all knew what she meant. Only then did Sasha notice the gun strapped into the holster at Dee's waist. What the...? She was getting more interesting by the second, although that didn't change anything. Dee was still going to stay down here with Prima and Rodney.

"Those bastards out there threatened me and then blew up my house. If you're going after them, I'm going with you." Dee squared her shoulders and stared right at Sasha. "You've got a partner whether you like it or not."

Sasha started to argue and then glanced at the gun again. Honestly, up against vampires it wouldn't be much good unless she'd loaded it with silver, which wasn't likely. Then again, if things were going south, the humans could be as big a problem as the vampires. Anarchy had a way of raising its nasty-looking head in situations like this, and that was a lesson she had learned firsthand. She nodded as she quit arguing. "Anybody else jumping on this bus?" She looked over at Rodney and Prima. They glanced at each other and then shook their heads.

"I've seen enough for one day," Prima said. "I don't need to go back out there. Ever."

Rodney waved his hand toward his command center. "You and I both know I'm more helpful from here."

"All right." She looked back at Dee. "Let's get out of here."

"Hey, beautiful." Rodney came over and put a hand on her arm. "Before you go, I brought you something you might need." He tugged her over toward the refrigerator. "You just need to know the right people who happen to owe you a big favor." He opened the door.

She gasped. "Oh God, I think I love you."

He laughed, reached in, and handed her one of the packets of blood. He had laid in a dozen, if not more. "Here, power up, and then get out there and kick some ass."

Sasha grabbed the gift and ran back to the bathroom. As grateful as she was, she didn't want to imbibe in front of them, especially Dee. Two minutes later, she returned feeling like someone had given her a new life. Power surged through her, and with her hunger fully sated, she was laser focused.

She patted Rodney on the shoulder and pushed up on her toes to kiss his cheek. "I don't think I love you. I do love you."

He winked. "Ah, you just want to get in my pants."

She laughed and gave him a second kiss on the cheek. "Maybe in another life."

She dropped to her heels, walked toward Dee, and waved a hand toward the big metal door. "Let's go."

❖

Dee couldn't believe she'd just gone toe-to-toe with a vampire and won. She also didn't know what she was thinking. Challenging Sasha when she knew she could crush her like a bug was way outside her norm. It felt right, though. In fact, it felt imperative. She had to go with her. It was a strong feeling with no rational explanation. Maybe she was picking up on some of Prima's psychic vibes. She just knew she was compelled to be at her side when she left the bunker.

At the same time, she certainly didn't want to return to the city. It had scared the bejesus out of her earlier, and now she was demanding to go with a vampire? If she closed her eyes she could still see the insanity, and trying to make sense out of any of it was impossible. Why was she wading right back into it, in the dark, with the vampires? Damn feelings that pushed in directions she didn't want to go. She was obviously losing it.

Or was she?

Something about Sasha made her want to be more than she was, and a little voice in the back of her head whispered that's why she'd opened her big fat mouth. Feeling more courageous had her now racing through the darkness in a lame attempt to keep up. The woman could run like an Olympic athlete, while Dee was a plodder who would be lucky to finish a 5k in anything that resembled a decent time. It would be a miracle if she got back to where the car was parked without impaling herself on a fallen tree. And hell's bells, it sure seemed like they were running a lot farther than when they'd trekked in. Granted, she'd come here in the daylight, which was probably skewing her sense of distance. Maybe.

Finally she could make out the shape of the car in the distance. Thank God. Her lungs were about to burst. Sasha wasn't even breathing hard, though Dee fell into the passenger seat huffing and puffing like a three-hundred-pound asthmatic. She ran a hand through her hair. Did she look as haggard as she felt? If they survived this thing, whatever it was, she silently promised herself to spend more time out running and less time punching away at her laptop.

That thought made her laugh out loud, causing Sasha to cut her a look. She shrugged. "Yeah, I get it. Not exactly laughing time, but you had to be inside my head to appreciate it."

"I'm not following you."

"You wouldn't be alone. My family's been trying to figure me out for years. Here's the deal." She gave herself a second to breathe smoothly so she wasn't gasping between words. Or gasping quite as noticeably anyway. "That run through the dark woods just kicked my ass, and I was thinking about how I need to work out more. Then I thought about what was happening out here and realized how stupid that was. I should be worrying more about simply staying alive and not about whether I can do a decent trail run. In the dark. With a vampire." She couldn't help it. She snickered again. "Sorry."

For a moment, Sasha stared straight out the windshield into the darkness that stretched as far as she could see in front of them. "I do understand. Sometimes when it seems the darkest and the bleakest, we have to take a moment to find the humor. It's what keeps us from falling into despair so deep we'll never recover. We have to hold on to hope no matter what the universe throws at us."

Dee heard the deep emotion in her words and realized that something had happened to this woman. Not just being turned into a vampire. No, it was something far more personal, and it had left a deep, lasting mark. "Yes. Exactly."

Sasha turned the key and the car came to life. She didn't put it immediately into gear. Instead, she stared out into the darkness beyond the windshield. "We can't let them win," she said softly.

"Pardon?" She wasn't following the abrupt change in direction at all. Must be oxygen deprivation. They'd been talking about running and keeping despair at bay with humor, and now it sounded more like they were going into battle. Then again, maybe that was exactly the way she should be thinking. Especially given what she'd seen earlier. Also a hazard of being a writer with ADD. Her thoughts jumped around all the time. It worked for her, and most of the time she swore it made her a better writer. Right now, though, it would probably be advantageous if she could focus on what they were soon to face, like Sasha appeared to be doing.

Sasha turned once more to look at her. God, she was beautiful. How on earth could she possibly be a vampire? They were monsters, right? Everything she'd ever studied portrayed them as ugly, dark, and evil. They shouldn't be lovely, smart, and interesting.

Sasha said in a matter-of-fact manner, as if Dee should already know this, "They want to take over."

"They? As in vampires like…" It came so close to slipping off her tongue, and she didn't want to say something stupid again.

"Like me," Sasha said. Damn. Nothing slipped by this woman.

"I didn't mean it like it sounded." How did she put her foot in her mouth every five minutes when she was around Sasha?

"There is only one way. You either are a vampire or you are not a vampire. I am. You are not. So, yes. I mean they as in vampires."

Dee couldn't argue the point and was still busy trying to figure out a way to get her size eight out of her mouth. If all else failed, she'd employ a technique she constantly used in her writing: diversion. The proverbial bait and switch. "What do you mean they want to take over?" She'd gotten momentarily stuck on the *they* part and missed the takeover piece.

Sasha began backing up the car, though the automatic-headlight switch must have been turned off because no lights came on. Dee couldn't see for crap, but it didn't seem to faze Sasha. She expertly backed from between the trees and onto the forest service road, where she drove steadily and with confidence despite the fact they had to be at least four hundred yards down the rutted dirt road. If she'd been driving, she'd have wrapped the car around a tree after about twenty feet. Or probably more like ten feet, she was that good.

Neither of them spoke until after they came out of the trees and pulled onto the empty highway. How quiet it was. No oncoming traffic. No one behind them. This wasn't like driving on the freeway, where cars constantly flowed in both directions. At the same time, she couldn't remember traveling on this highway without at least a few other vehicles.

Sasha finally switched on the headlights and, as she did, spoke to Dee's question. "A segment of my particular population is embracing an ideology that is pushing them to relegate humans to the minority category."

Dee was usually pretty sharp, but right now she felt a little dumb. This wasn't clicking, or as her brother liked to tease, she wasn't connecting the dots. "What do you mean, relegate to minority category?"

Though she was expecting to hear a note of exasperation or the tone of voice one used on a small child who required a slow and detailed explanation, neither was apparent. "Vampires have existed longer than any other creature on the planet, yet they have always been relegated to the shadows and to the whispered folklore that made them—us—out to be monsters."

"Can't blame humans for that really."

"And why not?"

That made her stop and think for a second. "Well, come on. You do use humans as food, right?"

Sasha nodded slightly, though her eyes remained on the road. "Indeed, but I would posit that humans are no different. Do you not use animals as food? I certainly did when I was human, without ever giving it a second thought. Doesn't that make humans just as much monsters as vampires are said to be? I would suggest that killing to survive makes no one a true monster. Killing for the sake of killing, yes. Killing for sustenance, no."

Okay. She could understand her point, sort of. Still, killing humans to survive wasn't really the same, though she suspected that the vegans and vegetarians of the world would be firmly in Sasha's ethical camp. The ideology of vegans and vegetarians aside, it was hard to completely wrap her head around Sasha's logic. Consuming animals for survival had been around since the beginning. It had never been acceptable to use humans for the same purpose.

"For argument's sake, say I agree with you. Why then are these vampires out there trying to kill every human in sight? That doesn't sound like anything related to survival. That sounds a lot more like a band of serial killers out for thrills."

That's the way it had seemed to her when they'd been out earlier. What she'd seen had been horrific. The six o'clock newscasts reported that last night thousands were dead just in Spokane. She had no idea what was happening elsewhere and was pretty sure she didn't want to know.

"It's all about survival of the fittest. Just like any superior herd of cattle, they want to breed for the finest. They're culling the herd by eliminating the weak. They've developed and introduced an airborne toxin that will take out all those too weak to survive. They're creating the ultimate herd of cattle, but instead of bovine, it's made up of humans."

A chill went up her spine. It suddenly made a twisted sort of sense. "That's messed up. How long has this been going on?" In her head nobody, vampire or human, could pull off something this massive without years of planning.

"For millennia. The very earliest vampire writings talked of the rapture, the time of the vampire rule. It has finally arrived."

That was shocking, creepy that in the background a faction was plotting to destroy the majority of a species and use the rest as dinner. "We're fucked."

This time Sasha shook her head. In the glow of the dash lights, her face radiated strength and determination. "They have been planning and plotting for thousands of years, but I am ready. I have been ready every day for a hundred years."

The Elders sat on the lush sofas and side chairs, each holding a crystal goblet filled to the brim with deep-red blood. A coppery scent wafted through the air that was pleasing to the group gathered here. Katrina too held a glass, though not a single one of them realized it had been poured from a different decanter. It was something none of the arrogant bastards needed to know. Seven Elders in total ranged in age from over two thousand years old to the youngster, who was a mere three hundred and twenty. They had much in common despite the great variance in their ages. Each was beautiful and elegant, and anyone who might walk into the room would guess that the eldest was no more than forty-five. All of them also mistakenly believed themselves to be untouchable.

She was banking on the depth of that false security. Though they were not particularly happy about having to come to her because of the inconvenience it caused them, none of the assembled even gave a second thought to the wisdom of meeting with her in this West Coast city that was far different from their usual meeting places. Even with the shift in protocol, they all showed up. An invitation issued and accepted. As the old saying went, they all had a horse in this race and wanted to be there when it was time to cash in their winning ticket. Little did they know that she held the only winning ticket in this competition.

They had just spent the last hour discussing the strategic strikes in North America, ranging from Miami and San Diego to Seattle and

Boston, as well as most of the major cities in between. Canada had seen hits in Vancouver and Toronto. It was truly a thing of glory. Planning this all had been one thing. Seeing it in reality was orgasmic.

Imre stared at her over the rim of his goblet. He wore an expression she knew well, had seen so many times over the centuries. Of all the Elders, he was the one she had to watch. A long life and a brilliant mind made him dangerous.

They'd been close since the moment they met. On the day she'd been introduced to him, she'd instinctively understood he was the key to her ultimate success. He was the vampire all looked up to. If he was her ally, they would all fall in behind. She used every skill she possessed to get close to him. She was his friend, his lover, his confidante. It didn't mean she liked him. On the contrary, she loathed him.

The woman who had been her mentor and maker had firmly believed in keeping friends close and enemies closer. During Katrina's years of captivity, she had watched and learned. When she'd demanded the gift that granted her immortality, she'd taken the knowledge those prior years had given her and used them. The lessons had stood the test of time. She might have hated her maker with an intensity that still carried heat, but her mentor had been a master manipulator and Katrina a stellar student. She smiled at Imre and held up her goblet in a mock salute.

Imre smiled also and winked at her. When no one was looking, he'd whisper in her ear that they should celebrate in the bedroom. Not bloody likely. "Let us toast our impending victory." He held up his glass, as did everyone else in the room except Eli. Imre didn't give her individual credit for pulling the trigger that had put all of this into motion. Not that she expected him to acknowledge her. If nothing else, he was predictable and consistent. He took credit for everything she'd ever accomplished. She'd always believed he was the one who had given birth to the term "narcissist." What he didn't realize tonight as he sat there with his self-satisfied grin was that this would be the last time he would ever slight her.

The assembly of vampire Elders was toasting with the warm, fresh blood of the housekeeper who didn't quite make it to the other rooms on her assignment sheet. Her absence wasn't an issue, for the hotel would experience a great many no-shows tonight. Her services in the housekeeping department were no longer needed, whereas she was providing Katrina a very valuable service.

Eli had prepared the feast for her guests to her exact specifications. Tonight their blood had a little extra kick, and it wouldn't take long now to witness the beauty of that kick. She truly wished this send-off could be more spectacular. Unfortunately, this would have to do. Even without the fanfare, it would have the same result, and she'd be free once and for all from their condescension and control. Imre's perpetual smirk would finally be wiped from his face. As the humans liked to say, soon there would be a new sheriff in town. Maybe she'd even have a pretty gold badge made. She smiled, sipped, and waited.

She cut her gaze to Eli who, as usual, was staring at his laptop screen. He wasn't paying attention to any of them; he was focused on the reports coming from the battlefields. A smile that really wasn't joyful played at his lips. It was the expression she was waiting for. "Eli?"

"Yes." He didn't take his eyes off the screen. She would like to be standing behind him and watching as the genius of their plan reached fruition. At the moment, he had the best ringside seat.

Instead of moving over to Eli where she could also watch the laptop, she continued to stand near the windows and sip where she could keep one eye on her guests. They were so full of misplaced greatness as they too drank and congratulated themselves. They talked of their plans and the glory that awaited them on the other side of this war. They talked of how they would rule over both the lesser vampires and the humans who survived. She wanted to scream. Instead she smiled.

"All is well?"

Eli nodded without looking up. "Everything is perfect."

Eventually, their glasses nearing empty, the terrible truth started to dawn on her guests, one at a time. Eyes were beginning to glaze, and complexions, already pale, were becoming blizzard white. Much like those silly game shows on television, it was like someone slowly pulling back a curtain to reveal what was behind it. As much as she'd like to be out there already tracking down the mouse she sought, she didn't want to miss this event. It was actually better than she'd imagined. It was so good to be her.

She held her goblet close to her face and inhaled the scent of untainted blood while watching them spiral down to the damnation they deserved. Mouths opened in silent screams, another beautiful side effect of the tasteless compound Eli had slipped into the blood he'd poured into each of the crystal goblets. The beautiful and expensive stemware had been brought in especially for this meeting. Some might treasure the hand-blown goblets, but Katrina planned to smash each one. She could almost feel her rush of excitement as she broke them into hundreds of pieces. Unfortunately, her glorious plan was thwarted. Glasses began to drop to the marble-tiled floor as they slipped from hands that had lost all muscle tone. They shattered as they fell, also shattering her final reward for this part of the plan. Oh, well. That would have been icing on a cake that was already fantastic.

Imre's gaze met hers, and she caught the dawning realization in his eyes. "You bitch," he said as blood trickled out of the corner of his mouth. She smiled.

She held up her goblet still half full of the untainted blood and tipped it slightly in a mock toast. "I think you mean, you brilliant bitch."

"You won't get away with this." His teeth were now as red as the blood flowing from his mouth.

"Oh come now, Imre. You're smarter than that." She raised a single eyebrow. "I've already gotten away with it." She waved three fingers at him. "Nighty night, you bastard. May you burn in hell forever."

The whole thing was over in less than ten minutes. Eli had finally left his station at the laptop and now stood behind her with one hand on her shoulder. She wanted to shrug it off. "It worked even better than on our test subjects."

Indeed it had. They'd tried it no less than five times, using those they'd turned especially for this project. Lab rats, so to speak. It worked quicker and more efficiently on the old ones, which made her smile. This plan had come together even better than she pictured. It was glorious.

They were gone. Every last old one. Every single pompous ass who'd stood in front of her and blocked her path to greatness. Everyone who had treated her like nothing instead of the master she'd become. They had underestimated her one time too many. Well, now she'd just taken care of that, hadn't she?

"Come on. Pick up all their cell phones and let's go," she said as she turned toward the door of the suite. As much as she'd like to stand around and revel in the success of her plan, it was in reality only a tiny piece of the bigger picture. She still had much to do. "We need to find that little bitch and then get out of this place. I want to be home when the final glory comes to me."

Eli gathered up the cell phones he found in pockets and bags, tucking each of them into a messenger bag that he slung over his shoulder. They were important and would prove very useful in marshaling the resources of the dead masters. They were no longer in charge, she was, and all their contacts would now be hers.

"Are you ready?" She glanced back at him. All of a sudden she was anxious to get out there and experience the revolution for herself. She thought of another revolution a hundred years ago and thousands of miles away. She'd been on the inside of that one too, a private guard of a different kind of royal family ousted from their tsarist autocracy and sequestered under house arrest. She hadn't cared about the collapse of the old regime or the Bolsheviks, and she sure as shit didn't care about the infamous Rasputin. No, all she cared about was the rush of excitement the civil war gave her and the chance to seduce the beautiful princess who in the end captured her heart and her body. For almost twelve months every night was filled with excitement and the gentle touch of a woman who made her heart pound. She'd wanted it to go on forever, and in a perfect world it would have. It was all a long time ago, and this was a war that would have a completely different ending.

Another time and another place, and no one would ever capture her heart again. Outside the doors of the hotel a revolution of her making was rolling through the night, and she wanted to step into the middle of it, throw her arms wide, and let the force of it fill her. Her focus was on the days ahead, and once she made her final peace with the past, the future was hers.

Eli adjusted the strap of the bag and nodded. "I'm locked and loaded." He was smiling as he spoke. The success of what had just occurred seemed to have infected him as well. He appeared to stand taller, his expression more focused. Good. She needed him to be on his A game for the rest of what was to come.

Katrina ran a hand through her hair, squared her shoulders, and walked on four-inch, four-thousand-dollar heels out of the hotel room toward the bank of elevators at the end of the hallway. She could hardly wait to get out of there. It was going to be a magnificent night.

CHAPTER SIXTEEN

Sasha hadn't given much thought to her companion as she'd run from Rodney's bunker. Vaguely she'd been aware of Dee's labored breathing and heavy-footed gait, clear signs of someone who wasn't a seasoned runner. Given that the woman made her living sitting in front of a computer, her huffing and puffing was a good clue that she didn't push away from it as often as she should.

Still, once they were in the car, and despite Dee's audible effort to get her breath back, she remained ready and willing to stay right with Sasha. That both surprised and impressed her. In her long years, experience had taught her that few were very comfortable in the company of vampires. The humans who were aware of their existence seemed to be fine in short stretches, but if exposure to them went beyond half an hour or so, they grew nervous and fearful. Probably afraid they'd become dinner, which in many cases was a legitimate concern.

Rodney and Prima were exceptions, of course. They had been friends of hers for some time now, and she could be with them all night and never notice even a twitch. They trusted her and it went both ways. She was seeing the same thing in Dee tonight. Perhaps that's why Prima had been so quick to introduce them. At first Dee had displayed that same expression of disbelief that every human had once they learned the truth about their preternatural counterparts, and that was expected. For Dee, it passed quickly, replaced by something else that wasn't easy to define. Interest? Respect? She couldn't quite put her finger on it. Whatever it was, she liked it.

Just as she liked having Dee in the car with her now. Sasha had help out in the city, as she'd called in the troops, so to speak. Or more accurately, called them via text. It was the twenty-first century, after all. The key vampire players were unresponsive, and that was deeply concerning. She couldn't dwell on that and had to shift to Plan B. While not the old and experienced ones, those she was able to reach out to were armed and ready to help. It was also useful to have a human ally. Or, in her case, allies. Sheer vampire power couldn't win this battle. It would take cooperation between vampires and humans like the world had never before seen to stop what was being put into motion. It meant coming out of the shadows once and for all. She really hoped she could pull it off and that the human population was ready to accept what they'd been denying since the beginning of time.

No, she refused to think that way. She was going to pull it off, and that was that. Her own people might have betrayed her, but no one knew that she too had a rabbit in a hat, and tonight she planned to pull that rabbit out. She had to. She didn't have any other choice.

That was okay. Perhaps it was time. Actually, as she thought about it, there was no perhaps about it. It was time and probably had been for a long while. This whole disaster in the making had to end. It couldn't be allowed to happen. Beyond that, justice was due her, and she intended to grab it with both hands. She would relish it even as she hated that thing inside her that drove her to seek it out. Justice had been denied her in many ways, and she'd moved on in this altered existence, spurred by the belief that one day the scales would once more be in balance.

She cut her gaze over to Dee, who stared out the windshield into the night. No clouds blocked the stars that sparkled like Christmas tree lights in the velvet-black sky. If things in the world were normal, it might be a romantic drive. Normal wasn't anywhere in the equation, and tension etched Dee's face, signaling an alertness she would need in the coming hours.

When Sasha had driven through the woods without lights, she'd been aware of Dee's anxiety. She could almost feel her fear as she waited for impact with a tree. It never came, and yet the tension had not left her body. She remained as tight as a tuned cello.

Even after they reached the highway, for Sasha, lights weren't necessary. She could have driven right into the heart of the city without needing them. Nonetheless, she turned had them on and immediately felt their calming effect on her companion. It was odd that she had even considered doing something like that. Normally, those around her simply had to deal with her decisions. So what if they couldn't see through the darkness? It wasn't about them. Growing up in a royal family wasn't conducive to considering the feelings of others. She didn't mean that in a nasty way either. It simply was what it was. She didn't accommodate, yet that's precisely what she'd just done. What was she thinking?

Easy. She was thinking that this beautiful and interesting woman next to her was risking her life to help her and, in a larger sense, the world. To risk her life for people she didn't know and never would. Complete strangers, some good, some bad, and yet without hesitation, she had run with Sasha into a night promising danger. It was impossible not to respect that action, not to find it fascinating and, frankly, alluring. She had never known anyone like Dee, had never been drawn to anyone like her.

"Where are we going?" It was the first thing Dee had said in at least ten minutes. They'd been riding in a somewhat easy silence. As easy as it could get, considering what they were driving into.

"To the city."

A text had come in not long after she'd plugged the phone into the car charger. It was still building up to a full battery, but it was getting there, making her feel connected once more. The car was doing its part, and the small portable charger Rodney had given her made sure she would stay in contact. No more dead smartphone battery. The text she'd received had been brief, which was fine. In a few succinct words it told her everything she needed to know. Those words would guide her journey forward. She smiled.

"I pretty much got that. What else is going on here?"

She didn't realize Dee had turned her attention from the highway and was now watching her. A ripple of something she couldn't quite define, or didn't want to, flowed through her. It wasn't unpleasant. She didn't have to be evasive. It was easy to be truthful with Dee. "I've been waiting a long time for this day."

"It's night."

She actually laughed. "I know, I know. The writer in you pays attention to all the minute details. I'll amend that to say I've been waiting a long time for this night."

"How long?"

She glanced over at Dee, who was watching her intently. In the dash lights, her eyes glittered. "You don't pull punches, do you?"

"I'm sorry. You're right. It's my writer's curiosity that makes me focus on the details that gets me into trouble all the time. You don't have to answer. I'm pushing for personal information that's none of my business."

Sasha didn't hesitate. "I've been waiting a hundred years."

"Wha…" Dee slapped a hand over her mouth. When it dropped, she asked in a hushed voice, "How old are you?"

"About a hundred and twenty, give or take. You know, in my day, a lady didn't give away her true age."

"No shit?"

"I shit you not." Why was she finding this conversation so entertaining and so easy to roll with? They were heading into a war zone, and this was no time for levity.

"Wow. You look fantastic."

She wasn't expecting that. "For a hundred and twenty?"

"For any age."

Warmth flowed through Sasha, reminding her of another time when sweet words had gone to her head and ultimately to her heart. Her youth and inexperience had made her vulnerable, and she'd fallen hard for a pretty face and even prettier words. She'd paid a hefty price for letting her first love fool her. She had never made that mistake again, and she wouldn't now.

"I appreciate your kindness." That's all it was. Another woman being charitable to her, helping the vampire retain a touch of humanity.

Dee was shaking her head. "Not kindness. I just call it as I see it."

Sasha detected an honesty in her voice she hadn't heard in a long time. Dee's words weren't like the ones spoken by the voice in her past. She'd been too young and naïve to understand back then, to hear their shallowness, and her weakness had undone her. What she heard now with the clear understanding of an experienced woman was night-and-day different. Dee was true. Her past was lies.

Dee put a warm hand on her arm, comforting even through the thick leather of her jacket. "What are you thinking? It's like you're a million miles away."

She glanced at her before returning her gaze to the road. She didn't see the highway that was a long ribbon of black, but a country dirt road lined by snow-covered trees. She answered honestly. "Not a million miles away. More like a century."

❖

Despite the urgency of their trip, the conversation Dee and Sasha were having was going far deeper than she'd intended, but it was just the way she rolled. One thought turned into a question, which turned into another question, and so on. It was the same way with her novels. A very simple observation could take her down a trail that ultimately ended up becoming a full-blown book. Or a novel could be going one way, and then all of a sudden it took a left turn that Dee didn't see coming, and the whole story changed. Yeah, it was like that.

Right now an off-the-cuff question had led to another and another because the woman next to her was incredibly interesting. Dee wasn't naïve enough not to realize that part of her interest was the draw she felt toward her. It had been undeniable, even before she ran into her naked outside the bathroom. That was pretty intense, although Sasha was even more alluring once she slid back into tight leather pants. That kind of vision was usually relegated to fantasy. It was pretty cool when fantasy met reality and took her breath away.

Dee was afraid, though, that she'd taken her curiosity a little too far, because Sasha had suddenly gone awfully quiet. As hard as it was for her to do, it might be time for her to close her mouth as well. She'd done enough damage, and they still had the whole night to get through. God only knew what was out there waiting for them. It was scary in the daylight; it had to be downright terrifying now that the night allowed the vampires to roam freely. She almost snorted. Funny how quick she'd shifted from nonbeliever to completely on board. It was kind of the "once you've seen it, you can't unsee it" situations.

Dee stayed quiet as long as she could while waiting for Sasha to say something. "I really was sincere when I said you look great."

"I appreciate your candor."

"But?" Something under her words made Dee wish she'd kept her big mouth shut. She really did suck at social interactions.

"But I don't thrive on compliments."

Okay. That wasn't exactly what she was thinking. Besides, someone as beautiful as Sasha had to be accustomed to routine compliments. Dee got them on her writing. That was part of being a best-selling author. People wanted to be around her. To ask her about her writing and how she got her ideas. If anyone mentioned her looks, it was usually to ask how she got her hair to stand up like that or about the various colors she liked to use just to shake things up.

She squeezed Sasha's arm lightly and then let her hand drop away. "Just an observation. I'll try to keep it in check."

"Don't. Not because of me. I find your candor refreshing."

"Where did you go just now?" She probably shouldn't ask, but she once again couldn't help herself. Sasha had a faraway look on her face that was too intriguing to let go.

She might have gone too far this time because there was a lengthy silence. Then Sasha started to talk. "I was remembering my home and my family."

"You're not from here." It wasn't really a question. Something about her radiated a vibe that was most definitely not Pacific Northwest.

"No. I was born far from here, and I haven't seen my family in a very long time."

She sensed the hesitation in Sasha and felt a little bad for pushing. It was hard not to, because damn if she wasn't fascinating as all get-out. "Sorry again, it's the writer in me. We ask questions when it would be better if we just shut up."

"After we get through tonight, I'll tell you all about me and my family."

Cool, she thought. She said, "So, where are we going? When we left, you didn't really say." It was time to take the conversation onto neutral ground before she had to take her foot out of her mouth yet again.

"The city."

She almost said "duh" and then caught herself. "Yes. You said that earlier. I guess what I'm asking is more specifically, where in the city and why? It's a pretty big place. Can you narrow it down?"

"I have to see a man about a horse."

Obviously Sasha had a plan she didn't want to share with Dee. She couldn't broadcast her mistrust any clearer if she tried. In a way Dee didn't blame her. They'd known each other about ten minutes. Just because Dee's instinct was to trust her, she couldn't fault Sasha for being more cautious even if it did hurt. "A horse?"

"It's something my father liked to say. I've got to meet someone."

"Are they going to help?" One guy wouldn't be enough to stop the tide of what she'd seen earlier. Just because the whole thing might be way out of her wheelhouse didn't mean she was reading it wrong. It would take an army of men, women, and every other preternatural creature they could bring over to their side to stop what was happening.

"More than help, he's going to pull the rug right out from underneath the ass who put this entire mess into motion."

She still wasn't convinced. "Hard to believe one guy can put a stop to even a tenth of what I saw today."

"He won't."

So why were they on their way to meet this man and his horse? Getting a straight and coherent answer out of Sasha was proving to be a challenge. No worries. She was up to it. "I don't understand."

"He won't stop anything. I will."

Katrina had answered the first calls that came in on the phones in Eli's bags. Each one made her smile grow. On the roof of the hotel's parking garage with Eli standing next to her, she could see all over the city. It was an excellent vantage point to observe her plans in action. A light wind blew across her face, and above her the sky stretched a canopy of twinkling stars.

After being banished to the shadows for eons, it was refreshing to stand tall and open. It reminded her of when she was human and could come and go as she pleased. Of course, in those days she could actually stand in the sunshine and run outside all day long. She missed the daytime, sort of. Back when she was human, she was a nobody. A scrawny little street urchin who had to scrabble just to eat. She shuddered, thinking about the things that had happened to her as she'd survived on the Moscow streets. Poverty was not a pleasant memory. Nor was her weak, pathetic mother and alcoholic father. Life was better on the street than going back to the hovel that passed as her childhood home. If not for the beautiful woman with the long golden hair who took her in, she'd have died young out on those cruel streets.

She'd believed at first that she'd been dropped into kindness and luxury. She soon found out that things were not quite as rosy as one would have thought inside the walls of the beautiful home on the Moskva River. From the outside it had been like a palace to Katrina. The first time she walked up those steps, she'd believed that she was going to be a princess. In a way, she was. She had everything a young girl could want. Beautiful dresses, combs for her hair, perfume, and a feather bed. She was taught to read and to write, to speak as a noble rather than a pauper. There was always plenty of food and fresh, clean water to drink. That was the beauty.

But the darkness came when the sun fell, both literally and figuratively. She was no longer subject to the kind of abuse common to young girls on the street or the fists and kicks of a drunken father. No, her body was untouched in that way. She was wanted for something more than her nubile flesh. It was her blood her hostess desired. No, needed like an alcoholic needs a drink. Bought and paid for with a life off the streets.

For ten years Katrina submitted to the whims of her benefactor. She wasn't a literal prisoner yet was captive nonetheless. Having experienced the luxury and relative safety of the grand house, she couldn't return to the horrors outside it. More accurately, she didn't want to return to the streets and realized that an opportunity existed if she was patient. She stayed year after year—learning, maturing, and planning—until the day she knew it had to end, one way or the other. She was not a goat there to be milked. She had grown into a woman—strong, tall, and beautiful—and she had repaid her pseudomother/mentor a hundred times over for everything she had given her. The day had arrived for the present arrangement to end.

And it did. She thought it would be at the point of the wooden stake she'd made and secreted in her room for almost two years. It had taken her that long to work up the courage to stand up and make her move. Surprisingly, it was far simpler than she'd anticipated. She had built up the confrontation in her mind until it was something of great magnitude. The reality was far different when she stood before her benefactor in the grand salon. In an instant, everything flipped. She didn't have to kill her. Not that night anyway. For her wish to be free was granted and, along with it, a gift: immortality. Her mentor, her soon-to-be maker, had simply been waiting for the day Katrina came to her. As she would later learn, it had been a test of sorts.

She had taken to the gift as if born to the darkness instead of two pathetic excuses for human beings. Inside of a year she grew more powerful than her maker, and it was then she used the wooden stake. She no longer needed her, and the vampire who'd so freely preyed upon a child had a debt to pay. Katrina took great joy in exacting the payment. By then, no one questioned the death of the eccentric noble who lived in the beautiful home, for they all believed Katrina was her daughter. She let them, just as she let them transfer all the noblewoman's wealth, property, and titles to her. She had felt like nothing in the world could ever stop her, and indeed nothing had in the subsequent years.

She felt much like that tonight. For a very long time she'd had to play the game the Consortium dictated. It was for the benefit of all of them, they told her. It was for their safety, they told her. It was the only way, they told her.

Well, she had something to tell them: Fuck You. Her first strike was to take one hundred percent control of her life. With their bodies on the floor of her suite just waiting for the light of day to turn them into dust, strike one was an unqualified success. She would now do as she pleased, when she pleased, and how she pleased. No more consultation with the Elders, who couldn't get past their own histories to see the future.

Step two was rolling in like an incoming snowstorm. The humans would soon bow to her. At least the humans who survived. Then she would assemble the best and the brightest, and once and for all they would discover how to give her back the daylight. If the scientists working for them now could figure out a compound to incapacitate the majority of the human population, then they could figure out how to let her walk in the sunshine once more. It would be done, and then nothing would ever stop her again.

"Have you found her?" She'd made this Eli's number-one priority after they were able to discover the toxin that was perfect to launch their initial attack. She hadn't needed him to work on that after they isolated the necessary chemical. It then became his mission to find her.

Eli was standing next to Katrina, his head moving left to right as he scanned the city below. "Yes."

The excitement generated by that single word made her tingle all the way to the tips of her fingers. It was almost as exciting as the day she put the wooden stake through her maker's heart. Almost. "Where?"

"She'll be at Duncan Gardens in—" He glanced down at his

watch. Such a pretentious piece that he wore. His concern about his clothing and accessories was an unnecessary waste of time and effort. They were always together, and no one paid any attention to him when she was nearby. "Twenty minutes."

"Duncan Gardens?" She didn't know what it was or where it was. She was here now only to settle the score, not sightsee. Actually, that wasn't entirely true. The air force base was worth a look. With its fleet of planes and young, nubile airmen and women, it was a treasure trove of resources. She was going to be able to leverage all of it to her advantage.

First things first. Dropping that bitch was number one. Then she'd marshal the loyal out at the base to keep the momentum going. It was a big world out there, and just because she'd steamrolled both Spokane and Seattle didn't mean the rest of the world would fall in line as quickly and easily as she'd like. Regardless of any roadblocks, it would happen. With all the resources becoming available, it was only a matter of time before everyone came into line.

"Where is Duncan Gardens?" It better be close.

"Up in Manito Park."

"Not helping," she snapped. He was being purposely difficult, and she didn't appreciate it. Though she'd never shared with him the reason behind her obsession with making this meeting happen, he was nonetheless aware of how important it was to her.

He took her by the shoulders and turned her a hundred and eighty degrees. She was now looking south toward the section of the city known as the South Hill. "Up there."

CHAPTER SEVENTEEN

When they reached the center of the city, Dee spoke up, and what she said didn't really surprise Sasha. "Doesn't it seem kind of quiet to you?"

Sasha shook her head. "No. This is what I was expecting."

Dee turned to her. "Really? I mean when we were out earlier today, it was like mania had struck everywhere. There was military around every corner, and bodies and..."

"It was horrible."

"Yeah. It was horrible. Even with my imagination it was beyond anything I could make up."

A chill went through her. "I've seen something very much like this before."

"What? You've seen this happen before. How can that be? When? Where?"

Flashes of the scene in a town in the northern regions of Canada came to her. The beautiful town surrounded by forests and rivers had nearly been obliterated. "Five years ago a small town in northern Canada was besieged. At the time I couldn't figure out what was going on. So many dead, and survivors turned. It wiped out the entire town."

A frown darkened Dee's face. "I never heard anything about something like that."

"A machine was in motion, and I don't think word of it leaked to any news media. I didn't understand at the time. I believe I do now."

"You want to share with me? I don't get it at all. I don't get any of this."

She'd seen the aftermath firsthand, and what she'd seen had

stayed with her. "It was beyond terrible. It was an abomination. Just as it is now."

"Spit it out. What happened up there?"

"I believe it was a testing ground for what you're seeing here. Almost everyone in that town was either killed or turned. It all makes terrible sense now. They were seeing how it would work before they set it loose on everyone."

"That sounds like a Hitler move, and I still don't understand."

"What's there to understand?"

Dee was quiet for a moment before she asked, "How did you find out about it when no one else in the world knew? Unless you were part of it."

Sasha snapped her head around to look at Dee, and at the same time a shot of anger surged. It was mixed with feelings of hurt that Dee would even consider her that callous and cruel. "No. I would never be part of something like that. I know what it's like to be erased, and I would never do that to anyone." She didn't add that she would cheerfully erase one person, because that was her secret to keep.

"So tell me about this town and what it means to this…" Dee motioned out the window.

"Forces have been at work far longer than you can imagine. Their goal is complete domination, drawing down the mist that separates the vampires from the humans so the vampires can rule."

"Why? I mean I now know that we've existed side by side for centuries, and even though it's still hard to grasp, I'm getting there. Everything has gone along just peachy, so why are they attacking now? It doesn't make any sense. Why not let sleeping dogs lie, so to speak?"

"Think about all the power struggles when kings and queens ruled countries. How somebody was always in the shadows who felt they were better and more entitled to the throne. They would do anything, including murdering husbands, wives, brothers, sisters, even children, all in the name of gaining power. In a nutshell, that's the current thought pattern of those who head the vampire universe."

It was the easiest way she could think of to explain a situation that was multi-layered and incredibly complicated. It was also an accurate way to explain it. The vast majority, ruling or not, felt they were far superior to humans, though they all started their existence in just that form. Century after century of existing on this planet had infused them with arrogance that had finally reached the point of explosion.

Sasha had suspected this day would come sooner rather than later. She'd seen it happen when she was a human. As a vampire, she'd been watching it build. She'd been blindsided when her family was destroyed in the pursuit of power, and after she'd realized what this new existence provided her, she'd vowed never to be in that position again. It became as important to be ready for the day it arrived as it was to be prepared to exact revenge. The two were not mutually exclusive.

The backdrop of her company had given her the perfect vehicle to put her in her current position. She'd always been smart, and the security firm enabled her to use her intelligence and monitor the pulse of both the human and vampire worlds. It wasn't a perfect plan, as evidenced by the recent knowledge of her two employees' deceit, but it was a good one nonetheless. Sasha's cell phone rang, and she glanced down, shocked to see it was Crystal. She pulled the car to the curb on Riverside, put it in park, and placed the cell phone to her ear.

"Crystal." This should be interesting. She tapped the fingers of her free hand against the steering wheel.

"Sasha, I'm sorry, so sorry."

She would have told her to go to hell, except for what Crystal said next. It shocked her into silence. She listened, and after she ended the call, she shook her head and smiled. All of a sudden she was, as a couple of her best protection detail operatives liked to say, locked and loaded. The decades of preparation were about to pay an unexpected dividend. She hoped so, anyway. She'd also learned along the way that no matter how well prepared a person was, complications could always throw the best-laid plans into turmoil.

"Who was that?"

"One of the traitors."

"Traitors?"

Sasha realized Dee hadn't been privy to the information Rodney had shared with her. "Two of my top employees were in bed with the Consortium, and that's how they found me."

"That's fucked up." Dee was staring at her with a look of determination and perhaps a bit of outrage. She liked the feeling of camaraderie it created.

"It most certainly is, but fortunately one of them has more of a heart than greed. They paid them a lot of money to turn on me, and the one who just called, Crystal, said it felt like blood money that left her feeling dirty. She just gave me the location of the other traitor. I'll deal with him later."

"What about Crystal?"

Sasha wasn't sure. She still believed Crystal was good at her core. She didn't usually extend second chances, that was an invitation to death. However, these were extraordinary times and called for extraordinary measures. "I'll figure that out after we deal with the Consortium."

"If you say so. But what can we do now to stop this?" She pointed out the window.

Sasha turned to look at her. Crystal and Rory had already shaken her trust. Then again, she'd always had a touch of hesitation with those two, particularly Rory, and that was her bad. She should have paid more attention to her misgivings. But maybe the woman sitting in the passenger's seat actually had her back. She hoped she was right and not just mistaking lust for trust. Then again, sometimes a person had to go with blind faith.

"You have to understand the landscape."

"So enlighten me. I think you'll find I'm sharp enough to follow."

"I have no doubt of that." In the little bit of time they'd been together, it was easy to pick up on the intelligence that had certainly helped Dee become a successful writer. "It goes something like this. The Consortium is made up of Elders who rule the vampire world together. One for all and all for one. It is the Consortium that has declared war on the humans. They already possess vast wealth and power, only it's not enough. They want everything."

"How do we fight them?"

"If all goes well, it won't be a long battle because they don't know I've been watching them since the day I escaped my maker, and I too have been making plans. For every move they've made, I've counter moved. My father liked to play chess and taught me well. I've used those lessons to gain the greatest advantage and have a couple of surprises up my sleeve. I'll be the one declaring checkmate."

❖

Dee's fear faded as excitement set in. Something about the way Sasha talked instilled more confidence than fright in her, despite what she was seeing the farther into the city they got. She caught motion out of the side of her eye that made her turn and look. Two young men, pale and dressed in the typical jeans and hoodies favored by the young, were racing toward them right now. As they'd talked while parked at the curb, the two had come out of Riverpark Square, their heads moving right and left as if searching. It became clear that's what they were doing because the moment they spied them sitting in the car, they jerked around and began running toward them. The speed with which they moved rivaled any world-class race.

"Go, go, go," Dee said with an urgency that made her heart beat fast. She didn't think Sasha had noticed them yet.

Sasha had to have heard her, yet instead of putting the car in gear and driving away, she opened the door and got out. She was wrong about Sasha not noticing. With her feet slightly apart and her back straight, Sasha stared at the two men as they ran directly at her. She didn't move, didn't flinch.

"Sasha!" Good God. What was she doing? If she got killed, Dee didn't even want to consider what would happen next.

"Stay in the car," Sasha snapped without turning to look at her.

No shit. Dee had felt brave and all when she stood up and said she was coming out here with Sasha. Now that she was here and watching death race toward her, bravery flew right out the window. No way was she getting out of the car, and in fact she hit the door locks. The click made her jump, and it occurred to her that as she'd locked herself in, she'd locked Sasha out. She started to hit the button again and then stopped. She could quickly unlock the door for Sasha, but if this went south, they were going to have to work hard to get to her.

The two reached Sasha in only a few seconds, yet it seemed like the scene was playing out in slow motion. Sasha held out her arms as if inviting them in for an embrace, and it struck Dee as both odd and surreal. The embrace didn't happen. Instead she grabbed them by their hair and smashed their heads together. Both of the men had at least six inches on her and should have been bigger and stronger than Sasha. They weren't, and she crushed their heads as easily as if they were overripe tomatoes. Dee choked down the bile that rose in her throat.

She figured Sasha would return immediately to the car once the men dropped like rag dolls to the pavement. Instead, she pulled a wicked-looking knife from some pocket inside her coat, knelt down, and plunged it first into the taller man's heart and then into the second guy's. She wiped the blood off on the last guy's shirt and returned it to the invisible pocket. Only then did she turn around and start walking back to the car.

Dee stared. This had to be some long, dark nightmare. She'd never seen anything like that. No way could any of it be real. At the car, Sasha pulled on the door handle and, when it didn't open, rapped softly on the window. The sound shook Dee out of her mini trance, and she hit the button to release the locks. The click sounded, and Sasha opened the door. She dropped into the driver's seat. Without saying anything, she turned the key still in the ignition and brought the car to life.

As they pulled away from the curb and the crumpled bodies grew small, Dee reached over and put a hand on her arm. Yup, it was real. No nightmare. Sasha turned her head to gaze into Dee's eyes. It was as if she could read her mind. "This is really happening. Everything you thought you knew and understood is gone. You won't be able to return to the world you lived in before."

"A girl can hope." She kept her hand on Sasha's arm. She really wanted to believe this was a momentary madness.

Sasha turned her eyes back to the road. "Before this is over, we're going to need that hope, but you have to redirect it. We have to hope my plans work, or we're all going down."

Dee didn't have a clue what she meant, and it didn't sound great. Sasha kept alluding to some great plan. The problem was she wasn't coming clean with what it was. Dee didn't feel very confident.

Still, sitting with her hand on Sasha's arm and feeling the strength in it kept total despair at bay. Now that they were away from the two bodies, she could think more clearly about what Sasha had actually done, and it was simple. She had saved Dee's life. Those two were planning to do to her what she'd seen done to some when they were out earlier today. It hadn't been pretty.

"Thank you." She took her hand away from Sasha's arm at last, though she didn't want to. Instead, she wanted to move closer, hold her hand, anything to simply be near her. Something about Sasha was like a siren's call, and she didn't want to resist. She couldn't remember ever feeling this way about anyone, and sure as heck not in the middle of a world war. Then again, this wasn't exactly the kind of world war anyone—well, anyone human—was expecting. A nuclear bomb, perhaps from a hostile country, but certainly not a tsunami of vampires taking out her friends and neighbors.

"For what?"

"For saving me."

"I need you."

Sasha's comment was short and to the point. No emotion, nothing personal. Dee didn't think she really intended it that way. Buried deep in those three words was something much more, and it warmed her heart. If she survived this ordeal, she was pretty sure there was a book in it somewhere. In the middle of end of days, people being killed, her understanding of the world forever changed, she was excited, all because of this one woman. Nobody would believe it, but all this would make one hell of a novel. It would be even better if it made one hell of a life.

"I've got your back." Dee's courage was returning, even if what she'd just seen made her shake from head to foot.

"Thank you." Sasha finally turned and gave her a quick, meaningful look. It made her warm all over. She sat up straighter in her seat.

Dee took a couple deep, steadying breaths. "What's up with the knife? I thought you had to use a wooden stake to kill vampires. That's what they do in all the movies and books." It was a good idea to get back on neutral ground before she said or did something totally inappropriate. Of course, she wasn't all that sure what constituted inappropriate behavior with a vampire.

"Don't believe what you see and read in fiction. For the most part it's a lot of crap. Folktales have a kernel of truth in them, though. Where it goes astray is that what gets written down leaves out most of the facts. A wooden stake does work very efficiently. A silver knife in the heart also does the trick. Easier to carry around a silver knife. Easier to kill with a knife."

"I thought silver killed werewolves. Oh, wait, are there werewolves too?" She'd been so amazed at finding out the reality of vampires that she hadn't given thought to any of the other preternatural creatures she liked to read about. It couldn't be true. The world couldn't have that much going on around them without anybody knowing about it.

Sasha nodded slightly, dispelling her belief that there wasn't more to learn. "Beyond the mist that obscures your view you will find another world filled with beings that defy human understanding. More than vampires are waiting for their turn to be seen and heard. There are many, and you can be certain they're all watching to see how this turns out."

"No way." Her mind was being blown, and she couldn't go there right now. If she had to consider the implications of what Sasha was telling her, she'd shut down. It was better to stay focused on the immediate threat, and that was the vampire invasion. One preternatural entity at a time. "About the silver thing?"

"Silver through the heart of a vampire is like a shot of ricin. Just a tiny exposure is fatal. Very effective with the least amount of effort."

"Werewolves too?"

"It does, indeed, work on werewolves."

A sudden thought struck. "How can you touch one and not destroy yourself?" She'd pulled that baby out of her coat and used it like a seasoned pro. She was carrying it on her body, and if what she was telling her about its potency was true, how could it not affect her at all? It didn't make sense. Like anything made sense at the moment.

"Valid question. My knives were custom-made a very long time ago. The handles protect me from the touch of the silver, and I have a sheath for the blade when not in use. I never actually touch the silver."

The woman kept getting more interesting. "I need to get a silver knife." She'd feel a lot safer with one of those inside her jacket, and unlike Sasha, she didn't have to worry about the touch of the silver poisoning her.

"No."

"Why not?" She was a little offended by the quick snap of an answer. Why shouldn't she have one strapped to her body? She was strong and capable and could take care of herself. Who was Sasha to tell her what she could and couldn't do?

Sasha turned dark eyes on her as she said, "They will kill you before you could get close enough to use it."

❖

DRAWING DOWN THE MIST

"We need to stop back in the room." Katrina realized that the meeting they were about to convene would be far more interesting if she changed her outfit. She looked fantastic as she was currently dressed, but this particular rendezvous called for something special, and she had brought it with her for just this moment. She'd been waiting quite some time to be able to wear it.

"We don't have time." Eli was looking at his watch and frowning. "I don't know exactly how long it will take us to get up there."

She agreed that sooner was better than later. It didn't change the fact that she was going in as she'd always envisioned. "It doesn't matter. We will make time." It was irritating to have him contradict her. He knew better, and to have him blurt out something like that now made her want to slap him. She didn't, because he shut his mouth and followed her like the good boy he was most of the time. Wise move.

Back in her bedroom she quickly changed into black pants and a form-hugging black shirt that showed her perfect curves, then went to the closet and spun the dial on the small safe. She'd set the combination as soon as they'd arrived so that the special items she'd brought would be safe until she needed them. Now was the time.

Five minutes later she stepped out and said, "I'm ready."

Eli, usually very stoic, looked surprised. "Are you serious? We're not going to a party."

"I have my reasons, and they are need-to-know. You don't need to know."

He shook his head and walked to the door of the suite. "Whatever you say, Boss. Let's get the car and drive up to the park. We may be able to make it on time."

She didn't really care if they were late. This was about her time and nothing more. When she summoned someone to a meeting, they waited for her regardless of how long it took for her to arrive. The repercussions if they didn't were well known. "Why are you being so hormonal tonight? It's not like you, Eli. Just do your job and keep your mouth shut. If I want your opinion on what I choose to wear, or anything, for that matter, I'll let you know."

Their car was sitting in the circular drive, one of the few staff still in the hotel having already brought it down. A few humans who hoped for alliance with the vampires and the potential perks that would entail remained. Katrina appreciated that, for she would find a place for the faithful beyond existing as food for their betters. At least until her minions could develop a cure for the effects of sunlight. Once that happened, they'd be cattle and nothing more.

Eli held the passenger's door open for her and then went around and got in behind the wheel. He was staring forward, his fingers tapping on the steering wheel. "How do you know what I'm really like? You've never cared."

Katrina snapped her gaze to him. "What is wrong with you?" If she didn't need him to get her to the meeting place, she'd break his neck right here and now. She didn't tolerate this kind of insolence. "You're acting stupid tonight and it's getting tiresome."

"Absolutely nothing is wrong with me. Quite the opposite in fact. I've never felt better than I do right now."

"You're behaving like one of those asses we left up in the suite. Their arrogance got them killed. Don't think for a second it couldn't happen just as easily to you."

"Killing me wouldn't be a good plan tonight."

Her anger with him began to ratchet up, and it wasn't just the talking back. It was also his tone. He wasn't going to go quietly—that seemed clear. "And why not?"

"You need me."

She opened her mouth to argue, but he actually had a point, as much as she hated him for it. The map program on her smartphone could certainly get her to the meeting location, but she had more to do during the next few hours than the fun and games that awaited in the flower garden. She did, in fact, need him to help coordinate the final assault. He was the detail guy, and before she could dispose of him, she needed everything to fall into place. Afterward, well, that was a different story, and he would be sent on posthaste.

The fact that he was right in this moment angered her even more than his sudden temperamental attitude. "And you need to remember who I am." She wasn't going quietly either.

His eyes stayed on the road. His words were cold. "Trust me, I never forget."

CHAPTER EIGHTEEN

Sasha appreciated Dee's vocalized desire to be armed and her willingness to take on the vampires that were around every corner. She was, however, naïve and didn't truly understand what they were up against. Driving through the heart of the city didn't fill her with confidence either. Things had progressed far more than she'd believed when they'd first left Rodney's bunker. The two that came at them on the street weren't an anomaly, and they were certain to encounter more of them sure to attack in the same frenzied rush. Dee couldn't understand the drive and quickness of her kind. With the newly turned, the desire to feed was fueled with an intensity that made them difficult to stop. Dee, or any human for that matter, wouldn't have a chance.

At the same time, she couldn't remember another instance when someone had offered to fight at her side. That included both humans and vampires. Oh, sure, she had her company, and through the years she'd had loyal, powerful employees who had her back. They were, however, employees who were paid to watch and protect. She had been walking a solitary path for decades.

Dee was different. She could have stayed behind with Rodney and Prima, and no one would have thought less of her. Rodney was a master when it came to the art of camouflage. Even with his incredible technical savvy, he'd managed to mask his tech usage so effectively that, to date, no one had come close to tracking his whereabouts. He'd developed a program that even pinged his cell-phone usage off towers miles away from his bunker. He was one human she had tremendous respect for, and he would have kept Dee safe.

Instead, here she was driving into the heart of the madness and asking for a silver knife. Part of her wanted to give Dee one. The other part, the more experienced part, knew that would be sending her to her death or, worse, putting her in a position to be turned. In all her years, she'd never turned another. She'd been pleaded with, offered millions of dollars, and been threatened, and she'd still refused them all. Even those she'd cared for. Especially those she'd loved. It wasn't what one did for a lover if they shared any true affection at all. Well, to be more precise, it wasn't what she'd done for those she'd really liked. She hadn't loved anyone since before she'd been turned. She wasn't sure she could love anyone again.

After a long silence, Dee said, "I think you're underestimating me. I'm not totally incapable."

"No. I'm not underestimating you. I'm confident you're quick, smart, and capable. I could tell that the moment we met, but you have to realize that you don't know what you're up against. It's like the old saying about bringing a knife to a gunfight. These things are not human, and their abilities exceed anything you've ever seen before."

"These things? Are they different from you?"

Ouch. That hurt, and the feeling was unexpected. Normally she couldn't care less about being considered less than human. She'd had a lot of time to get used to it and didn't totally disagree. Coming from Dee, it had a bite she couldn't have anticipated. The answer she gave her was honest. "No. They aren't different from me."

"Then I don't see the problem."

Sasha certainly did. "You saw how fast those two back there were, right?"

"Yes. So what? I might not be able to smash their heads to jelly like you can, and I get that. To quote you, what *you* have to realize is that I know where the heart is, and I can use a knife or a stake or whatever you give me. I can do it."

Katrina sighed as she saw a woman, or what used to be a woman, race on foot past the front of the car close enough she could have reached out and tapped the hood. She only braked because she didn't want to be slowed down by running over her. "Did you see how fast she was going?" She pointed to the vampire now racing up Post Street.

"Stop. I'm telling you I can do this. You're not going to be able to save the world all by yourself. I can help, and you'd be stupid not to let me."

Another ouch. Normally being called names rolled off her. She simply didn't care enough about who was spouting for it to matter. With Dee, it suddenly mattered. Still, she planned to hold her ground. She refused to put Dee in danger. "It's complicated, and I'm not doing it all by myself."

"Not all that complicated from my point of view. Stop the vampires, save as many humans as we can. Get the world spinning in the right direction again. What am I missing here?"

"I'm a vampire. What about me?"

Dee put her hand on her arm again, and once more, her touch sent a rush of warmth through Sasha. She liked the way it felt, and there was no changing that. "You're different in a way that really matters," Dee said.

She thought about what she was planning to do before the night was over. Did it really set her apart from the ones they'd be hunting? The truth was a little hard to admit to the woman riding next to her, but she did it anyway. "I don't think so."

❖

Sasha's tone made Dee really look at her. Maybe she was being naïve. After all, she'd just found out about the existence of vampires, and here she was making a call that sounded like they'd known each other for years. It was one of those immediate things, a connection that didn't have a good explanation and that people had a tendency to distrust.

Why not believe it? After all, everything in her world had taken a giant step to the left. Everything in everyone's world had taken that same giant step. Half her neighbors were probably gone by now, her house was a pile of rubble, and she was riding through the city with a gorgeous vampire. Take all that together, and she had no trouble buying into instant attraction and the feeling of having known Sasha for a lifetime. It was all good, and she decided not to fall victim to distrust. She was going to say screw it and trust her one hundred percent.

"I'm sticking with my instinct. You're not like them. Not at all."

She pointed out the window to a female vampire who was feeding on a woman who'd made the mistake of wandering out into the night. How many times throughout the city was this same scenario playing out? It made her sick to even consider what the answer might be.

Sasha glanced at the macabre scene outside the window and sighed. "No, in many ways I am not like that. Do not mistake me for human, though, because I am very much a vampire and have been for a hundred years. Don't forget that fact."

"Trust me. After what I saw a couple of minutes ago, that's not going to happen. It still blows my mind, that hundred-year thing." Dee couldn't help it. The writer in her wanted to know the story. The way Sasha fought, she had to have been some kind of soldier. Housewives and daughters didn't fight like that.

A long silence stretched out as Sasha continued to navigate the streets that were cluttered with empty cars, along with a few of the military vehicles Dee had seen earlier in the day patrolling the streets. She worried they were going to be stopped. It didn't happen, as it appeared what was left of the military was more focused on the vampires. Shots rang out behind them. She didn't turn to see. The world seemed to have already come to an end. The one thing that gave her hope was the occasional faces she'd seen peering out of the windows of the downtown condos and the houses they passed as Sasha drove south. All wasn't lost yet. She hoped.

Sasha finally spoke. "I came from a very special family, and because of that, we were targets."

"For the vampires?"

Sasha shook her head. "No. Targets for those who wanted to take everything from us, and they did."

"Are they vampires too?" She was stuck on that idea. It was incredible to think that might be the case.

Again she shook her head. "Only me. They are long turned to dust." Her words were so quiet Dee almost didn't hear them.

The sadness in Sasha's voice made Dee wish she could put her arms around her and hold her close. The obvious love she had for her family was clear, and she had no doubt that losing them had to be a difficult burden to carry. She thought of how she'd feel if her family was dead and gone, leaving her alone in the world. The possibility turned her cold.

"It must have been hard to stay young and watch everyone you knew grow old." It was impossible to imagine.

Sasha glanced over at her, and the tears in her eyes glistened in the dash lights. "I would have cherished being with them as they grew old and died normal, natural deaths. That's not what happened."

Dee almost didn't want to know but couldn't help herself from going all the way. "I know you said you'd share your story later, if we survived. Tell me now, please. What happened to them?"

"My family was executed."

❖

The drive to the park on the city's south side was relatively quick. It was just a couple of miles from the hotel, and thanks to Katrina's grand plan, very few cars were on the streets to slow their journey. Another sign of how right everything was with her vision.

A short distance past the massive hospital that rose from the lower part of the hill, a large sign told them they'd arrived. The main part of the park identified as Manito consisted of a mass of sloping green grass, a large duck pond, and covered picnic areas. A moderate parking area was designated right off the north border, but Eli drove past it and through the park on one of the narrow roads that appeared to traverse the park. He made several turns until they came to another parking area tucked between the hills that gave the park such an interesting character.

"We're here." He got out and came around to her side of the car. He'd been blissfully quiet for most of the drive and was once again acting like the obedient Eli she demanded. She was glad he'd thought his behavior through and gotten himself back in line. She really didn't want to have to train a new assistant until she was firmly placed in her new position.

After he opened her door, she stepped out and glanced around. From where they were parked she didn't see anything special. Wasn't this supposed to be some grand garden? The jewel of the city? A few roses grew up to their left, and that was about all she could see. If this was what people around here thought of as a special garden, they needed to set their expectations higher. No wonder she'd never been inclined to come here before. No wonder she'd never thought to look for her here. This wasn't the kind of place she had grown up surrounded by. Of course, who knew where she'd been in the intervening years, and this could appear to be paradise in comparison to some.

"Are you certain we're in the right place?" She sniffed, moderately impressed by the pleasing scent of flowers wafting through the air. Perhaps there was more than was currently meeting her eyes. She doubted it, given that she was rarely wrong about anything or anybody. It was one of her gifts.

As she stepped out of the car, three men raced at them. Not now, she thought as she stood her ground. They stopped a few feet away and quivered. Their eyes darted around like animals on the hunt. Essentially that's exactly what they were: hungry and looking for a meal. The young irritated her, even if she had made them. They were simply too needy, and she wasn't teacher material. She might have given them life immortal, but making it stick was up to them. She preferred the style and grace of older vampires, like Eli. He was perfect for her purposes. She'd gifted him with immortality, and he'd been a loyal servant ever since. It wasn't something she'd taught him. On the contrary, she'd left him to his own devices. If he made it, wonderful. If he didn't, oh well. He had not only made it; he'd flourished. Now, he complemented her style with his own, and it worked for both of them. He was handsome, grateful, and obedient, his earlier moment of sass aside. Given the war they'd just waged on the humans, she'd give him that as long as it didn't happen again.

"Stay." Her one word had the desired effect. It always did. Everyone responded to her commands, human and vampire alike. That was only one of the reasons she was the perfect person to be on the throne. That's the way she thought of this anyway. A return to the days of royal rule. She hadn't been born of royal blood. At this point that didn't matter. Her long life had gifted her with everything she needed to be worthy of a crown, and thus it would be. Those asses back in her suite had thought it would be them, a council of vampires, sharing the power. Stupid, that's what they were. She wasn't. Stupidity had cost them everything.

The recently turned vamps stood with their arms hanging and their mouths working. It was like watching a trio of snapping turtles. It wasn't attractive. It never was. The cravings were the most intense in the first few days. It felt like the body was on fire, and the only thing to ease the hunger was to feed the fire with blood. Fresh, warm human blood. Old, young, male or female—it didn't matter as long as the heart was pumping and the blood flowing. She still remembered that feeling even all these years later. The newbies in front of her wanted to move, to search out that rush of fresh blood, but they didn't.

She stared at them long enough for them to completely internalize her supremacy. It was a little like imprinting baby animals. Because she took the few minutes necessary to do this, they would always know her and respect her. They would become part of her legion. Young, strong, and helpful. Best of all, disposable.

"Go back," she commanded them.

They turned as one and returned in the same direction they'd come. Their arms still hung at their sides, and they shuffled their feet. "Oh, for God's sake, you look like zombies. Have some pride, boys. Run!"

They did, picking up speed until they were running fast, their arms swinging at their sides, and then they disappeared from sight. Soon enough they would find what they sought, and within twenty-four hours they would be ready to do whatever work she gave them. It was just the beginning. There would be dozens, hundreds, thousands more in the blink of an eye. It would be like the red tide flowing in from the ocean. She smiled.

She turned her attention away from her future soldiers and back to Eli. "Where is she?" No other cars were in the lot, no one else in view. Anticipation of what was to come was growing too strong to ignore.

He said nothing, just turned and began heading to the end of the parking lot. There he walked up several concrete steps and stood at the top, presumably waiting for her to follow his path. He should have waited and walked with her instead of expecting her to follow like an obedient puppy. Her annoyance with him was beginning to grow again.

Keeping her anger in check, she followed his path. She would have time enough for him later. Once she arrived at the top of the steps and stood next to him, she understood. Ten or twelve steps down on the other side and hidden from view when standing in the parking lot spread out a garden worthy of the finest English manor. Even in the darkness it was clearly magnificent, and for just a moment, she was impressed. The air was filled with the scent of thousands of blooms. She particularly liked the fountain that was the centerpiece of the garden.

"She'll meet us there." He pointed to the fountain she'd been admiring.

Despite her appreciation of the design and the work that had gone into the garden, she wasn't impressed with its suitability as a meeting place. An uneasy feeling settled over her, and she frowned. "I don't like it. Too wide open."

"I get your hesitation, but just remember, it's the same for her. Once we're down there, no matter what direction she comes from, we'll be able to see her. It's wide open. No way to get close and still stay hidden."

Katrina studied the garden more intently. Eli was right. No one could stage a surprise attack if she was standing by the fountain. Everything was open and visible inside the garden. Tall shrubs surrounded the exterior, which gave her pause. Then she decided they were far enough from the fountain not to be an issue. Only flowers swept up close.

"Let's go. How much time before she gets here?" Katrina started to descend the steps and walk the concrete path to the center.

Eli glanced at his watch. "If she's on time, five minutes or less."

Five minutes? She'd been waiting far more than five decades for this moment. Three hundred more seconds was nothing. All her irritation with Eli faded away as energy buzzed through her, and she was smiling as she almost ran to the fountain.

CHAPTER NINETEEN

The look of shock on Dee's face was pretty much what Sasha expected. Her next question wasn't. A little insulting but not unexpected or illogical. If the shoe was on the other foot, her thoughts would roll the same way.

"They were criminals?" She did like the note of disbelief in Dee's words. That took some of the sting out of the insult.

Sasha smiled because it was so absurd to think about anyone in her family as a criminal. Her gentle, fun-loving sisters. Her delicate, bright little brother. Never. Not in this life or the one they went to. They were waiting in heaven for her, not that it was the direction she was likely to go after the life she'd lived. She had committed some sins she didn't think she could ever atone for.

"No, they were not criminals. They were royalty."

Dee's head whipped in her direction, and she stared at her with big eyes. "No way. Who are you? I mean, really, who are you? Why, all of a sudden, do I think Sasha Rudin is a made-up name?"

This was a conversation she'd had with very few over the years, and she did mean very few. Even Rodney and Prima had no idea of her birth family. She had to think if she wanted to share it even now. Dee was so smart and so alluring. She made her feel alive in a way she hadn't for a hundred years. Sasha was drawn to her like no other person ever. Not even her lovers. The few she'd taken to her bed had been fun. They'd made her feel less empty, though never quite erased the emptiness. She glanced over at Dee and made up her mind.

"I was born Maria Nikolaevna in 1899."

"You're Russian. Now that you say it, I can hear a ghost of an accent. It's cute." Dee was nodding and then abruptly grew still. "Wait. Maria, as in…"

"Yes."

"Holy crap. How did this happen?" She waved her hand at Sasha in a way that seemed to encompass everything. She got it.

"Let us just say that history is not always written exactly the way it went down." Sasha pulled the car to a stop around the side of a greenhouse building in Manito Park. She motioned toward herself. "Case in point."

"Wow, weren't you like twenty, twenty-one or something like that? I'm trying to remember my history, but you've kind of blown my mind, and facts have flown out the window."

"I was nineteen."

"Holy crap, nineteen? That's insane."

"Yes." She remembered how mature and adult she'd considered herself back then. How she'd known that the love she felt for the other woman had been the real thing because she was old enough to know true love. It was going to be the kind of love that lasted forever. What a fool she'd been, and how she'd paid. "A vampire was part of the firing squad. She'd been part of the guards who'd watched us during our captivity, and she was there when they gunned us down."

"She turned you?"

"Worse. Before she shot me and before she turned me, she'd been my lover."

Dee was shaking her head. "That's not right. Not in any world. Not in any time."

She wasn't wrong, and in intervening years that truth had become a heavy stone on her heart. Particularly considering she wasn't even the youngest in her family. She didn't want to think about that night or the basement or the sound of the gunshots right before they ripped into her. Or of the woman she'd grown to trust and love who'd carried her bleeding body from that room. She'd thought she'd come to save her. She'd been mistaken about many things that night. It wasn't life she'd given to her; it was hell on earth. It wasn't love she wanted from Sasha; she'd demanded obedience and servitude. She'd hated her for it then, and she hated her just as much now.

Sasha brought her thoughts and emotions back to this place. "No, it was never right. But we have to move now. No time to revisit the travesty that was poured down upon me and my family."

Dee looked out the window at the massive park, now dark and foreboding, even though it was one of the most beautiful places in the city. "You know, I do get it. We've got vamps to take out. We've got human lives to try to save. Tell you what, Sasha. We get out of this alive, you have to tell me the whole story. I mean, you have to have met that guy, Rasputin, right? That's some kind of crazy."

Crazy didn't even begin to describe the last few years of her human life. No one could possibly imagine what they'd gone through. The memory should have faded, given the years that had flowed by. That wasn't the way it was. She still remembered it all. Every last second. Sasha took one of Dee's hands. "If we make it through, you have my promise. I will tell you everything. Even about Rasputin. He was a strange and interesting man." She brought her hand up to her lips and kissed it.

❖

The shot of electricity that jolted through Dee when Sasha's lips touched the back of her hand was as powerful as the best orgasm she'd ever experienced. She wanted to yell "do it again" and caught herself before the words passed her lips. Not the time or the place.

Instead, she kept her cool, or thought she did anyway, and said, "I'm going to hold you to it." Yeah, she sounded calm and collected. Sasha would have no idea she'd just rocked Dee's world with that kiss. She only wished it had been her lips rather than her hand.

"Deal."

Dee looked out the car window and wasn't sure why they were here, of all places. Seemed kind of weird to her. Sasha moved with a confidence that suggested she had a firm plan in mind. It would be nice if she shared this master plan. So far that wasn't happening. Not that she could really blame her. After all, they didn't really know each other, and how would she even know she could trust Dee.

She looked outside the window at the night that was more ominous than she could ever remember and questioned whether they would live through this siege. Or rather, if she would live through it. She was relatively certain Sasha would live to fight another day. Everything she'd seen today told her it was truly war on home soil. She'd always figured it would be because some inept politician said the wrong thing to the wrong unstable leader, and boom, the nukes would fly. That wasn't even close to what was happening here, and she knew that millions of people out in the world just like her had been totally blindsided. Nobody in their right mind could have ever seen this coming.

Since when did folktales and horror movies actually come to life? At this point, the bigger question was why didn't everyone know they weren't alone in this world? It wasn't a fair fight. If they'd known, then maybe they'd have been prepared for what they were up against. Better yet, maybe they could have found a way to coexist. The phrase "why can't we all just get along" popped into her head.

She almost laughed out loud. People of different backgrounds, religions, and beliefs had a hard enough time making it all work. How on earth would it have worked with humans and the not-so-humans? The preternatural kept out of sight for a valid reason, and she couldn't blame them.

She glanced over at her companion and knew that if there were many like Sasha, or Maria, or whoever she was, Dee could make it work. She was drawn to this woman, and not because she was beautiful or intriguing, but just because. Sure, she was easy to look at. That was only the book cover. There was so much more beneath that thrilled Dee. She thought of the old love-at-first-sight thing, and while that was a leap she wasn't willing to make, it still had that feel to it. They better get out of this alive, because she really wanted to know what was beneath this feeling she had for Sasha. She wanted to know each and every page inside that book.

For the moment, however, she needed to focus on the here and now. "Why are we here?"

Sasha said nothing at first. Then she sat up tall and said, "Two reasons: information and revenge."

Information and revenge in the deep, dark night in the middle of a massive park that was closed and most likely overrun by young, hungry vampires. Again she almost laughed. The park rules said it was closed after dark. Given the state of the city right now, it was stupid to even consider that any rules could or would be enforced. Exactly how many vampires were traipsing through the roses and flowers and trees as they sat here talking? No, back that thought up. She didn't want to know.

Sasha might be a righteous vampire, and thus being at her side was cool. Clearly those waging this war were not cut from the same cloth. There was nothing righteous about what they were doing, and to be at their side was as far from cool as one could get.

Sasha had told her their journey was to gather information, which was a great idea. The more they could collect, the better off they'd be. That wasn't what got Dee out of the car, however. It was the comment about revenge. She wanted to know exactly what Sasha meant and toward whom it was directed. From the look on her face, Dee definitely would not want to be on the receiving end of that. Somebody had pissed her off in a big way, and she suspected that revenge would be on an equally big level. Somebody was going down, and she was glad it wasn't her. But did she really want to be there to see it? Then she thought of something her grandmother used to say: in for a penny, in for a pound. She glanced over at Sasha, and it was an easy decision. In for a pound.

"What do we do now?" Dee shut her car door and stood waiting for directions.

Sasha looked at her over the hood of the car. "You need to get back into the car and lock the doors. Here are the keys." She tossed them over, and Dee barely caught them.

"No way." She didn't move to open the car door she'd just closed.

"This isn't your fight. You'll be safer here."

"The fuck it isn't. This isn't only about your need for revenge. My house, my neighbors, my friends? What about all of that makes it not my fight? At this point I think safety is overrated anyway."

Sasha stared over the hood of the car at her, clearly wanting to argue with Dee. She couldn't. Dee's points were valid. "You walk out there with me," she pointed in the direction of Duncan Gardens, "you are putting yourself in real danger. You saw what those two downtown were like. This will be worse. I may not be able to protect you."

Sasha's arguments were just as sound, and Dee thought for only a second. "I'm willing to take that risk."

❖

Katrina stopped breathing the moment she caught movement out of the corner of her eye. She didn't even have to turn her head to know who it was. She recognized the cadence of the walk. It hadn't changed in a century. "At last," she murmured, more to herself than anything. Her fingers buzzed.

She whirled around and there it was, the face she hadn't glimpsed in a hundred years. The same feeling she'd experienced on that long-ago day when she'd come through the garden to see the princess and her sisters sitting on the garden wall rolled over her now. That night too the moonlight had cast a warm glow onto her pale cheeks and her long, shiny hair. In those days the paleness was a result of the restrictions she'd been under as a captive. Tonight it was because of the life she'd led since then, one that meant she lived in the darkness just as Katrina did. It didn't change a thing, not all the years or the betrayal. She had loved her then, and the feeling was still there as deep and intense as always.

She had taken the night duties guarding the tsar and his family on a lark. Her thoughts were that it would be fun to see history as it was made from the inside, and the bloody war raging in the country was going to be like one of today's buffets. Easy sustenance was everywhere, and the fun she'd anticipated was delivered. What she hadn't expected was the beauty of the young princess, the lightness and joy she brought. Katrina had been hardened to the world long before she'd been turned, and for that brief bit of time when she'd been loved by Maria, she'd experienced emotions she hadn't known existed within her. When Maria rejected both her love and her gift, hope withered and died, replaced by a deep desire for vengeance. The hardness that had defined her life as a child returned tenfold.

Her chin came up while the look of shocked recognition that she'd waited so long for didn't happen. Maria, or rather the reinvented Sasha, came toward her and Eli with a determined stride, her shoulders back, her long hair whipping in the light breeze. Behind her hurried another woman, tall and dark-haired, and clearly human. She could smell the blood that roared through the human's body, and it made her ravenous. She pushed her urge to the back. She would have time enough to feed when this was done.

What she wanted to witness, what she'd waited so long to witness, was some kind of reaction from Sasha. She had to know that Katrina was here to settle what should have been taken care of all those years ago. Rejection wasn't okay, not then and not now. Those who dared turn their backs on what she offered had only one avenue open to them: death. Nothing about that had changed in the ten decades since they'd seen each other.

Call her the Grim Reaper, because she had come prepared to make this Sasha's last day walking on this planet. She'd gotten lucky when she escaped back in Russia, first from the firing squad and then from Katrina. That luck was running out tonight. Once this was over, she and Eli would call their pilot and take her private jet back to Seattle. She could then peacefully watch as her troops did the work necessary to bring the world to its knees.

When they were about twenty meters away, Sasha stopped and said something to the other woman. At that point, Katrina could see the woman's face clear enough to realize she was the troublemaking writer. How this Dee person had turned out to be with Sasha was a story she'd love to hear, though it was unlikely. She didn't intend to give either of them enough time to explain, and really, it didn't matter one way or the other. Except now that she thought about it, she was rather pleased they were together. Two problems in one place. Two solutions in one place. This was going to be a good night.

When Sasha turned back around and started walking again, the writer did not. She stayed where they'd stopped, her eyes on Katrina and Eli. She smiled. Did Sasha really believe the woman would be safe a whole twenty meters away? In the old days, Katrina had been impressed by her intelligence and common sense as much as she'd been by her beauty. Maybe she'd lost all of that in the intervening years. Too bad. She preferred her prey to be sharp. Made the game much more fun.

"Maria," she said when Sasha got within ten feet. She liked goading her with the name of the woman she'd fallen in love with back in the mother country.

"Maria died a hundred years ago."

"Not to me."

"Especially to you."

"I'm surprised you came. You did know I'd be here."

"I was banking on it."

"Why?"

"You owe me."

Katrina laughed. "I owe you? Oh, that's rich."

"You took everything from me. I want it back."

"What? Like this?" She fingered the necklace she'd put on before they left the hotel and smiled broadly. "Well, yes, I helped myself to a few things. After everything I'd done for you, I was entitled. You and your spoiled sisters would never be in a position to wear anything like this ever again. Your foolish mother thought sewing them into your dresses would protect them. Her big secret. We knew, we all knew, and I for one saw no sense in letting good jewels go to waste. In case you're curious, I have more like this, and I've enjoyed them immensely over the years. I think of you every time I put a piece on."

Sasha's gaze swept over her, and she detected contempt in her gaze and her words. It wasn't the reaction she was expecting. "I don't care about the jewels. I never did. Mother, yes, but me—no, I never needed them and never will."

Her fingers dropped away from the diamonds. A note in her voice made Katrina believe she meant what she said. She was profoundly disappointed her bait didn't have the anticipated effect. "If not the jewels, then what can I possibly give you back?"

This time Sasha smiled. Her expression held a cruel edge that in her previous life she never could have pulled off. She'd been too sweet. "You really don't get it, do you?"

"Enlighten me."

"You took my world from me then, and now you're trying to do it again. Not going to happen, Katrina. Not again."

Blah, blah, blah. Apparently in the intervening years she'd become tiresome. Too bad. Once when she was young, Sasha had been a pure delight, and she'd been more than happy to introduce her to the pleasures of loving another woman. It had been a wonderful time that she'd hoped would continue forever.

"I'll take whatever I want." Her earlier feeling of attraction was beginning to fade, replaced by lust. Blood lust. Again she caught the tantalizing scent of the human's blood as it rushed through her veins.

"Think again."

She'd gotten cocky since the last time they'd seen each other. Good for her. Too bad it wasn't going to help. She'd glimpsed that strength back in the old days and always wondered what she'd be like if she grabbed it with two hands.

She raised a single eyebrow. "Oh, please enlighten me. You know me well enough to know you don't stand a chance."

Shocking her, Sasha turned her attention away from Katrina and to Eli. "You have what I need?"

"Absolutely." He tossed a flash drive in her direction, and Sasha caught it. As soon as she did, he tossed the bag with all the cell phones at her. She caught it as well.

"What the fuck?" Katrina whirled to look at her trusted confidant, almost speechless. Almost. "What have you done?" she screamed.

He laughed. "Payback's a bitch, isn't it, Boss?" His face was filled with self-satisfaction, and she intended to claw it off.

"What are you talking about?"

"My family, you arrogant bitch." Now rage transformed his face into one she'd never seen before. "You killed my family, and now I'm going to watch while they kill you."

She was going to rip his throat out, but before she went after him, she whirled back around to face Sasha. Sasha and her scribbling companion were nowhere in sight. Her scream filled the quiet night air.

Chapter Twenty

As much as Sasha wanted to exact her revenge at this opportune moment, she did the right thing and waited. It took every ounce of her self-control to turn and flee. This was bigger than her, and she couldn't afford to waste time or lose the element of surprise. She moved with the speed that came to all of them, and in this instant she was more grateful for it than at any other time. With the flash drive safely in her pocket and the bag of cell phones slung across her shoulders, she grabbed Dee around the waist and had her back at the car in a matter of seconds. They were racing out of the park before Katrina had enough time to fully react. It was exactly what she had been banking on. If she and Eli hadn't been able to catch Katrina off guard, she could never have matched her in speed or strength. Sasha knew she was good. She also knew Katrina was better.

"What just happened, what do you have, and where are we going now?"

Sasha looked over at Dee. "Which answer do you want first?"

"Take your pick."

"We've got to get these back to Rodney." She patted the bag still around her shoulders, although she actually meant both the bag and the flash drive. They were critical to the plan.

"Why?"

"They're going to save you and everyone else."

"You have got to start answering in full paragraphs so I can understand. How can a flash drive save the world from any of this?" Dee pointed out the window at the activity on every corner. It wasn't the good kind of activity that should be happening in a place this nice and had picked up in intensity in the short time they'd been up at Manito Park. In fact, it had picked up at an alarming rate.

Sasha glanced over at her as she maneuvered through the city, trying to return north to the highway that would take them to Rodney. Again, she had to make a judgment call. Trust her or not? She put her hand over Dee's, unsure what she was seeking. The sensation that flowed through her was strong and hot and reached all the way to her heart. It was trust.

"I got my hands on the Consortium plans, and I enticed Eli over to my side not long after." She thought briefly of the traitors in her own network and wondered for a second if Eli's information would be tainted by that betrayal. He'd been working with Rory and Crystal. She weighed her earlier conversation with Crystal and went with trust. Rory and Crystal hadn't been aware of her arrangement with Eli. They had simply been feeding Katrina all she wanted on Sasha, so the information Eli had just handed off to her would be valid and helpful. He was working his own angles for his own reasons, just as she had been doing. As long as she got what she needed, it was all fair play.

"It's more than a flash drive. It's information and access. We've been working on countermeasures to every plan they've devised for years. And have been waiting with our ducks in a row for quite some time. All I've needed since this showdown started was the final call on what they planned to use to bring the humans down. The phones are an added bonus. They should be quite helpful."

"You've been waiting for this? Wow. I still can't figure out how the human race can be so incredibly oblivious. I'm embarrassed on behalf of all mankind."

"Don't be. Vampires are really good at blending in and making you believe whatever they want you to. The practice goes back as long as humans have been around." She'd actually had the same sense of incredulity when she'd been turned, wondering how she'd never noticed. How she'd never realized what Katrina was, particularly given how intimate they'd been with each other. She'd had enough time to come to understand the skill of her kind in the intervening years.

"I suppose you're right, but I still feel oblivious. I thought I could really see the world and the people in it. I thought it was what helped to make me a successful writer. Boy, was I wrong."

"Think of it more as being aware while not completely tuned in. Now you are. After this, you're going to see everything differently. You're going to be better armed."

"Oh, isn't that the truth. Now that I've seen it, I can't not see it! I'm pretty sure nobody will be able to miss it from here on out. Things are going to change on the third rock. Now, explain to me again how you and Rodney are going to save the planet?"

This time she didn't hesitate. Her trust issues had been resolved. Sasha told her everything.

Dee's head was still spinning as they paid absolutely no attention to speed limits on the way back north with the precious cargo still hanging on Sasha's body. Once she understood what was in the works, she was as anxious as Sasha to get back to Rodney. Only one question remained with no time to ask it. Sasha once more had the car parked in the trees, and once more they were running through the dark woods. This journey back, she did a little better. Maybe she could be a trail runner.

About the time she was patting herself on the back for her smooth footing, she stumbled and tripped, though she managed to stay on her feet with her eyes on Sasha's back. Her ankle burned and would hurt for days. Following the sure-footed vampire through the woods took a lot of concentration, and when they arrived at the entrance to Rodney's bunker she was immensely relieved. Then they were back inside and dashing down the stairs to the big metal door, which opened before they had a chance to pound on it.

"You've got it?" Rodney's eyes were flashing with what? Excitement? Yeah, she was pretty sure that was excitement, and why not? He was about to become one of the saviors of the humans they counted themselves among. Pretty cool, if she did say so, though she wasn't going to say it out loud. They hadn't actually saved anyone yet, and Grandma had always told her not to put the cart before the horse. Grandma had a lot of those snappy sayings.

"I do." Sasha tossed him the flash drive that she'd pulled from her pocket. "It's the money shot," she said.

"Hot damn," he muttered as he spun away. "I don't know about you ladies, but I say let's fry some vampire ass." He stopped, turned, and looked at Sasha with a contrite expression. "No insult intended."

A little smile turned up the corner of her mouth, and the look of hope in her eyes matched his. "None taken. There's a fair amount of vampire ass I'm very anxious to fry."

Without warning, Prima shoved a hot cup of tea into Dee's hands. "Drink this," she commanded.

Neither thirsty nor hungry, Dee tried to hand it back. She was keyed up for this vampire-fry-ass thing. "I'm okay."

"No, you're not. Whatever happened out there has taken a toll. You look like somebody beat the tar out of you. Now drink this or else."

Dee looked at her friend and cocked her head. "Or else what?" Prima didn't typically mete out threats of physical violence. She was more the conscientious-objector type.

"Or else I'll have to call in reinforcements." She nodded toward Sasha, who was hovering over Rodney's shoulder as he navigated the many files on the flash drive. "Don't think I won't either."

Dee had the urge to resist again just because she wasn't totally opposed to seeing what Sasha might do. The thought of having Sasha's hands on her body was most decidedly exciting. Then again, maybe now wasn't the best time to press it. Nobody needed a distraction. If Sasha and Rodney did save the world, well, then perhaps she could revisit this scenario with the lovely vampire.

"Fine, fine, fine," she muttered as she put the cup to her lips. "I have a mother, you know."

"Don't act like a child."

She stuck her tongue out at Prima before she took a sip. Surprisingly, the tea was quite nice. She wasn't sure what Prima had put in the clearly custom brew, but it was sweet and bitter all at the same time and filled her with a boost of energy she didn't even realize she needed. She hated it when Prima was right. Then again, Prima usually was, and no, she didn't actually hate it when her friend was right. She liked it quite a lot.

"Better?" Prima had her hands on her hips and was looking at her like her mother used to when she was being particularly naughty.

"You know it is."

Prima gave her a knowing smile and a nod. "Why yes, I do. Dr. Prima at the ready."

"I'd call you a bitch, but you'd know I mean it in the most loving way possible."

"Of course you would. Who doesn't love me?" She spread her arms wide. "I'm infinitely lovable." Dee glanced over at Rodney and in her heart knew he'd wholeheartedly agree with that statement. She hoped when this was all done, the two of them could spend some quality time together. Despite having just met Rodney, she was convinced they were meant for each other.

"This is going to work out, right?" Her ADD mind did one of its lightning jumps from therapeutic tea to vampire apocalypse.

Prima turned her gaze on Rodney and Sasha. A frown darkened her usually bright face. "If those two can't save us all, then we really are doomed." When she turned back to look at Dee, the frown was gone, and brightness reilluminated her face. "I have a good feeling about this. I think they're going to do it."

Despite everything she'd seen both earlier in the day and once night had fallen—the blood, the death, the creatures that were running with such abandon—she couldn't help the feeling of hope that embraced her as well. Part of it was Prima's confidence. Part of it was the way Sasha had reacted at Duncan Gardens.

If she'd understood what was written between the lines, and she was sure she did, the woman she'd seen standing at the fountain was the same one who had not only had a hand in gunning down Sasha's family but had subsequently turned her into a vampire. And that was after she'd made Sasha believe she was in love with her. All she'd done was cruel on so many levels that Dee wondered how Sasha had been able to stand before her and not tear her apart. Dee didn't think she'd have that much restraint. She'd have gone ballistic the second she was in her face. Sasha had been amazing. She'd focused on saving people she didn't even know instead of avenging her family and herself.

She watched now as Sasha and Rodney spoke in low, urgent tones. She detected excitement underneath as well and had the impression that whatever the man, the vampire, had given her, it was a game changer. Would he survive what had happened? She had the feeling he wouldn't. She also had a feeling he didn't care. He'd gotten his revenge.

"Got it!" Rodney threw a hand up in the air, and Sasha slapped his palm with her own. "Hot damn, we got 'em."

"Yes!" The look of triumph on Sasha's face was bright and glowing. Real hope bloomed inside Dee.

Rodney jumped up from his command center chair and pointed at Sasha. "Start making the calls, my clever friend, and I'll get the syringes ready. Take that, you bloodsucking assholes!"

❖

Eli stood with his legs apart, glaring at her. Katrina had never seen such a look cross his face. It wasn't defiance. It was hatred so clear and intense that, had she been a mere mortal, it probably would have seared her skin. Instead, it only served to increase the fury that engulfed her. He had no right to do what he'd done, and oh, he was going to pay in ways he couldn't imagine. There would be no quick death. He would suffer.

"You fool," she screamed as spittle hit him in the face.

He slowly shook his head. "Oh, how wrong you are. That was the least foolish thing I've ever done."

"You're dead." Her fingers twitched at her sides.

"Fuck you, Katrina. I've been dead for a hundred years, and there's nothing you can do to me now. I've been dead since the day you slaughtered my wife and my daughters."

That remark momentarily cut through the red haze of fury, and she had to think. Sometimes they all blended together—the people, the meals, the places. It seemed like Eli had been at her side forever, but as she now thought about it, Katrina realized it had been only shortly before Sasha's betrayal. He had been there with gun in hand when they destroyed her family, just as she'd commanded him to be. He'd been there when they realized that Maria hadn't died from her bullet wounds. He'd been there when Katrina gave her a second chance. And he'd been there when she'd turned her back on everything Katrina had offered her. He had been there for it all.

All along she'd believed that he was unwaveringly loyal to her. With all they'd gone through together, she had no reason to believe otherwise. Now she was stunned. How could she have missed the blackness in his soul all these years? She was better than that.

"I'm a very good actor." He answered her unspoken question. "I played you. For years, I've played you, and you have always been such an arrogant bitch you never noticed."

If he'd truly been her enemy all this time, there had been many opportunities over the years to take revenge. "Why now?"

His smile was not sweet. "Sasha's idea, and a damned good one, if I do say so. She always was a smart woman. A century to think about it has made her even smarter."

Now the fury inside her morphed to something like molten lava. "She knew?"

"Not about you. I kept that little gem close to the vest and only just let her know. About your plans, well, yes, she's been in the loop."

"How long?"

"Since before we took over Kramer's empire. He was the match that lit the fire."

"He was the key I needed to make all this happen. To finally track down Maria." She waved her hands in the air, then realized her actions made her look as though she was losing it. No way was he going to get her to melt down. She dropped her hands and stared at him.

He raised his eyebrows. "That's what you were supposed to think. Hate to break the news to you, darlin', but you're not quite the genius you like to believe you are. I manipulated you, and now you're going to watch everything you wanted crash and burn. You aren't going to be the queen of anything."

"No!" She couldn't help it. All her good intentions to stay calm disappeared. This creature was going to die. She was going to rip his head from his body and drink his blood.

He smiled broadly, and this time she thought she saw joy in his expression. "Oh, yes. Better get your white flag ready, Boss, because you're going to have to wave it if you want to stay alive. Then again," he shrugged, "you probably won't survive this no matter what you do. You can wave a white flag all night long, but in the end, it's going to turn crimson."

A trickle of fear entered her heart, and she hated him all the more for it. "You will pay for this, you bastard."

"As I said before, Katrina, fuck you. I've been paying for years and waiting for the right time and place to make you pay for what you did to me. Well, it's finally time. It's your turn to pay up."

"I will tear you limb from limb. I will make you suffer in ways you can't imagine." Her mind was racing with what she intended to do to him. She could envision his blood dripping through her fingers.

Slowly he pulled a syringe out of his pocket and held it up so she could clearly see it. "Not going to happen, Boss. You can't stop it now. The train has already left the station. She's going to take you down like the rabid bitch you are, and I'm going to join my family. *Hasta la vista!*"

Before she could reach him, he'd plunged the needle into his arm and pushed the plunger all the way down, smiling the whole time. He was still smiling as he crumbled to the lush green grass of Duncan Gardens. Shocked, she watched his body literally melt into nothing. In less than thirty seconds, it was as if he'd never been there. Katrina stood alone in the gardens under the glowing moon and a canopy of stars in a velvet sky.

CHAPTER TWENTY-ONE

Sasha stood once more in her small bedroom and stared at the egg sitting right where she'd left it at sundown. "I'm sorry," she whispered. "I'm trying to make it right, and I will, I promise."

"What are you sorry about? What are you trying to make right?"

She whirled, shocked to see Dee in the doorway. She hadn't heard her approach, which wasn't like her at all. She always heard the movement of anyone and everyone. Another perk of what she was. Was she losing her edge? Then the truth hit her hard. Their invisible connection let Dee move into her personal space without disruption. She could deny it all she wanted, but the reality of it was impossible to ignore. In her very long life, no one had really held a spot in her psyche like this woman was managing to do in what felt like minutes. Even though she'd believed she'd been in love with Katrina, the woman had never affected her the way Dee did. She should be upset, but she wasn't.

Life had thrown her curves that no one in their right mind could have ever imagined, and she'd rolled with each and every one of them. Her life of privilege had been taken away in an instant, yet she'd managed to make peace with that time in her life. She'd had her family and she'd even found love, or so she'd thought at the time. She'd made the best of every bad situation.

Even when that love had turned on her and made her what she was today, she'd found a way to live with that too. It hadn't been easy. Of course, revenge was a pretty good motivator, and it had kept her charged decade after decade. She'd never expected to feel about another person the way she did right now. Despite everything happening in the world above them, she wanted to survive because she wanted to walk side by side with Dee, hold her hand, and kiss her lips. It didn't make any sense, yet there it was. Denial wouldn't change a thing. She was falling for a unique and beautiful human.

"Sasha?"

She realized she'd been staring off into space and shook away the introspection. "Sorry. I was talking to myself. Silently anyway."

"I get that and it's cool. What I can't figure out is what you have to be sorry for. You're saving us. You're saving everyone. You're the last person who should say they're sorry."

She turned her gaze back to the egg and then walked over to pick it up. "This belonged to my family what feels like a million years ago. Everything we had was taken away and scattered throughout the world. It was like vultures swooped in and picked our bones clean. I've spent so many years looking for things like this and bringing them back together. I think I believed doing that would bring my family back together. I think I believed it would make me feel whole again."

"Things." Dee seemed to be grasping what she wasn't saying so well.

"Yes, they are just things, not the people I loved. They're gone, and spending so much energy on reclaiming our possessions won't change that. Things such as this egg represent my father, my mother, my siblings, but they don't bring them back. I've been chasing ghosts, and I'm so tired."

"That's nothing to be sorry about. None of it was your fault, and there's nothing wrong with wanting things that remind you of them. You're right on one thing, though. You don't need the egg or anything else to remind you of your family. They're in your heart and always will be."

"Yet I'm still here." The bitterness she felt was intense. It was as it always was, a deep sense of betraying her family by not dying in that basement with them. Their lives flowed out in rivers of red on that floor, and hers should have too.

"And I'm glad you are."

"I should be with them."

"You're meant to be here."

Something about those words hit her, and she studied Dee. She was sincere. It helped close the crack that had been in her heart for a hundred years. Not all the way, but enough to instill a touch of peace. "Thank you."

Dee laid a hand against her cheek, and Sasha leaned into it. "Thank you. Everyone who survives this will thank you."

"I let her go."

Dee dropped her hand away and studied Sasha intently. All of a sudden, the light seemed to come on. "That woman in the park."

"That vampire, yes."

"But you got what you needed from that guy, right?"

"I got what we needed. I didn't get what I wanted."

"And that is?"

"Revenge."

Dee wanted to hug her. It was just her way of comforting those she cared about, and even though Sasha was talking of revenge in the dark, kill them fast kind of way, something seemed broken in that one word.

"She was the one who made you what you are." It wasn't a question because it was crystal clear to her. The conflict inside Sasha made sense to her. She could feel it as if it were her own.

"Yes."

"Then let's go back." The words almost fell out of her mouth. Definitely one of those speaking-before-the-brain-engaged moments. Even so, once the words were out there, she was okay with them. Sasha needed to make it right, and if that meant revenge against that thing in the park, that's what it was going to be. She sure didn't have trouble with taking that one out of the equation.

Besides, she was confident Rodney was on top of whatever their plan was to save the world. He was most decidedly pumped, and besides mining the flash drive, he was at this moment filling three syringes with what, she wasn't quite sure.

Sasha had handed the bag off to Prima, who had pulled a series of phones from inside and then lined them up on the table, putting them at the ready for Sasha. Before coming back here to the bedroom, Sasha had used each one of them to make calls. Most were short and sweet. A couple took a little longer. When she was done, she'd excused herself. Dee had waited a moment before following.

"No, we're not going back. We have things to do here first."

She respectfully disagreed. "Okay. I'm done with being in the dark. Come on." She took Sasha's hand and tugged on it. "Explanation time."

Back in the main room, Sasha looked over at Rodney and nodded. "Dee and Prima need to be brought in."

"Good call." Rodney dropped into his chair and made a complete three-sixty turn.

Sasha nodded at both Prima and Dee. "Tell them."

He was smiling. "All righty. First and foremost, you must all know that I'm a rock star and I got it nailed." He looked up at Sasha. "Thank your pal, Eli, next time you see him."

Sasha's expression darkened. "Just tell them." It didn't escape Dee's notice that Sasha blew right past the mention of Eli, and she had a sinking feeling she knew why. She'd lay odds that the handsome man she'd encountered at Duncan Gardens would never be seen again. Hopefully his demise was on his own terms.

"Okay, okay. They went with KED."

Sasha nodded, and a light entered her eyes. "Good. We've got them."

Both Rodney and Sasha sucked at explaining what was going on.

"What is KED, and why is that good? You two are horrible when it comes to cluing us in."

Rodney turned his chair until he was looking at Dee. "We nicknamed it *knock 'em dead*. KED. In simple terms, it's an airborne virus that attacks the human immune system. The kicker is, it's selective and affects only some of the human population. It's all in your DNA. Some it kills. Some it doesn't. That's how they designed it."

"A kind of survival of the fittest," Sasha added. "Rather ingenious of the bastards. Some die immediately, some it takes a bit longer, and some are immune."

It hit Dee forcefully. "In other words, it's getting rid of a lot of threat by killing a large segment of the population and ultimately creating a herd of the finest cattle. Cattle, of course, being the humans the vampires want to feed on."

"I knew you were smart the first moment I met you." Sasha put an arm around her shoulders.

She didn't feel very smart. She felt scared. She'd been out in the city breathing in whatever it was they'd let loose into the air. If what Sasha said was right, just because none of the three humans in the room succumbed right away didn't mean they were immune. "We had to have breathed the fumes in when we were outside. We could still die." Her heart sank. So much for having time to investigate her attraction to Sasha.

"Au contraire," Rodney said as he got up. "Nobody in this room is going to die."

"How can you be so sure? We were out there. We breathed the tainted air. We're probably dying right now." She didn't want to die. She didn't want Rodney or Prima to die.

"We're prepared." Sasha squeezed her shoulder again. "That bitch didn't get the drop on me this time. I'm a lot older and a whole lot smarter than the last time we came face-to-face. She underestimated me and my buddy here. You'll survive this because we have you covered."

"Locked and loaded." Rodney held up a small vial of a golden liquid. "You thought I was just living down here being all paranoid and stuff. The crazy guy that thought someone was out to get him. Ha. Joke's on all of you. Someone was out to get me and you and you." He pointed to Dee and Prima. "While you've been up there living under Big Brother's nose, I've been a busy guy, and this is going to save your lives and everyone else's. So come on over and step up. Doc Rodney has the cure."

"What does it do?" Enough weirdness had invaded her life over the past few days that she wasn't jumping into anything without questioning first.

"This—" Rodney held the vial upside down as he pulled the plunger on a syringe he'd inserted into the small rubber cap, "is a twofer. First, it will render you immune to the virus."

"And the twofer part?"

He put the vial down, held the needle up, and pushed the plunger until drops fell from the tip. "Two, any vampire who has the poor judgment to try to take a little sip of your blood is in for a really big surprise."

Dee waited for Rodney to continue, but apparently he wasn't going to spill the secret until they asked. Seriously, he was awful at this. Prima beat her to it. "Oh, for heaven's sake, Rodney. What's the surprise?"

This time Sasha smiled as she looked into Dee's eyes. "It renders human blood toxic to a vampire. One sip and it's the last sip they'll ever take."

❖

Katrina was so shocked for a moment she didn't move. Then she screamed and kicked at the dust where Eli had just been standing. All that remained to even hint he was there was a pair of shoes and a pile of clothes. "You bastard! You dirty, fucking bastard! How dare you do this. How dare you take your own life. You were mine!"

It was incomprehensible. Eli, trusted and privy to her every secret, her go-to man in any and all situations, was a Judas. To have him turn on her like this was as bad as Maria refusing her affections. He had escaped her wrath, and she couldn't do a thing about it. Maria or Sasha or whatever she wanted to call herself would not win. Eli might have passed along critical information to her, but in the end it wouldn't make any difference. It was already too late. Nobody could do a thing to stop what was happening. All they had to do was look around this city and they would know. She would succeed.

The virus had been let loose in every major city in the United States. Humans were dying by the tens of thousands, and vampires were rising as they never had before. It was like Mardi Gras in a very bloody and preternatural way. It was marvelous and thrilling and perfect.

Still, she needed to do some damage control. Eli had tossed Sasha the phones, which was a small problem. She needed to reach out to her counterparts, and those phones were the most efficient way to make that happen. Still, the loss of the phones wasn't a showstopper. Back in the hotel suite her laptop was still sitting on the desk. Inside it was a treasure trove of information.

Kicking at the dust one more time, she whirled and ran back to the car. This wasn't her city, and she didn't know her way around that well. She was stuck driving herself back to the hotel, and she hadn't driven herself anywhere in years. Why would she, when she had Eli to do all the work? The upside was that she had a memory that most would kill for. It was no problem for her to retrace the route here without a single wrong turn. It was more challenging to figure out the car, given how long it had been since she'd driven. Things had changed in the interim. Finally, she got it and was driving out of the park.

At the hotel, she raced back to her room. At the door she realized that she didn't have the keycard. It had been with Eli. Her frustration was immense, and for a second she was frozen. All it took to open the door was one powerful kick. It crashed open, the door falling to the floor with a loud bang. Inside, she leveled another kick at one of the bodies that lay in her way as she tried to get to the desk. Her rage was massive by the time she sat down and flipped open the laptop cover. Her fingers flew over the keyboard as skillfully as Eli's had done. She was pulling up files with all the phone numbers she'd need when her cell phone rang. The sound of the ringer made her jump.

"Yes." Her curiosity was too great to let the call go unanswered, though that was her first instinct. Too much work to do to be bothered with unimportant calls.

"Meet me on the Monroe Street Bridge. One hour."

The call ended before she could say another word. Well, well, well. That was unexpected. Slowly she put the phone down and smiled. Yes, she would definitely be there in an hour.

CHAPTER TWENTY-TWO

It had taken less than ten minutes to make the calls. The conversations were quick and pointed. Eli's gift of the bag full of phones made Sasha's job easy, and Rodney had a long list of numbers already programmed into his phone. Once all the players were in place and the wheels of the cure in motion, she'd used Eli's phone to put in one final call. Out of all of them, it was the one that meant the most. Everything was going well except for one thing: Dee had refused to allow Rodney to give her the injection that would make her immune. Sasha was having a hard time understanding or accepting her logic.

"Explain to me again why you won't take it?" Sasha was staring at Dee and working very hard not to hold her down so Rodney could give her the shot that both he and Prima had already taken.

"Simple. You're going after her."

"Of course I am."

"I'm going with you."

"This will protect you."

"It won't protect you."

Sasha stopped and thought about what she'd said. In so many ways it didn't matter. Once she took care of Katrina, her job on this earth was done. If she died, her demise was a hundred years overdue. "You could already be infected. We have to stop it. We have to protect you."

"None of that matters."

"It matters to me. You're more protection to me if you're immune." She'd say whatever she needed to in order to keep Dee safe. In this short amount of time, she'd become precious to her, and she wanted her to live out her life without having to worry about what Sasha's kind had done to the humans.

"No, I'm not. We're running out of darkness, and if you're going to kick her ass, you're going to need strength. I can give it to you."

"I don't understand…" She stopped talking and stared because suddenly, she did understand. The realization of Dee's intent horrified her. "No! Absolutely not."

"My choice." Dee just stared back at her.

"No, it is not."

Dee put her hands on her hips and challenged Sasha. "You need fresh blood to be as powerful as possible. I can give that to you. She's not going to beat you."

"Rodney brought me packets. They're in the fridge. I don't need you."

"Got her all stocked up thanks to friends in high places," Rodney added.

Dee kept her gaze on Sasha. "Oh, right, and you're going to carry them in your pockets just in case. That's bull, and you know it. I'm your best chance at success."

"Absolutely not."

"Absolutely yes. Let's go get this over with. We've got a vampire to take down. You've waited too long already for this. Let's go!" Dee almost ran to the door. She didn't look back.

"You're going to lose this one," Prima told her. "You haven't known her as long as I have. Short version: she doesn't back down once she digs in."

"I like her spunk," Rodney added. "Kind of reminds me of someone else we all know and love." He looked pointedly at Sasha. "Take this," he said as he pressed a small device into her hand. She glanced down and realized it was the remote that would open the big steel door. "You better follow her before she gets herself killed out there."

"I may kill her myself," Sasha muttered as she followed Dee out of the bunker.

❖

Dee knew she was right. She also knew that Sasha wouldn't rest until the woman from the park was toast. The best shot Sasha had to make that happen once and for all was to fortify herself with Dee's blood. Yeah, it sounded creepy, and the last thing she'd ever imagined herself doing was being the Holy Grail for a vampire, but hey, part of life's great journey was doing strange and unusual things. It would make for a good story for her family fifty years down the line. If, that is, she actually survived the night to have a family down the line.

Sasha wasn't totally wrong in saying that she was going out unprotected. She'd seen what was out there, and even though Rodney and Sasha had put a machine of salvation into motion, the solution would take days, weeks, or even years, depending on how widespread the toxin's effects were. With something so invasive, a great deal of damage could be done in that amount of time. She just hoped they ended up saving more than they lost.

Truthfully, she didn't wish to be one of the lost either. She also didn't want to lose Sasha. She had heard the finality in her voice earlier when she declared that living beyond tonight didn't matter. In a way, she understood. Sasha had lost everyone who'd ever mattered to her. She'd had to walk the earth as a solitary creature for more time than she should have.

Until now. The draw Dee felt toward her was so strong it was like an invisible steel band. How many of her friends had she watched as they fell in love and discovered life partners? How many times had it happened to her? That would be a big, fat zero, until now, and though it was most assuredly crazy that it was this beautiful vampire who made her believe in happily-ever-after, that's what had happened. Nice and normal love would be cool. Then again, when had Dee ever settled for nice and normal? Her family would resoundingly say never. No sense in changing character now. She was what she was, and she liked who she liked.

She was already outside in the woods when she heard Sasha's light step behind her. "Let's go kick her ass."

Sasha put a hand on her shoulder and turned her so they were looking at each other. "It's my fight."

"We can do a quid pro quo later. Tonight I'm your wing woman. Some other night, you can be mine."

"You don't have to do this."

It was true, she didn't. "Don't have to. Want to." Dee wanted to get going fast in the direction of the car.

"Why?"

She looked down into Sasha's expressive eyes. She studied her face and smiled. "Because you're the most exciting woman I've ever met, and I don't want to lose you now."

"Vampire."

Dee shrugged. "Vampire. Woman. Semantics." She pressed her lips against Sasha's. The kiss filled her with such joy she didn't want to stop. She did, bringing her head up and cupping Sasha's face with her hands. "Got it?"

Sasha just nodded. "Good. Then let's do this." Dee turned away and, for the third time in one night, started running in the direction of the car. She was going to have some seriously sore quads come tomorrow.

❖

Katrina's fury only increased by the time she stood in the middle of the Monroe Street Bridge. Despite her having dialed every number in her computer files before coming here, not one of the calls was picked up. It didn't make sense. Not only should they have been waiting for her call, but they should also have been ready to roll. Something had apparently gone very wrong. Damn Eli. This was all his fault.

In a fit of rage, she threw the laptop through the window of the hotel room. The glass shattered as the computer flew out into the night. Shards of glass fell to the floor, glittering in the lamplight. Her hands shook, and all she could think about was revenge. This was *her* doing, and she was going to pay. Her fury built as she made her way the few blocks from the hotel to the Monroe Street Bridge.

The normally heavy traffic was quiet. Not a single car went either north or south. In fact, the entire city was uncharacteristically quiet, thanks to her handiwork. At least something was going right. Out there in the darkness, her soldiers were multiplying. It was as she wished and as she needed.

For the moment she could focus on what was to come. She waited away from the covered benches in the center of the bridge. They contained beautiful and interesting elements of design, but standing near them was impossible. The strong smell of urine and alcohol lingered deep and heavy. In addition to the stench, the view was obstructed. It was imperative that she have full sight of the bridge, and she could get that only by standing outside. She watched the north and south access. *She* would be coming from one or the other direction. She did not expect anyone from the water side. The falls below were raging, and the white water sent spray up and into her eyes. It was beautiful if one was into that sort of thing.

"I didn't think you'd come."

Katrina had turned away from the spray and watched as the woman walked her way with slow, easy steps. Even after all these years, she recognized the stride. She knew how she moved, how she looked. She'd watched her for hours as she'd strolled in the gardens and the fields with her sisters and, on rare occasions, her brother. When he was there with them, he was treated like delicate china, unlike the girls, who were strong as well as beautiful. In her heart, one was more beautiful than the others, and she'd quickly been able to capture her affections. The circumstances for the sisters were dire, yet it hadn't mattered. She'd never expected to fall in love and be loved in return. It had been a unique and magical time.

Everything had changed when that love was betrayed. In all her years she'd never been turned on before. And no woman had ever walked away from her. Not successfully, anyway, and that record would not be broken now. Her beginnings on the street had taught her that no slight can go unpunished regardless of how long it took to deliver the fatal blow. She'd waited a long time for this, and after the hiccup earlier tonight, she planned to savor the current victory.

"Of course I would come. I've been looking for you since you killed my family and made me into this thing." She waved her hands up and down in front of her body.

"And I've been looking for you. Who's the blood donor?" The way her words made the lines harden around Sasha's mouth gave her some satisfaction. She liked that she could get under her skin.

"You don't need to worry about her."

Katrina laughed. "You think I'm worried? Oh, little Maria, you're just the same, aren't you? You change your name, your hair, your clothes, and none of it makes a difference. You're still the little princess worried about everyone else. Daddy's perfect little girl."

"I've changed more than my appearance, and that should concern you. I gave up perfection the day you sank your fangs into my neck."

Katrina shrugged. "I have nothing to worry about. By this time tomorrow, I'll have the world in my hands. You're the one who should be alarmed."

This time Sasha laughed, and it wasn't a good sound. There should be alarm in her voice yet instead she heard glee. "You have no idea how wrong you are, Katrina. That's why I told you to come. I've stopped everything you tried to do. I've got people in place to counter you at every turn. You won't have anything in the palm of your hand tomorrow or any other day."

Katrina shook her head slowly from side to side. "You're way too late. It's happening, and nothing you can do will stop it."

Sasha's gaze didn't waver, and she still couldn't detect anything that resembled fear. "Nothing? Are you sure?"

A sick feeling hit her in the stomach. "What have you done?" She didn't want to believe her and desperately wanted to wipe the smug smile off her face. This meeting was nowhere near how she'd imagined it as she'd walked through the chaotic streets toward the bridge.

"I knew what you were up to. I've been following the Consortium's activities for years. We've been ready and waiting for you to make your move. The only surprise? That you came here, but I suspect it was because you finally found me. Tell me I'm wrong."

Her hands clenched and unclenched. "I will kill you."

"You killed me a hundred years ago."

"You've been an ungrateful bitch since I met you. You never appreciated anything I did for you, and when you would have perished alongside your family, I gave you life. I gave you a chance."

Now she did see Sasha's expression change, only it still wasn't fear that darkened her eyes. Hatred beamed from her eyes like a lighthouse beacon. "No. You gave me nothing but misery, and now it's time to pay. Karma is here to give you a big slap."

Her nails bit into the palms of her hands, and blood dripped to the concrete sidewalk. "You can't touch me. I will destroy you." Katrina launched herself toward Sasha at the same moment her onetime love raced toward her.

CHAPTER TWENTY-THREE

Every decade of suppressed rage roared to the surface as Sasha charged straight at Katrina. Her anger was a fire that would be quelled only when one of them was dead. And it wasn't going to be her.

She reached for Katrina's throat, craving to rip through her flesh and silence the voice that had whispered in her head for more than a century. She wanted this over right now. Before she could strike and dig her fingers into Katrina's cool flesh, Dee screamed, "Don't."

That single word coming from Dee's lips stopped her. It didn't stop Katrina. Her forward momentum brought them crashing into each other like Rocky Mountain elk locking horns, and Katrina's nails bit into Sasha's skin. The pain was searing as blood flowed down her neck. That Katrina drew first blood was unacceptable, and Dee's warning forgotten, she was spurred forward and slashed out with her own hand. It connected, and now blood flowed across her hand and down her arm. Had it been human blood, it would have been warm. It wasn't. It was as cool as her own that dripped down to stain her shirt.

Out of the corner of her eye she saw two figures running toward them. Recognition dawned, along with shock. Rodney and Prima. They must have followed her and Dee. She should be furious with them. However, she was glad. Both of them had taken the serum Dee had refused, and that made them powerful allies in this fight. They would be immune from a vampire's bite and, better yet, would transfer a killing punch should Katrina try to feed from them. It was the kind of help she could use.

Dee had jumped on Katrina's back, her arms around her neck as she tried to get her to let go of Sasha. She didn't appear to realize that she was like a fly trying to slow down a lion. Sasha's strength was massive, and in most situations she would be the champion. That was far from a given this time. Katrina had age, strength, and fury on her side. Sasha had righteousness on hers. She believed righteousness would win out. She had to believe it. She also had to save Dee before she was hurt.

"Get off me!" Katrina threw Dee against the bridge balustrade like a rag. Dee screamed, and Sasha feared she was hurt. She didn't intend to loosen her grip on Katrina and couldn't check on Dee. It was a risk she couldn't take even to protect the human who was fast becoming important to her. She prayed Dee wasn't seriously injured.

Katrina was fighting like a tigress. She spun with a move that freed her from Sasha's grasp as if she were nothing more than a three-year-old trying to hold on to her mother's leg. She wasn't expecting the move, and she paid for her lack of anticipation. "Damn you," Sasha cried as she went down on one knee. Pain shot up her leg, and she was relatively certain she'd just shattered her kneecap. She ignored it and jumped back up to her feet.

"You're a fool. You always were." Katrina laughed and then whirled again as first Rodney launched at her and then Prima. Sasha believed they had numbers on their side, and between them they would be able to take her down. It was four against one. No way to fail. They would have her any second.

She was wrong.

Katrina hooked her arm around Rodney's neck in a lightning-fast move that broke it. The snap was sickeningly loud on the otherwise quiet bridge. She then whirled around, grabbed Prima by the neck, and tossed her over the balustrade, where she tumbled into the swiftly moving river below. The way the river was running over the falls, she would be dead in minutes as her body was smashed against the massive rocks that rose on either side. The two were taken out in a matter of seconds.

"No!" It was the last straw for Sasha. This bitch had helped kill her family. Had held a rifle and pulled the trigger over and over again until their blood ran like a river across the basement floor. Murder wasn't enough to satisfy whatever twisted pleasure drove her, and she'd next taken away Sasha's chance to be reunited with her parents, her brother, and her sisters in the afterlife. Katrina had not changed in the intervening years. She had just killed two kind, decent people and hurt someone she was beginning to care deeply about. Enough was enough.

The horrible laugh that seemed to echo and amplify in the still night air gave her chills. "Give up, little princess. You never had a chance against me. Not then and not now. No one does." Katrina moved lightning fast to grab her around the neck and pull her up and off her feet. "You were always mine to do with as I please."

Sasha reached for her, hoping to be able to wrap her hands around Katrina's neck. "I'll destroy you." Rage was an excellent motivator.

"That ship sailed a long time ago. You've got nothing left. Your friends are dead, your girlfriend worthless." Her fingers were digging into her flesh, and the breath was beginning to leave her. She feared that Katrina might be right and that she really was going to win this battle.

"You're not going to win." Her words were barely a whisper, and blackness was beginning to crowd her vision. "I will not let you." Big words that required action to back up. She prayed that she could find it in time.

"I've already won, you little fool. I always win."

Dee shook her head with as much vehemence as she could, trying to clear the stars threatening to take her away into oblivion. Never before had she felt anything like the power of the vampire who was holding Sasha off her feet. She was not going to black out. As her vision cleared, she could see that the crazy one was more than simply holding her up. She was about to rip Sasha's head from her body.

That wasn't going to happen, not as long as she was still breathing. Dee was going to destroy her, and that was saying a lot for a person who abhorred violence. Even the gentlest person could be pushed too far, and this was that day for her.

North of where the two vampires battled, a crumpled form lay in the middle of the road. It took a second for her to register that it was a man. It took another second to hit that the man was Rodney. Even from here, she could tell he was dead. She wanted to puke. Again, she sucked it up and took quick stock of her options.

Quickly she scanned the bridge for Prima, and another wave of nausea struck when she couldn't find her. Only two possibilities existed:

Prima had gotten away or had been tossed into the river. Her heart wanted to believe in the former. Her intuition told her it was the latter.

The realization that Katrina had killed her old friend Prima and her new friend Rodney chased away any lingering stars that flitted around the edge of her vision. Her head was clear, her thoughts coming into focus. No way was this bitch going to take everything from her.

She settled her gaze on the two locked together in battle. From the look on Sasha's face, time was almost up. If she didn't do something and do it now, they were all going to die. Two too many had already lost their lives tonight. This had to stop.

She put her hand to her throat and fingered the silver necklace while she searched for a game plan. It always calmed her to touch the star-shaped pendant. Her mother had given her the necklace when she published her first book, even though it hadn't sold that many copies. It hadn't made a lick of difference to her mother whether she sold a hundred books or a hundred thousand. She always called Dee her shining star and thus gave her the necklace to remind her of how proud her family was of her. Now, the touch of the silver gave her strength.

Suddenly, she stilled her fingers. Something Sasha had told her earlier came back to her, and as it did, she knew exactly how to end this once and for all. She could almost see a scenario in her head. She yanked the necklace free without bothering to unclasp it. *Thank you, Mom.*

The star held firmly between her thumb and forefinger, Dee lunged at Katrina. Rather than trying to drag her away from Sasha, this time Dee pulled her arm back and screamed. At the same time, she put every ounce of power she possessed into plunging the sterling-silver star into Katrina's neck, puncturing the flesh and pushing it as far in as possible. Blood spurted out, hitting her in the face, but still she didn't let go. She pushed and pushed on the piece until she couldn't shove it in any farther. She felt soft tissue, blood, and bone.

"Die, you awful bitch. Die!" Tears were running down her cheeks, and she hoped she wasn't too late. She wished she'd figured out what to do sooner.

For a moment nothing happened, and then Katrina crumpled to the ground, her face a mask of agony, her hands dropping away from Sasha's neck and going to her own, where she clawed, trying to get at the piece of silver. A gurgling sound came from her throat. Dee thought she could make out a single word. "No."

"Yes," she spat into her face. "Yes. Die, you piece of garbage."

Sasha had been right. Sterling silver was a kiss of death, and the proof was in the dissolving body of the vampire who had caused the deaths of who knew how many. Who had destroyed Sasha's family. Who had destroyed her friends. She wanted to do more than simply watch her dissolve into a pile of ash. She wanted to dance on the remnants of her body.

Her glee turned to concern when she realized that Sasha was also on the ground, unmoving. Had her heroic actions been a little too little and a little too late? Had she been too slow to make a difference? She dropped to her knees and grabbed Sasha, holding her close. Her arms were limp and her head lolled. Blood coated her neck. Dee held her close, sending up a silent prayer. At first she couldn't tell if Sasha was still alive, and then she saw the rise and fall of her chest. *Thank you, God.* She was breathing.

She kissed the top of her head and murmured into her hair. "Don't you dare die on me. Don't you dare."

Tears flooded down her cheeks when she realized that off in the distance, the sun was beginning to come up. This was bad. Very bad. They were a long way from the car. Wiping away the tears with the back of her hands, she dredged up her courage and strength. It was all she had left to fight with. Calling on a surge of energy way beyond her normal range of ability, she picked up Sasha and began to move in the direction of the car. It was on the north end of the bridge, and the battle had ended on the south side. She might have been able to pick Sasha up, but running with her was out of the question. Her weight-bearing exercises consisted of gym machines, not carrying hundred-pound women for blocks. What to do? She kept cutting her gaze to the sky and wondered how the daylight could be approaching at the speed of a commuter train. It wasn't fair. After everything they'd done, the universe was conspiring against her. With a whole lot of effort, she managed to carry her in the direction of their vehicle. Dee felt like the unconscious Sasha weighed more like two hundred pounds, and she was huffing and puffing before she made it ten feet.

As the first ray of light hit Sasha's face, she screamed and her eyes flew open. Smoke rose from the spot where her once-smooth complexion was now burned and blackened. Dee dropped Sasha's feet to the bridge floor and slung an arm around her waist. Her shoulders no longer screamed in protest. "Come on," she told her. "We've got to get you out of the light. Can you stand?"

Sasha's legs buckled and she almost fell. Dee didn't let her go. "Leave me," Sasha whispered. "Go somewhere safe. This isn't over yet."

"I'm not leaving you anywhere. Move your damn feet. We didn't make it through all this to have you die on me now. Move it."

As if taken off guard by the command, Sasha straightened a little and obeyed her. The rapidly dawning sky burned her face and hands, smoke rising like a campfire. She didn't make another sound until Dee unceremoniously dropped her into the back of the SUV. Furiously she searched for something to shelter Sasha and finally settled on putting her in a fetal position under the carpet padding that covered the entire hatch area. She had to get Sasha to slide over so she could pull it free, but when she did, she was satisfied at how it protected her. The whole time, Sasha never uttered a sound despite the blackened skin. Dee wanted to cry. She didn't have time to cry again. She had to be the strong one and get them out of here.

By the time she reached the wooded area where they'd been stashing the car while at Rodney's, she figured she'd set a land speed record for north Spokane County. Given the state of the world at the moment, she hadn't worried about a county sheriff's deputy or state patrol officer pulling her over. She wasn't even sure how many of them were still alive, and if they were, she suspected they had more to worry about than a random speeding vehicle on a deserted highway.

She jumped out and ran to the back. She'd parked the car in deep shadows so that Sasha was as protected as possible. Sasha wasn't moving, and only a thread of a breath was evident. She was losing her.

"Oh no, you don't," Dee declared. She could think of only one thing to do, and it was the one contingency that had kept her from taking the miracle cure earlier. The only problem was, she didn't know how to accomplish this life-saving mission. It required a sharp instrument, and she had nothing. Then a thought occurred to her. She began to dig through the pockets of Sasha's leather coat and was rewarded when her fingers touched something hard and metal. The silver knife she'd seen her use on the young male vampires.

Briefly she wondered why Sasha hadn't used it earlier and then let it go. It didn't matter. Saving her life now, did.

"Don't be a wuss," she muttered to herself as she took the knife out of the sheath. It was long and wicked-looking, and it made her shudder. "Now or never." She drew the incredibly sharp blade across the soft skin of her hand, and the pain made her breath catch. Blood immediately came to the surface, deep red and warm. She put the palm of her hand to Sasha's barely open lips. "Drink or else," she warned her. She didn't really know what *or else* meant, but it seemed like the thing to say. It had worked on her earlier when Prima had made her drink the energy-restoring tea, and she hoped it worked now on Sasha.

At first it seemed her grand plan would fail, and then slowly Sasha's hands came up to press Dee's palm closer to her lips. Thank the gods, it was working. After only a few moments of accepting Dee's gift of blood, Sasha began to look better, and her eyes opened. In them was something Dee couldn't quite describe, but it made her shiver with excitement. Or maybe it was blood loss. No, she'd go with excitement.

After about a minute, Sasha pulled Dee's hand away. "I can't stay out here. I have to get inside. There's a coat in the cargo bin."

Sure as the world, inside the built-in cargo bin was a long, hooded coat, perfect to keep a vampire protected from the sun's rays. Being with a vampire put a whole new spin on the term "sun's harmful rays." She draped the coat over Sasha before she helped her out of the car, making sure every inch of skin was covered. For a second neither of them moved. Then Sasha leaned over and kissed Dee on the lips. The thrill it sent through her was pure magic.

Sasha pulled back and looked her in the eye. "Thank you for saving my life. Now run."

And they did.

EPILOGUE

Fifty Years from Now

Sasha finished typing and sat back as the last of the pages spewed from the printer. Writing it all down was like living it all over again. How she remembered each and every moment, as though it had just happened instead of half a century ago. Some of it was very good. Some of it very bad. When the printer stopped, she gathered up all the pages, put them in a tidy stack in the middle of the table, and slowly set the blue and gold egg on top.

For over an hour she sat and stared at the manuscript. On the pages she'd tried to capture the essence of Rodney and Prima, long dead but never forgotten. She still missed them, even after all these years. Both had died protecting her, and for that she had done her best to preserve and honor their memories. Rodney's body had been recovered and his ashes spread in the woods he so dearly loved. Prima's body had washed ashore two weeks later in Long Lake, the massive lake north of the city fed by the Spokane River Katrina had thrown her into. The only comfort was that they were able to send her home to her family. A vampire war memorial had been erected in the center of the city, and on it were engraved the names of the warriors who never stopped in their fight to save the human race. Two of those names were Rodney and Prima. It wasn't much, but every time she stood and gazed upon it, she smiled, for she remembered them for the unique and wonderful individuals they had been. She and Dee had helped in every way they could, though she'd never really felt like she'd contributed enough, given what Rodney and Prima had done both for her and for humanity.

Still, she'd tried to accomplish what she could, and in her heart, she believed they'd be proud.

The war that Katrina had put into motion didn't end on the bridge that night. It was the beginning of the end, but it took months for the serum to reach around the world, and in the interim, many died. She'd made thousands of calls to get the information out. It was Rodney who had made the real difference. He had used all his genius to get the formula out to everyone. He'd made it available on a global basis before he and Prima even got to the bridge. No one else in the universe could have accomplished such a feat. It had saved the human race, even though the final tally of those lost was in the millions. What he did had ensured that the survivors were in the tens of millions. In Sasha's book, that was a win.

Katrina's goal, in addition to destroying Sasha for spurning her, had been to become the ruler of the world. It was a foolish goal, though completely in character for her. Katrina had always thought big. Her ego had given her the courage to seduce a princess and succeed, but in the end, it had brought her down. Katrina's blind spot was herself.

Sasha had believed that once Katrina was destroyed, she'd find the peace that had always eluded her. Funny how that wasn't the way it worked out at all. The revenge she'd fixated on for decades hadn't come in the way she'd envisioned. She wasn't the one who'd killed her maker. In fact, she'd almost died in her hands. It was Dee who changed it all. Smart, beautiful, and funny Dee, a gentle, beautiful soul who wrote books that millions waited to read. A kind and gentle soul who advocated peace. A warrior when the situation called for it.

In the end Sasha did find the peace she'd been searching for since the day her family stood in front of a firing squad. It was simply a different kind of peace than she was anticipating, the kind that came from unconditional love. She'd always believed her preternatural state made her unlovable and unworthy of love. She'd thought that once she witnessed Katrina's demise she would be ready to join her family at long last. It hadn't happened anywhere close to the picture she'd had in her head of an unlovable, unworthy vampire. Every day of the last fifty years, Dee had made her see the exact opposite. She had been loved, and she had loved in return.

Together they stood side by side through the fallout of the war, the ultimate reconciliation of the humans and the surviving vampires, and the world that finally gave space to all creatures: human, animal, and preternatural. The remote Rodney had pressed into her hand on that last night had been the key to his underground bunker, and it was there they worked in safety for months. He had left them everything they needed.

The airborne toxin that Katrina had let loose had finally dissipated and its effects weakened to the point it was no longer a threat. The vampire nation was crippled by the war, and the Elders who survived adapted and became allies to the humans. Because of the serum Rodney had distributed, the vampires had no choice but to work with humans if they wanted to survive. It was precisely the opposite of the world Katrina was trying to create, and it still made her smile.

They were finally able to leave the bunker behind and make a life in the new world. They created a home where they lived and loved. Dee wrote her novels that after the end of the siege became deeper and more impactful. Sasha rebuilt her business, and when the day came to walk away, she turned it over to her most trusted ally. Dreams she'd long ago given up on came true.

Her smile faded as she looked over at Dee, who was dozing on the sofa. She had to finish the account of World War V, as Dee liked to call it, and soon. An urgency that made her heart bleed was pushing her forward. Neither had said it out loud. Both knew what was coming.

"It's a full moon tonight, isn't it?" Dee's eyes were still closed. "I could always feel the change in the air on full-moon nights. You think I might be part werewolf?"

Sasha looked out the French doors to the patio beyond and the big round moon that was spilling golden light down on the red bricks they'd picked out together. "It is a full moon, and no, I don't think you're part werewolf. Pretty sure we'd have noticed before now if that was the case."

Dee laughed lightly. "True enough. Can we go outside and sit for a while?"

"Of course we can." Sasha left the table and went over to pick her up, blanket and all, and walk outside, remembering a long-ago night when Dee had carried her in her arms. Tears burned at the back of her eyes, and she blinked them back.

It was a warm summer night, and even ten years ago, Dee would have been wearing shorts and a sleeveless shirt in this kind of weather. Now, Sasha tucked the blanket tighter around her thin body. "This all right?" She sat her on the rocking love seat where they'd spent so many evenings sitting next to each other and talking about anything and everything.

"It's perfect. Sit with me." She patted the seat. "I just want to be here with you for a little while." She closed her eyes once more.

Sasha sat down beside her and put her arm around her bony shoulders. She pulled her close. "I love you." Tears welled again in her eyes, and she couldn't hold them back any longer. They were hot as they spilled down her cheeks.

"Back atcha." Dee let her head drop to Sasha's shoulder as she patted the top of her leg. She left her hand there. It felt as light as a butterfly.

For a long time, they said nothing, just sat together letting the love seat rock back and forth, back and forth. The air was clear and clean, a light wind catching Dee's fine hair and blowing it around her face. In the distance, a dog barked and a bird swooped low over the yard.

"I love you," Dee said.

"I love you more." It was their private joke.

"I have to go now." Dee's words were barely audible.

The tears flowed harder down Sasha's cheeks. "I know." She held her tighter.

She knew the minute Dee had left her, yet she didn't move. There was no need. All the arrangements had been made. Everyone knew their part and what was to be done after. There was nothing left for her to do except for one thing.

Her chin rested on the top of Dee's head. Quietly she said into the darkness, "Mama, Papa, Olga, Tatiana, Anastasia, Alexei, I'm coming home at last." She kissed Dee's hair. "And I'm bringing someone very special with me."

Sasha sat on the swing holding the love of her very long life in her arms and watched the sun rise over the mountains to the east.

About the Author

Sheri Lewis Wohl grew up in northeast Washington State, and though she always thought she'd move away, never has. Despite traveling throughout the United States, Sheri always finds her way back home. And so she lives, plays, and writes amidst mountains, evergreens, and abundant wildlife.

When not working the day job in federal finance, she writes stories that typically include a bit of the strange and unusual and always a touch of romance. Her novel *Twisted Whispers* was a 2016 Golden Crown Literary Award winner for Paranormal/Horror, and *Twisted Screams* was a finalist for a 2017 Golden Crown Literary Award.

Sheri and her K9 partner, Zoey, are a nationally certified K9 Search & Rescue team. She also likes to participate in local triathlons and puts her acting chops to use every chance she gets. You can catch her in televisions shows such as *Z Nation* and *Grimm*.

Learn more about Sheri at her website, www.sherilewiswohl.com, her blog, sherilewiswohl.wordpress.com, and on Twitter: @sherilewiswohl and Facebook: @SheriLewisWohl

Books Available From Bold Strokes Books

A Chapter on Love by Laney Webber. When Jannika and Lee reunite, their instant connection feels like a gift, but neither is ready for a second chance at love. Will they finally get on the same page when it comes to love? (978-1-163555-366-6)

Drawing Down the Mist by Sheri Lewis Wohl. Everyone thinks Grand Duchess Maria Romanova died in 1918. They were almost right. (978-1-163555-341-3)

Listen by Kris Bryant. Lily Croft is inexplicably drawn to Hope D'Marco, but will she have the courage to confront the consequences of her past and present colliding? (978-1-163555-318-5)

Perfect Partners by Maggie Cummings. Elite police dog trainer Sara Wright has no intention of falling in love with a coworker until Isabel Marquez arrives at Homeland Security's Northeast Regional Training facility, and Sara's good intentions start to falter. (978-1-163555-363-5)

Shut Up and Kiss Me by Julie Cannon. What better way to spend two weeks of hell in paradise than in the company of a hot, sexy woman? (978-1-163555-343-7)

Spencer's Cove by Missouri Vaun. When Foster Owen and Abigail Spencer meet, they uncover a story of lives adrift, loves lost, and true love found. (978-1-163555-171-6)

Unexpected Lightning by Cass Sellars. Lightning strikes once more when Sydney and Parker fight a dangerous stranger who threatens the peace they both desperately want. (978-1-163555-276-8)

Without Pretense by TJ Thomas. After living for decades hiding from the truth, can Ava learn to trust Bianca with her secrets and her heart? (978-1-163555-173-0)

Emily's Art and Soul by Joy Argento. When Emily meets Andi Marino she thinks she's found a new best friend, but Emily doesn't know that Andi is fast falling in love with her. Caught up in exploring her sexuality, will Emily see the only woman she needs is right in front of her? (978-1-163555-355-0)

Escape to Pleasure: Lesbian Travel Erotica, edited by Sandy Lowe and Victoria Villaseñor. Join these award-winning authors as they explore the sensual side of erotic lesbian travel. (978-1-163555-339-0)

Music City Dreamers by Robyn Nyx. Music can bring lovers together. In Music City, it can tear them apart. (978-1-163555-207-2)

Ordinary is Perfect by D. Jackson Leigh. Atlanta marketing superstar Autumn Swan's life derails when she inherits a country home, a child, and a very interesting neighbor. (978-1-163555-280-5)

Royal Court by Jenny Frame. When royal dresser Holly Weaver's passionate personality begins to melt Royal Marine Captain Quincy's icy heart, will Holly be ready for what she exposes beneath? (978-1-163555-290-4)

Strings Attached by Holly Stratimore. Rock star Nikki Razer always gets what she wants, but when she falls for Drew McNally, a music teacher who won't date celebrities, can she convince Drew she's worth the risk? (978-1-163555-347-5)

The Ashford Place by Jean Copeland. When Isabelle Ashford inherits an old house in small-town Connecticut, family secrets, a shocking discovery, and an unexpected romance complicate her plan for a fast profit and a temporary stay. (978-1-163555-316-1)

Treason by Gun Brooke. Zoem Malderyn's existence is a deadly threat to everyone on Gemocon, and Commander Neenja KahSandra must find a way to save the woman she loves from having to make the ultimate sacrifice. (978-1-163555-244-7)

A Wish Upon a Star by Jeannie Levig. Erica Cooper has learned to depend on only herself, but when her new neighbor, Leslie Raymond, befriends Erica's special needs daughter, the walls protecting Erica's heart threaten to crumble. (978-1-163555-274-4)

Answering the Call by Ali Vali. Detective Sept Savoie returns to the streets of New Orleans, as do the dead bodies from ritualistic killings, and she does everything in her power to bring their killers to justice while trying to keep her partner, Keegan Blanchard, safe. (978-1-163555-050-4)